THE BLOOD SOCIETY

B.B. PALOMO

Ember Sky
PUBLISHING

For more information, email authorbbpalomo@gmail.com

Published by Ember Sky Publishing, LLC

Edited by Emily A. Lawrence

www.lawrenceediting.com

Cover Design by Sarah Hansen, Okay Creations

okaycreations.com

Print ISBN 978-1-7350666-1-5

Ebook ISBN 978-1-7350666-0-8

To my daughter, Emberly. Always follow your dreams.

Contents

Prologue

"Sammy!" Strong fingers bit into my shoulder, shaking a dream from behind my eyes, yanking me out from a peaceful bliss. "Get up now!" The voice hissed.

"Dad?" His grip left my skin, but I could still feel the pressure of his touch like a phantom mark. I rubbed the sleep from my lids, clearing my vision of floating obstructions, bringing my father's panicked face into focus.

"Hang on tight, baby, it'll be okay," he said.

My father had already ripped my plush comforter back before my brain could focus on what he was saying. The mattress dipped as he leaned in to scoop me up like I weighed nothing, pulling me in painfully close. His heart pounded against my body, sending Morse code to my own chest, which was quickly replicating the same rhythm.

"What's going on?" I cried out. "I can walk!" I tried to insist, feeling much younger than my thirteen-year-old self.

He shushed me aggressively, not pausing to apologize as he normally would after getting short with me. My whining died in my throat. I pulled myself higher to see past his shoulder as he rushed out of my room and down the stairs.

The house was still dark but bright white light snuck through the glass paneling that sandwiched our heavy wood door, painting the floors and lighting a path. My father raced into the study, setting me down quickly to clear off his computer desk with a single sweep of his arms. I cried out as his things scattered to the ground, but if he noticed, no indication was given.

Isn't it morning? Why is he so scared?

His jet-black hair was disheveled from sleep, sticking up in every direction but down. The same soft gray sweatpants he'd always worn to sleep were matched with a wrinkled white T-shirt that looked like it had been quickly grabbed from the laundry basket. The bare bottoms of his feet slapped the floor as he rushed around the room. I peeked out the window as loud snaps echoed throughout our home. The sound of the emergency lights was unmistakable as each one was flipped on, explaining the light I had just seen through the door. The sudden brightness stung my eyes, but I forced myself to wait until my pupils adjusted so I could try to see what was happening outside. These were just for emergencies, so why were they on? The sky was dark except for the smallest sign the sun was trying to wake up, painting the very bottom of the horizon a soft orange.

"Get away from there!" My mother's voice was frantic as she rushed into the study and forcefully shut the double doors behind her.

"What's going on?" My heartbeat spiked as I ripped away from the window at her scold, sending anxiety into my throat. I had never seen my parents afraid like this. My parents weren't afraid of anything.

"We need you to hide, Sam, they will be here soon," she said hastily with a quiet ferocity I was unfamiliar with.

"Rachel, help me!" My dad struggled to tug the heavy desk backward.

My mother raced to him, pushed her back against the front slab, and used her legs to help shove it back up against the shelves that lined the walls of their study. As the legs moved off of an expensive Persian rug, rubbing against the old shiplap flooring, the sound of nails scraping against a chalkboard replaced the winded breathing coming from my parents. With every thrust, every scrape, a new wave of chills worked its way up my spine as I stood there, motionless, trying to make sense of what was happening.

A book fell from the shelf as my dad heaved his last push, knocking the desk as close as possible to the shelf. It landed on its spine with a thud, opening to some random page only to be kicked to the side as my parents hurried. My father reached down and whipped the rug back, exposing a hatch door. He fumbled clumsily with the recessed handle before catching it enough to lift the door open. The house had decades on my parents, and I wondered how long people had been prepping for some sort of doomsday.

"Are we under attack?" I asked, pushing back against my mom's hands as she tried to lead me into the dark hole. No one answered. Instead my father tried to assist my mom by ushering me with his hand to follow her physical command. My mother shoved me harder when I didn't budge, forcing me to stumble into my dad's arms. He pulled me close, not allowing me to struggle as he turned me to face the blackness and all but pushed me into the opening. The first step into what was really a little more than a crawl space creaked under my weight. I took another step down, almost slipping on the inch of dust that had accumulated over the years of disuse.

"Let me stay," I begged. "I can help!"

I hadn't realized I had a death grip on my father's arm until he ripped away from me, taking a moment to clasp my hands between his. He looked at me, unblinking, like he was trying to remember every detail of my face. His green eyes glistened against the limited light and though I had never seen him cry, I was sure that's what was happening. His callused skin against my own unworked palms lingered only for a moment more before he let go and took a step back.

"Do not make a sound and do not come out—*no matter what you hear*," he said without emotion.

His words cued shouting, followed by gunfire that erupted in shorts bursts at first before turning into rapid fire. I flinched with every bang as my mother forced me lower into the trap space with a broken smile. Her hands were softer than my father's as she placed her palm against my cheek, trembling slightly. Her blond hair was pulled back into a tight elastic, keeping her long locks out of her face. I stared into blue eyes that resembled my own trying to read them, trying to figure out what I should do.

"We love you so much, baby, it will be okay. Be quiet until the team gets here. Always be strong, my little dove," she choked out.

A single tear slid down her cheek as she closed me into the darkness. Only little slivers of light snuck down into my hiding place through the small separations in the flooring. The rug was thrown back down over the secret space, sending dust into my eyes and stealing a majority of the light. I tried to fist the dirt out of my vision while the desk was returned to its rightful spot, hiding the hatch completely. I quietly crawled to the only light not being blocked by the rug, reaching my hands out into the dark to feel for any obstacles. Small rocks cut into the flesh of my knees as I moved, but I stayed quiet even though I so badly wanted to call out for my parents. I reached the end of the space, trying to soak up the stripes of white that painted the ground and ignore the darkness I had just left. I told my parents I wasn't afraid of the dark anymore, but a part of me still shivered at the things they said went bump in the night.

My parents continued to move around the office, speaking in hushed tones, but I didn't know if it was because we were hiding or because they didn't want me to know what was being said. A loud crash came from the foyer. I tensed as my breath caught in my throat, subconsciously trying to silence any noise from my body completely. I dug to the deepest depths of my courage trunk and sat up on the bones of my knees, peering up through the cracks in the floor. The study doors swung open like they were possessed, plaster cascading down where they bounced against the walls before becoming still.

A creature I had never seen in person but knew well strolled in, its movements jerky as it searched its surroundings. My dad shoved my mom behind him even though they were both equipped with weapons I hadn't even noticed they grabbed. I couldn't see past the creature, but when my dad whispered to my mom that backup was on the way I wondered to myself why 'backup' was needed. We had guards out front that were always on watch. I only saw one. I knew my parents had handled a handful more on a good day, but the look on my parents' faces made me fear for what I couldn't see behind it.

Its head snapped up as if it was just noticing them standing there, ready to defend our home. It didn't resemble anything human; they never did. Even through the floors I could see the deep burgundy veins mapping their way through skin that appeared to be pulled too tightly around its physique. In the lighting, it seemed to be blanched of color, looking as though it didn't have a single bit of the blood I knew it was craving. Beside the ripped shorts that hung loosely what I could only assume used to be 'his' hips, he was naked, void of the clothing and hair you would see on humans. The vampire moved forward, studying my parents, each step sending dust down into my eyes, burning them until I could rub them clear again.

He jumped forward to only be blown back from the blast of the revolver comfortably gripped in my dad's hand. A blood-curdling howl pierced my ears, but it wasn't coming from the dead creature, it was coming from something behind him. The room was rushed. My dad grunted as he was slammed back into the desk, pinned between furniture and creature. My mom launched herself to the side to avoid being taken out by my father, rolling smoothly away and gracefully getting back to her feet in record time. She landed a solid kick to one of the creature's midsections, sending it tumbling down. The sound of bones cracking filled the room as my father pummeled his stake through the sternum of the beast who had him pinned. The vampire fell to the ground without another sound. Another one pressed forward and even as my dad joined my mother's side the look on their faces told me there were just too many.

Five more piled in, all attacking in unison, slashing at

my parents, who tried to fight them off but even being the best hunters in the business they were unprepared and outnumbered. A jagged scream pierced the air as my mother drove her stake into the heart of one of the vampires. She yanked the stake out as the creature stumbled back and collapsed. Two more turned to her and attacked in revenge as my dad fended off the others. She whipped to the right, avoiding the claws of one, but the other had prepared for her move and caught her. The scream that attempted to bubble out was cut short as the creature bit into her throat, lacerating her flesh as it pulled away without unlocking their jaws. Blood swam down her neck, pouring out of the wound like a faucet that had been left on, soaking into her ivory shirt.

"No!" my dad roared.

He ran his stake into the heart of the monstrosity he was fighting, shoving it back hard enough to take out another one fumbling for him around the corpse. Just as quickly he whipped around but failed to catch my mother as she was thrown down, landing just above where I was crouching. I caught my gasp in my hand and covered it with my other because I didn't trust it to stay put. My mother's body was shielding any light that was once coming through the floor.

I blinked as warmth pattered against my cheek. The smell of copper stung my nostrils, curdling my stomach. I knew what it was, but I couldn't move, couldn't wipe it away as it trailed down my face like the unshed tears I was holding. I was frozen. I tried to listen for her breathing, but I couldn't hear over the bees buzzing in-between my ears. The sound seemed to travel down my body until I was shaking in tune with its rhythm.

"*You!*" The sound of my dad's broken voice cut through

my fog. I wanted to move, but my legs stayed locked in place. I felt so weak and defenseless. He struggled against something, as I prayed he was killing every last one of the bloodsuckers up there. The unmistakable sound of a snap rang out as a body fell to the ground, shaking the floor. Bile rose in my throat, but the clasped hands over my mouth kept me from retching. I didn't need the sound of creatures rummaging through the office to tell me my parents lost their fight.

Glass shattered, sending fragments to rain over me through the floorboards. The reinforcements were here, I could hear them coming through the windows and the clear signs of fighting. Tears filled my eyes, spilling over and running down my cheeks. They were too late. My name was being called out frantically around the house, but I couldn't get my lungs to work. I couldn't bring myself to call out and be saved. I wanted to go with my parents, wherever that might be.

"Sam!" a familiar voice screamed out closer this time. "Oh my God." Alec's voice was weird to me, muffled by the water sloshing in my ears.

"I know," someone responded, disgusted.

"Jesus." Another person filed into the room with foot-steps following. "This is a massacre. Is it hollow here?" the voice asked, the floorboards creaking above me.

They must have moved my mother because light flooded into *my safe space*. I choked on a sob that welled up from my core. It was true, they were gone. I lost the ability to hold myself and fell backward, landing in dirt, letting the glass shards slice my hands.

"Sam?" Alec's footsteps creaked around my mom's body, looking down into the crack I sat under. "Sam." His voice cracked with relief as our eyes met through the floor.

Normally comforting, they did nothing to ease the pain that radiated in my chest, growing bigger and threatening to consume me entirely. Even my best friend couldn't change this. Things were never going to be the same. I was never going to be the same.

Chapter 1

BREATH ESCAPED me in quick gasps as my lungs struggled to push oxygen throughout my body. Dirty water dripped from rusted pipes, forming puddles along the dimly lit tunnel situated under an abandoned warehouse. It was an old trading path, one not known by most, but I had access to the original building plans, which made it easy to find. Lampenflora covered the decaying concrete path, mixing with the stench of stagnant water, making my stomach tighten and churn as I struggled to keep from slipping.

Water soaked through my boots, saturating my socks as I ran through the puddles. Their splashes echoed throughout the stone construction as the weight of my feet destroyed their holding cell. I could no longer be discreet. The tables had turned and now I was not the hunter but the hunted. I wanted to laugh to stifle the nerves rising in my chest. Every step I took was giving away my location and if I didn't act fast, I would be screwed.

This started as only the best of intentions. There are only so many hunters and jobs get turned down all the time. It had only gotten worse as our population dwindled and theirs increased. I figured I would handle this one. It was only supposed to be two vamps, however that quickly turned into a horde and now, despite promising I would not do this, I was running for dear life from one that turned out to be much stronger than the others.

My senses were on high alert, like a caffeine overload my body trembled slightly, disobeying my strict training. The light was finite and dim, straining my eyes as my pupils attempted to adjust properly. I tried to listen over the sound of my running, aiming to get a read on how far away the beast was. Each step shot lightning bolts of pain through my legs as they carried me forward impelled by the adrenaline that was coursing through my veins.

I allowed myself only a moment to slow down and cock my head slightly to listen harder for my target. Raspy unneeded breaths blasted out of dead lungs, closing in on me quicker than my legs could move. I ducked behind a nearby wall, the bricks slimy and cold against my bare arms. The abrupt temperature change sent goose bumps crawling up my shoulder as I pressed myself closer, willing myself to become invisible. I wasn't supposed to be on this mission alone. Who was I kidding, I wasn't supposed to be on this mission *at all*, but I had an act for bending the rules. No one knew I was here. No one was coming to get me if I didn't make it out of this alive. I should have been more than prepared, but this one was strong, and I, well, I was still healing.

Sliding my hand across my waist, I felt along the leather of my utility belt until my fingers brushed the engraved wood of my stake. The vampire was moving fast, splashing through the same puddles I had just run through. Unnatural grunts of frustration escaped from its mouth when it thought I had escaped. I stretched my senses out, trying to calculate its next move. My target wasn't using their animalistic ration to hunt me anymore. It was angry.

Potentially over the five dead vampires I had quietly staked before they realized they were under attack.

The movements trailing behind me stopped so rapidly I almost failed to notice the way the sound was sucked from around me. I made my breath shallow, pressing my tongue to the roof of my mouth, not wanting to make a sound until he got closer so I could catch him off guard. Cool air lingered in the tunnel, but a bead of sweat trickled down my forehead anyway, carving a pheromonal streak down my face. A sound of acknowledgment escaped his throat, followed by a guttural roar that bounced off the walls surrounding me.

Frustrated, I bit my lip hard enough to taste copper. It smelled me.

Gripping my stake, I swung around the corner, sliding through the water, and ended in a crouched position facing my enemy. The vampire I encountered was dressed in the carcass of an old suit, the fabric barely clinging together enough to stay on his body. It anticipated my move, throwing a quick jab to my sternum, hitting right on target and forcing me back. I managed to stay upright as it ran toward me. I escaped the swing of his clawed hand, moving just in time to only feel the wind of the swipe against my face. I swung around, using my momentum to kick him perfectly in the head, causing a low growl to rumble from his core.

A moment passed, neither of us moving. His eyes were like black orbs searing into me. Flesh was pale and pulled too tightly against his sharp bones. Blue capillaries mapped their way around an emaciated body as two snake-like slits vibrated back and forth with each short intake of breath. I never got used to it. They all seemed to have their own features, accompanied by the trademarked ones we had grown accustomed to. The moment passed before I could initiate a move first. The creature came at me, slashing his claws, left to right, with no contemplated movements. I pulled out my stake, narrowly dodging the attack, and pointed the petrified wood at the atrocity that stood before me.

He lunged at me as I shifted to the left, bending slightly to get a better angle. I propelled my stake forward and smiled as the sharpened tip connected with flesh, letting the momentum of the vampire's run force it through his sternum and into his un-beating heart. The penetration made a sickening crack, but I held still.

Warm blood coated my shirt as an ear-shattering scream protruded from the monster. I wished it were like the books. I wished it would turn to ash and disappear. Instead the creature crumbled to the ground in a heaping pile of unnaturalness. I reached out to retrieve my stake, having to use my foot to create counter pressure to slide it out. I brushed the weapon along my jeans, transferring the blood from the wood to my pants, and returned it back to my belt. I did a final sweep of the tunnel, counting my small blessings that there were no more, and I could rest. I laid small trackers down near each of the dead vampires, flipping on the switch and taking a second to watch the red orb move around like it was in a lighthouse. The hunters did this so the cleaning crew knew where each one lay, and that this location was cleared. A team would be by to pick them up for burning in the morning, or if they were in 'good' condition they would be brought back to be studied further, in attempt to find a cure.

I worked my way back to the built-in ladder, leading me up to the warehouse I had originally entered through. I added trackers to the last three vampires up here. My uncle would know I went out on my own now that these gave my location away, each one linking to my unique employee code, and he was not going to be happy. I hoped the number of bloodsuckers I took out would help ease whatever I was going to face in a few hours, a type of atonement for my actions if you will.

Who was I kidding? I was dead meat.

As I opened the rusted door, the chilled breeze that started to blow as the sun went to sleep across the horizon was a welcomed feeling. I knew it would warm up as soon as the sun moved high in the sky but relished in the weather October was bringing us. The air dried the perspiration that coated my skin and supplied a refreshing breath to my winded chest.

The door shut with a loud bang that echoed through the ghost town that used to be Brisbane, a small town outside of San Francisco. The full moon lit the street in beautiful white rays, battling the orange hue rising in the east as if it wasn't prepared to lose its turn to be seen. The sight almost let me ignore the decaying buildings and trash that littered the ground. It looked nothing like the city, resembling more of a forgotten wasteland than anything. The sunrises here were still unbeatable; though so were the deaths.

I worked my way back north. I could call for a ride, but then I'd have to turn my phone back on and see the missed calls I knew for certain were there. The walk back to San Fran would take forever, but with the sun making its appearance shortly, the buses would start on their daily routes and I could catch one for the remaining distance as soon as I hit the limits of the Protected. I knew I should be worried about more vampires, but I pressed on, almost begging one to jump out and find me.

Just one more for me to kill.

This was my life, my job. I was paid to rid the world of a new type of plague. One that didn't have a cure, and until recently didn't have a working Band-Aid. This was a *sickness*. Age-old diseases were no longer the most feared illnesses for humans, but rather a welcomed way out of the new world we lived in. A world of deserted communities and fear. People like me were the only thing standing between life and these monsters who needed our very essence to sustain their own.

Before I left the quiet, abandoned street, I took one last look at the warehouse. The windows were shattered, littering the ground with glass confetti. Bubble lettered graffiti was painted on the walls asking God for help. I hoped that gave the person some reassurance, especially since the chance was good they were gone now. I didn't know what the old world looked like before the vampires, but I dreamed of it with busy streets, like the ones in the city and people all over, not just in the safe zones we called the Protected, afraid that the day may be their last. A life of soaking up the sun and getting to explore the night. No curfews, no monsters, and no fear.

I guessed it could still be worse. Though people were condensed into zones, there was still food, plenty of work, and trades to help stimulate the economy. The Protected was set up to feel like nothing had changed, you could be safe there. We had the essentials. However, as soon as you ventured from that, as soon as you were past that imaginary line and crossed into the Deserted and the light faded from the sky, everything that I and the other hunters had been working so hard toward was gone. You were gone.

Disgust boiled in my chest, rising into my throat like angry froth as my achy legs walked me closer to the edge of civilization and my transit home. It was ridiculous speaking to no one, but I couldn't help but to whisper my feelings to the wind anyway, praying it would venture to whoever could make this all go away.

"Fucking vampires."

Chapter 2

I focused on the vein that pulsed in my boss's forehead. The angrier he became, the bigger the vein expanded, throbbing in unison with his inclining heartbeat. It protruded out further, making me worry about his blood pressure before it sank back into his head as he inhaled deeply.

"How many times are we gonna do this?" Todd, my dad's best friend and practically my uncle in non-blood related terms, placed his index finger and thumb on the bridge of his nose, rubbing it up and down to soothe the headache I knew I was giving him. "You cannot take off alone on assignments. This will stop." Spit flew from his mouth, landing in little droplets on his desk.

I wanted to argue but knew it would fall on deaf ears. Todd ran the company, making and enforcing the rules, for now at least. I had been warned more than once not to do what I did last night. I understood why he was mad about me disobeying the rules but didn't understand why he was *this* mad. I had completed the job with *mostly* no issues arising, following the same routine as I would have if I was on a team. Our taggers, employees who kept mostly to the rooftops to search for bloodsuckers, had shot trackers into two vampires seen nearing the Protected and the green light was given to the hunters to deploy a team. Sure, I wasn't a team and maybe that's why my request to go was declined, but take out the 't' and 'a,' do a little rearranging and *voilà*, there's the 'me' so that was good enough. Right?

Todd's face turned the same shade of red as his hair, which normally contrasted with the paleness of his freckled skin when calm, or more accurately when I wasn't around and for a second, I wondered if I had said any of that out loud. He dove right into reminding me of the dangers of hunting and going out to work alone. As he flung his hands to prove his point with animation, I focused on the silver name plate that sat perfectly centered on his desk to try and smother the smirk that pulled at the corners of my lips. *Todd Weathers* was written in bold font underlined only by his borrowed title of President.

"Are you even listening to me?" Todd snapped his fingers at me, the sound bouncing off the bare walls of his office and bringing my mind back to the surface.

I hadn't been, but nodded anyway, unintentionally encouraging him to continue on his rant. I fiddled with the company badge attached to the belt loop on my jeans, pulling the card from the reel and then letting it go, the sound calming. Samantha Cordova was written across the top in bold font even though I hated that name. Well, that wasn't completely true, I just hated being called Samantha. It reminded me too much of being alone. The left half of the card was consumed by my picture, taken as an intern as I refused to update it when getting hired on permanently.

The girl who smiled back at me looked just like my

mom. Long golden hair framed a heart-shaped face. Plump lips tugged up, pointing at what used to be a straight nose before it had been broken during a mission. My eyes were bright then, but I knew now those shiny baby blues had turned into a dull gray, devoid of the happiness they used to contain. There was no indication me and this girl were the same person, but Todd let me keep the photo regardless.

Lungs filled with air like someone was going underwater, pulling my gaze back up, and I knew Todd was about to flip his lid.

"I just don't get why I'm being reprimanded for taking out a group of tagged. That is literally what I am paid to do." I watched him deflate himself, content that at least I was engaging him. *Phew.* "The job was clean, no one got hurt, and they weren't left to go feeding on people for another night. It turned out fine."

"That's not what this is about, and you know it. Dammit, Samantha! Don't pretend like you don't understand the issue here. You're not ready to be back out in the field after what happened. It's too soon. Plus, the rules are clear, *hunters* can go out and last I checked that meant more than one." He sighed. "The rules are there for a reason, to keep *you* safe." Todd said it like there were only rules because of me.

"I think the dead vampires from last night would say otherwise." I scoffed. "I don't need any more time off. I need to work. Alone." I tried to convince him. "This is what I do, it's what I'm good at."

"I disagree. I think it would do you a world of wonders to take a break." His green eyes filled with concern, making me shift uncomfortably in my chair. I didn't need his pity. "Just until you're healed."

"I am healed." I stretched my arms out, displaying the

fading bruises and scar covered wounds writing their way across my body. They etched a permanent story in my skin, a tale about loss and pain.

"Not physically, mentally." He brought his index finger up to his temple, tapping it instead of making a circle, which I was sure he'd rather do.

His wrinkles deepened around his eyes, making him look older than the forty-six-year-old man he was. His age wasn't always this apparent. He still carried himself like a young man, like the man I remembered when I was a little girl. The one who would give me piggyback rides and tie my shoes. Even after the night with my parents, Todd was there, always trying to support me even though all I wanted was to push him away.

"I just don't know if you're ready. You have experienced so much loss, you haven't mourned. You could have taken months, as much time as you needed, but you refuse to do what's right—no, what's best for yourself. You're playing a dangerous game," he said.

"It's been weeks since Alec—" I tried to swallow the lump that formed in my throat, the pain shooting from my neck to my chest like a jawbreaker had been shoved down my esophagus. The thought of my partner, my best friend, about him being gone was too much to bear. Six long weeks had dragged themselves by, reminding me I was alone and that Alec was never coming back. "It's all I can do to—feel, feel anything but what I feel now." I choked.

My sleep was plagued with his memory, never ending nightmares recalling only the way he died. Replaying the scene over and over until my body finally graced me awake and released me from my dreams. I got him killed. If I had been more patient, if I had listened, he'd still be here with me today. I screamed out for him, the sound ripping through my throat, tearing out of me in such a rush it burned my windpipes as I lay in a pool of my own blood. His face, that beautiful face of his contorted in pain and terror as he was dragged back into the darkness realizing I wasn't going after him.

"Sammy?" Todd's voice tore me from my demons, their presence still lingering on the surface.

I blinked, trying to rid my eyes of the dryness that made them burn. My body had slouched back into my chair, my shoulders resting unevenly on the off-white cushion. Todd stood up, walking around his imported, mahogany desk, something he only did on rare occasions now. He placed a leathery hand over the fist I hadn't even realized I was clenching, squeezing it softly. I forced my muscles to loosen, relaxing my fist and breathing in deep.

"How about a deal?" He suggested.

I had a sneaking suspicion I wouldn't like what he had to offer. Todd was notorious for only betting if it was in his favor. *The house always wins,* he would say with a hearty chuckle. I looked up to hear him out anyway, knowing there wasn't really another choice. The smell of expensive cologne engulfed me now that he was closer, somehow comforting and distancing at the same time, reminding me of the man I knew and the very noticeable differences between us.

"You can go back out into the field"—he held up a hand at my excitement, halting me—"if you take someone with you, as it is protocol, a new recruit. How does that sound?"

"How does hearing my extensive vocabulary of unique curse words sound?" Todd shot me a look, but I didn't drop the tone. "Alec was my partner. I can't replace him."

"You're not replacing him, but I can't sit here and let

you do whatever it is that you want. Do you know what showing that kind of favoritism could do?" He offered like it was the worst offense imaginable.

"But a new recruit?" I whined as if I wouldn't be contesting it if it was someone better trained. "Isn't there another team that can take her?"

"Him." He corrected.

"Of course it is." I rolled my eyes.

"And no." He continued like I hadn't interjected. "Since the accident, everyone has been working to get more samples and acquire another live specimen," Todd said.

I knew he was talking about a vampire. They were hard to kill and even harder to capture. It took a relatively large team to get one alive. They couldn't be tranquilized because their blood did not flow like a human's any longer, making it little to ineffective, and trying to trap them was even worse with their strength being unmatched and only willing to be lured by a live person since that was their food. It took skill, patience, and almost always resulted in an injury or death to get one back to the facility and caged.

We employed a team of skilled scientists to backtrack what the government from before had done and work on unraveling the mistake it had caused. The old government was so desperate and careless to try and build a super soldier, a perfect warrior of war so they could be the power-house of the world, they would sacrifice and experiment on their own citizens. They wanted people who were faster, stronger, and more durable, but the plan backfired— because they succeeded.

They thought they had come up with the perfect serum, like steroids on crack. The participants were exhibiting more attributes than they had anticipated. Strength, speed, even the ability to heal at a faster rate than the healthiest

person but something went awry. They were hungry, yet
unable to satisfy the need with the food they were used to.
Then participants started getting sick…really sick.

The fever burned them up, seeming to set their
humanity ablaze and leaving them a shell of who they were
with only one desire. To feed on us. To them it was just a
failed experiment. They were fully prepared to put their
subjects down and call it a day, but before they could one
got out. All it took was one bite and the disease transferred,
spreading through their venom secretions with each new
victim. It transmitted like wildfire, killing some and
changing more. It was only thanks to D.O.V.E. and the
eventual vaccine, which was administered during regular
"preservation days" hosted by the company, that we weren't
all turned into bloodsuckers or their food.

Still, all the effort was almost too late. Our population
was a fraction of what it was before, humans living on top
of each other in the Protected zones, trying to stay alive.
The vaccine helped limiting infections, but its effectiveness
left much to be desired. It had to be administered regularly
and even then, trying to force every person to get it and to
stay within the lines of the Protected was difficult.

D.O.V.E. or the Department of Vampire Extermination
was practically law now. Created by my father, starting as
just a militia of people who wanted to save the human race,
had now turned into a multibillion-dollar company,
employing the strongest people to hunt and kill the biggest
threat to our race's survival. Starting small in California,
now facilities had been built in all the major cities, with
similar companies popping up in other countries, creating
safe zones as people moved closer to protection and
vampires got wise about their hunting grounds.

It was a gradual shift, but as D.O.V.E. expanded and

what was left of the world turned their backs on the government that had burned them so many times, the company was looked to for guidance. It started with 'best practices' and quickly turned into rules and taxes to stimulate a similar feeling of the world before. There were still struggles outside of the vampires, there were still the poor and rich, the classes often determined by how close you lived to D.O.V.E. and how close you stayed to the Deserted, though other things contributed like occupations and education, which seemed to be more readily available to people who were closer to the center of the city. The emergence of vampires had changed a lot, and a little, all at the same time.

I personally hated calling them vampires. It made it seem like those cheesy movies and books were fortune-tellers instead of works of fiction, but there was already a name for someone who drank blood, so it stuck. Hunters like me were always in demand as can be imagined. It wasn't uncommon for the job to literally eat us alive, but without people who were willing to hunt, there would be nowhere left to hide. It was rare that you ended up here by choice. Usually it was solely out of need, however there were still a good chunk of us who were gung-ho about saving the world and enjoyed the hunt.

Todd exhaled and I worried I had missed something he said, but when I looked up he wasn't looking at me, instead gazing into thin air like he was gathering his thoughts.

"You still think it was an accident?" I raised my brow. There were whispers the head scientist had made a big discovery, something that would change everything—a cure. As fate would have it, the vampire she was working on escaped their cage, killing her and our dream of a better tomorrow. Everyone banded together, determined to understand what she had found, but even five months later it seemed like she took the remedy to the grave with her.

"Sam." Todd closed his eyes, bending his neck to the side like it needed an adjustment. "You can't go around saying stuff like that anymore. Everyone wants there to be a cure and it makes people extremely uncomfortable when you accuse them otherwise."

"How does a vampire escape from a locked cage?" I pressed on, seeing the small shake of his head when I didn't leave it alone. I had felt like there was something off about the whole thing since the beginning, even dragging Alec into it before he…died.

"Why are you convinced it escaped?" His glance was fierce. "You know it could have happened while she was working. It was a freak accident and I hate it as much as the next guy, but we can't change what happened. Besides, you're trying to avoid the subject. You're lucky I am not suspending you for your recklessness. You couldn't have put yourself in a more dangerous situation. And what about your friends here, what about me? Could you imagine what that would do to us?" He questioned and I tried to imagine, but the feeling of remorse just fell flat. "Regardless, this is what I want. So, this will be done, with or without you. Your choice."

"Yeah?" I challenged, knowing I was treading on shaky ground. "Only for two more years. Once I am twenty-one, I will be inheriting this company and it will be my decision." I said it like I looked forward to it, but in reality, the thought scared me immensely.

Todd palmed invisible wrinkles out of his pressed suit before taking a seat. His face was relaxed, but the stiffness in his shoulders told me he did not like being reminded that he would legally have to relinquish his rights to this company per my parents' will.

The words sat in the air without any rebuttal or objection. The sunlight coming through the window was leveling with my face, making it hard to see. I squinted against the light and hoped it descended quickly, wishing silent luck to the teams on duty tonight. I glanced over at the clock that rested diagonally on a bookshelf that matched the color of Todd's desk. Curfew would be in full effect soon for the residents of the city. Just another way D.O.V.E. was trying to keep people safe, while teams started to deploy for their night shifts, heading toward the tagged to work to further shrink the vampires' population.

"If you don't take a partner"—he didn't stop as I flinched at the word—"then you leave me no choice but to schedule a mental evaluation and put you on paid leave until you are cleared by the doctors." It didn't seem like he took joy in what he was saying, but my mind still imagined him, cartoon faced, evil laughing at me.

Hurt blossomed in my chest, blooming like a fast-framed lotus. I tried to hide it, but I knew my face was distorted, giving away my feelings. Todd noticed, sighing sadly and lowering his tone, attempting to patch the damage that word seemed to do to me. It was probably silly for a word to evoke so much hurt, but the syllables merged together anyway, slapping me.

"Your safety is the most important thing to me," he said.

"Okay." I had lost and I knew it.

"Okay?" He didn't seem sure he had heard me correctly.

"Okay!" I repeated, annoyed.

He smiled at me, but I refused to return it. A knock at his door made us both turn, catching us off guard.

"It's open!" I yelled, earning me another hard stare from Todd, but I shot him a fake grin and an innocent shrug like it was a counterattack.

"Sir—oh, Sammy! Hey!" Alana walked in to give her report of the night to Todd, shooting me a head nod. "Teams Bravo, Delta, and Tango have all been deployed. We're about to head out on a call now. We're just waiting for James to get his gear and the residents to close up. The new recruits are assisting the police with curfew checks. No casualties to report."

"Thank you," Todd said. "You're dismissed."

Alana turned to leave, but no one missed the fact that his eyes were on me when he said that. I made a show of getting up and leaving so he'd know I didn't appreciate being passively told to go, but if he noticed he didn't say. The door closed heavily behind us, drawing glances from the office workers around the floor, who quickly cast them down as soon as I made eye contact with them.

"Hey!" Alana tapped me on the shoulder. "I haven't seen you. How have you been?" Her voice was unnaturally light; she was doing that on purpose. Normally she sounded rough. Combined with the fact she had a few inches on me and a 'don't tread on me' attitude, this was an obvious attempt to ease lightly into conversation with me, the *damaged* girl.

"Hanging in there." I laughed, but it sounded forced and fake. We used to be close, not as close as Alec and I were, but if I ever had a friend, she was it. Everything changed after his death. Now it was too painful to be around people. It was exhausting to have to put on a face to save everyone from me and the black cloud that had attached itself to my life. "You get a good gig tonight?"

"No." She chuckled. "Not like anything you would have gotten. Just going to take out a few loners and call it a night. It's surprisingly quiet right now, but you know how it goes."

"The calm before the storm," we said together, remembering an inside joke we had from training. She would tell me that when I was getting my butt handed to me by our trainers. I always fought better when I was mad.

Alana smiled, running worn fingers through her hair. It was cut short and gelled back, a look I would never be able to pull off, but she had no problem doing. She was dressed for the night. Black shirt tucked into the same black-colored cargo pants—standard-issue, all held together by a belt with a metallic buckle. Glossy, midnight combat boots squeaked as she adjusted her weight, still needing to be worn in before they were going to be comfortable.

"We should get together sometime. You know, if you have some time and catch up. I miss you." She looked away like she was embarrassed when she shouldn't have been. I should be, though. I knew I had withdrawn from everyone, even the few people I was closest with, and it killed me to hurt them, but I couldn't bring myself to drop the walls I purposely built. I couldn't get close to anyone again; their fate would only be death.

"Yeah. I'll get back to you because Todd was just saying I'd be able to go out on some missions, so I'm sure I'll be swamped soon, but we can find something," I lied and though she smiled, her dark eyes told me she saw right through me.

"Yeah, okay. Well, I better head out." She turned to leave, giving me a slight wave. "Those bloodsuckers are always hungry."

"Be safe!" I hollered back at her, meaning it.

I wanted to vent. I wanted to tell her how lonely I felt. How lost I was or even about how angry it made me that I wouldn't be going out today too, that I wasn't going to be driving my stake through as many cold hearts as I could, but I didn't. I watched her leave, knowing I had no plans to take her up on her offer. The only plan I had was trying to figure out a way to convince Todd this partner was better off without me, or with another team and that I was better off alone.

Chapter 3

I WASN'T BEING COMPLETELY honest. I did have another plan, though I wasn't overly willing to talk about it after the scolding I had just received from Todd. Without Alec here, I knew I was the only one who still felt off about the recent death of our head scientist. I didn't know her personally, never really wanting to dive too deep into the logistics of how things were being fixed on the back end, wanting much more to focus on fixing the things I could control.

The science lab appeared to be empty as I gazed through the small peephole window on the right-hand side of the door. I had run my badge through the reader twice, getting an angry red light each time indicating I was not permitted to enter. My nose pressed against the glass, my warm breath fogging the glass as I tried my best to see farther into the space.

"Are you looking for someone?" a soft voice asked behind me.

I turned to see Ruby standing behind me, juggling a lunch plate and a bag of chips with a soda can stuffed between her side and arm. Her almond hair was pulled back into a messy bun. Some of the strands had broken away, falling in careless waves around her face. Square glasses sat crookedly on her nose as she tried to scrunch her face and blow the hair from her vison. I didn't know her well, though I had seen her frequently because she was in a relationship with one of the security guards employed here.

Which was exactly why I needed to speak to her.

"You actually!" I smiled big, trying to seem more friendly than my reputation made me out to be. "Let me help you." I reached for her items before she could object, holding them for ransom.

She hesitated before walking past me and sliding her credentials, unlocking the door. I followed her in, depositing her items on a steel table as she walked to a desk cluttered with papers and pens, and a computer that sat dead centered, the screensaver bouncing back and forth from each corner. Other than the rest of the desks that seemed identical to the one Ruby stood by, the room was spotless. I walked over to the morgue freezers that lined the wall, peering around the corner to an empty cage, the cage where that vampire was before he attacked.

"Are you crazy?" Ruby shouted, as she snatched her food from where I had left it. "This is an autopsy table!" Her face turned five shades of green before she decided the chips were safe, but the sandwich that was on her plate was going to have to go. "You owe me a new lunch." She tried to sound fierce, but her tone came out soft, reminding me of a child's demand, and I had to suppress the smirk that threatened to pull up my lips. She dumped the food and turned back to me, hand placed solidly on her hip.

"I'm sorry, okay?" I pushed my lip out in a pout. "I'll

get you a new lunch, but I need a favor first," I said, diving into the real reason why I was here.

"That's rich," she said before sighing. "What is it?"

"You're dating Elias, right?" I asked, pretending like I didn't know. She raised her brow, clearly seeing my poor phishing attempt.

"Yes, what about it?" She frowned. "We already made sure it was okay!" she added quickly like I was the conflict of interest police.

"Oh, no, no." I waved my hands in front of me, realizing what she got nervous about. "I'm not implying it's a conflict thing or anything like that. I just meant I was wondering if you could get something for me." The words flew from my mouth and I looked over my shoulder like it was an illegal request. "A tape." I finished, looking back at her.

"A tape?" she asked, confused.

"Yeah," I replied simply, trying to pretend it was no big deal. "I just wanted to see the tape from that night."

"Couldn't you just ask for it?" she said, her look far away. I knew she was friends with the girl who died, and I felt bad for bringing it up, but I didn't know who else to ask since I wasn't exactly liked around here. I was either not liked for being too vocal or not liked for being Todd's niece. There wasn't a middle ground.

"I would, but…" I didn't know if I should tell her about me blocking Elias's path to be a hunter. It wasn't on purpose, not really. He had made a request to transfer to the facility and start training. I was asked if I thought he could cut it, and I answered honestly saying no. I had no way of knowing that my comment would block his path. I had more say then. Alec and I were a team everyone wanted to be around, and I guess they figured I would know better than anyone who was able to hunt. "I just don't think he would say yes to me," I admitted finally. Her eyes widened in acknowledgement. She must have heard about what happened. Maybe he told her that I ruined his dream.

"What do you think you'd find?" she said, surprising me.

"I'm not sure. I just want to see what happened," I replied, pleading with my eyes.

She looked away, sighing. I had no clue what she was thinking about, but I could see the emotions playing across her green eyes as she came to her decision. She brushed the hair from her face and pushed her glasses up higher on her nose. "All right," she said, the words hanging heavily in the air. "But it will probably take me a few days."

I nodded and thanked her, giving her a small wave when I left, hoping she didn't change her mind. I didn't know what I expected to see. I had no reason to suspect it was anything more than what it was, but a feeling still nagged at me, twisting my stomach in knots. To be so close to an end to this and have it slip through our fingers due to something as simple as negligence, I just couldn't come to terms with that.

I shoved on the heavy glass doors that led out of the ten-story building D.O.V.E. owned. The cool air was surprisingly fresh considering the condensity of the city. I filled my lungs before letting the door swing closed behind me, stepping out onto the sidewalk and into the quickly fading light. It would be dark soon and I needed to move before they started cracking down for curfew since I was supposed to be off for the night. The last thing I needed was Todd's goonies telling on me if I was forced to hunt.

A man who looked about my age, maybe a few years older, was to the right of me, examining our building. His face was scrunched up, eyebrows pulled tightly together, as he stared on. He looked like he was deciding if he should walk in or turn around and never look back. Probably a new recruit. I had seen that look on many faces throughout the years, people wondering if they really wanted to risk their lives to save others. It was a call to action most couldn't stomach.

"If you have to think about it, turn around." I offered unsolicited. He looked like he wanted to say something, his eyes shining against the last of the light of the day, but I had already turned to make my way home.

Parents ushered stubborn children into their homes, cutting off playtime and locking up tightly for the night as I walked down the street to Fifth Ave, toward the last convenience store before D.O.V. E.'s protection ended, where the Deserted started. A group of friends hollered out to a cab, trying to catch one of the last rides before transportation came to a grinding halt. The farther from D.O.V.E. I got, the more the environment changed, showing the safety net that D.O.V.E. provided getting thinner and thinner. Less of the houses were kept up, more having squatters than actual homeowners living in them, but they were still full of people who didn't dare venture out farther.

I preferred this part of the city. It wasn't so far out of the zone that I was concerned, but it was far enough away that it wasn't patrolled as regularly as the inner-city where there was a larger population, leaving me plenty of opportunity to hunt without Todd knowing—hunt off the record. I had made a vow to avenge the deaths of my parents and Alec, and I couldn't do that on the assignments I got from D.O.V.E. alone.

My building came into view, its deep gray stone contrasting against the chipping yellow paint. The corner streetlight was already buzzing with life even though the sun's rays still snuck through the buildings. At the bottom of the building was a little store, not quite connected to the building but close enough that it appeared to be a part of it. Mr. Becker, the owner, was dressed in beige slacks and a Hawaiian shirt. He stood at the door, desperately trying to get the metal gate to pull down, locking himself inside.

"I don't know why you don't hire help." I laughed as he startled slightly at my voice coming up behind him.

"Oh, honey, then I would have to share the profits." Mr. Becker didn't have to turn to know it was me. I snorted because we both knew he wasn't getting rich off this place. Sometimes I wondered if he kept it open solely for me because I never saw anyone else here.

"Tell you what, I'll help you close up, but you have to let me grab a few things first. Before you close out the register."

He scratched the gray five o'clock shadow that prickled his chin, the sound audible as he pretended to think it over. I smiled as he agreed like it was a hard decision and moved to walk under the half tugged down gate, only having to bend slightly at my five-foot-five height and pull it all the way to the ground. He handed me a padlock that I looped through the opening and knob in the floor, closing it with a click.

Mr. Becker walked with a slight limp, his back hunching further every year. Next to the register was a picture of him and his wife, Jolene, when they bought the store. The picture was in black and white, but you could still see them both smiling from ear to ear, her hanging on his shoulder with one hand and the other dangling keys for the photographer to see. I knew from talking to Mr. Becker that her hair was a dark shade of auburn, but in the picture those short curls looked like a deep black with a gray beret keeping the bangs from her eyes.

He rounded the corner and I made my way to the back where the refreshments were stacked neatly in a transparent doored fridge. I tucked two bottles of Coke into my elbow, pulling it close to my body to carry them as I walked farther back and retrieved a bottle of rum from the shelf. Balancing the items with ease, I headed back to the counter to deposit my things. Mr. Becker was removing his blue apron, folding it neatly to place next to the register like he did every day.

"You turned twenty-one?" He smiled at me. I was pretty sure he knew I wasn't, but he also never questioned the card I bought off of some high schoolers last spring when I tried to sneak into a bar. *Tried* being the key word since Alec caught me red-handed and any plan I had was foiled. It felt like every memory had him in it. Each thought that raced across my mind was accompanied by a painful pull in my chest and that simmering rage in my gut.

"You're walking home again?" He nodded to the window as the darkness rolled in like a creepy fog while stuffing my items into a brown paper bag.

"I can take care of myself. Besides, it's just around the corner," I reassured him.

"I know, but I still worry. You know I would walk you home. I am just—" He hesitated, so I finished the sentence for him.

"Old?" I pushed money toward him to pay for my things.

"I was going to say scared, but let's go with old...sounds better." He smiled and counted my money. Mr. Becker pushed back the excess change and slipped the rest into the register, which chimed when he opened it.

I grabbed the bag and walked toward the back door

that led into the alley to make my way back around to the front of the apartment.

"Don't forget your change!" Mr. Becker hollered at me.

"Don't forget to lock the back!" I hollered back, not returning for the extra money. This seemed to be our routine every few days. I envisioned him shaking his head the way he did and gathering the money to put away. As if on cue I heard that chime of the drawer closely followed by the sound of the door closing and the lock clicking into place.

I quickened my pace a little as the sun disappeared from the sky. I thought about what Todd had said, thought about Alec, those memories swirling around my head making my throat swell with unshed tears. I painfully swallowed them down, trying to push them to the deepest depths of my soul. I buzzed myself into the building. I didn't want to fight tonight.

I wanted to forget.

Chapter 4

My sunglasses did nothing to stop the fluorescent lights from waking up the drummer who had taken residency inside my skull, hammering out beats that made my stomach churn in protest. The night before I needed a little bit more numbing than I had expected. The idea of having to work with a partner reminded me of how much I missed Alec, and Alec reminded me of how much I missed my mom and dad. It was a vicious cycle of memories I both wanted to forget and yet remember at the same time.

I closed my eyes on the elevator ride up to the tenth floor, letting myself get lost in the lyric-less music that played on its ascent. The obnoxious ding that echoed through the metal death trap as I reached the correct floor made me want to turn around and call it a day, but it was too late. The stainless-steel doors opened, exposing me to the room and the workers buzzing around inside of it. I didn't know why seeing them running around, ushering assignments to their designated hunters, and completing their tasks made me so mad. Didn't they know this work was surrounded with death, and yet they laughed and greeted people like every time we went outside we weren't playing Russian roulette.

Can't turn back now.

The smell of coffee wafted through the air, tickling my senses, and for a moment I let myself think that today may not be *that* bad. I almost ran to the break room to pour a cup but settled for a brisk walk so I wouldn't draw any unwanted attention. On my way I passed through the office area, lined with cubicles and employees collaborating with other facilities, receiving and handing out assignments, all hard at work but in the safety the walls of D.O.V.E. provided.

The walls of the building were painted a bright, boring beige that I normally despised, but the color was oddly calming to my roaring stomach as I tried to not upchuck. Art lined the hall to the break room, pictures of shapes and colors with no particular thing standing out. It reminded me of the counseling session I was forced to attend after my parents died, the one Todd was convinced would be beneficial for my healing. The therapist showed me card after card of shapes and asked what I saw in each of them. I lied and would say a butterfly or tiger but really, they looked like nothing to me, nothing more than squiggly lines on top of each other. I didn't gain anything from going to the sessions. The healing I felt happened during training. I could let everything out when fighting, let go of all the pent-up emotions swirling inside of me.

I turned the corner, itching the spot I had just received my new dose of vaccine in, never really getting used to the routine. I got mine religiously. All hunters did since we were most at risk for getting bitten. I couldn't count how many times I had actually been bitten, probably enough to have to use both my hands. It was painful. The venom burned your skin, leaving it angry and red, but the pain didn't compare to the feeling of being too weak to avoid it for me.

The coffee was fresh. I grabbed a mug with the D.O.V.E. company logo on it; the name was spelled out, half on top, the other half on the bottom in basic print in a circular crescent moon. In the middle was a pair of fangs crossed out with an X and the bottom read *By the People, For the People* as a sort of mission statement, another add-on by Todd. I poured the caffeinated liquid into the cup, skipping the sweetener and cream, opting to keep it black. I clasped the mug with both hands, letting the warmth soak into my skin. The bitter drink coated my tongue, immediately easing my headache and shaking away some of the stiffness in my body from the lack of sleep. I never understood how people could have their coffee black when I was younger, but now I got it. I didn't think about anything other than how the drink tasted and that was a massive improvement from what usually swirled around in my head during the day.

Alec and I used to spend our breaks in here, hiding from Todd because I was always getting into trouble for one thing or another. The first time Alec placed his hand over mine in a way that was different than he had ever touched me before was in this room. My heart pattered all the way to my ears as I worried I was thinking into his touch more than I should. I had long had a crush on him, and in the typical student teacher way it wasn't appropriate, despite him only being four years older than me. It was the first time I felt like maybe he felt something more too.

A woman's high-pitched laugh made me wince, ripping me from my thoughts and bringing the musician back into my brain for an encore. I slowly peeked around the corner,

peering deeper into the break room, which was blocked off
by a wall. Two girls were sitting next to one another,
inhaling a box of mini, white-powdered doughnuts and
practically shooting the sugary goodness back out with their
cackling.

"Please tell me you saw her?" The girl was trying her
best to whisper, but it was not working. Her deep brown
hair was hacked off into a bob style cut that I could never
pull off, but somehow she made it look feminine. She wore
a pin skirt that was stretched too tightly around her body
matched with a red laced blouse. I recognized her as the
receptionist named Francine. "She's the *best* agent we
have?" She dragged out 'best' like it was some kind of joke.
I leaned in closer to try to hear her better. The girl next to
her laughed while combing slender fingers through her
shiny red hair.

"I honestly just think Todd takes pity on her because of
her parents. She is messed up in the head now." The
redhead finished her sentence by motioning finger circles
around the smooth skin of her temple. "There is no way
she's going to inherit this place, trust fund baby or not."

Francine shook her head frantically with approval, her
own fingers still clasped tightly around the doughnut,
pushing indents into the soft dough. She tried to break it
into smaller pieces, causing the crumbs to fall down onto
her skirt. The powder was easily visible against the black
fabric as she tried to brush the fallen pieces off but only
ended up blending the sugar in more apparent streaks.

"I know! And now her partner is dead…" Francine
trailed off to finish chewing her treat. "And everyone knows
she left him on purpose, because anyone as *good* as her
should have been able to save him. Less eye candy for us
now. Alec was so cute." They both sighed in unison.

Heat clawed up my chest and into my cheeks, bringing my skin to an uncomfortable temperature and though I couldn't see it, I was sure of the color too. At the mention of Alec's name, I saw red. I bit down on my tongue and yanked away from the wall just as someone was passing me, crashing into him, sending coffee and stacks of files flying everywhere.

"Do you have eyes?" I snapped, hearing the girls go quiet then chuckle while pinching my dark shirt and dragging it back and forth from my now sticky chest, trying to cool my burnt skin. I knew they couldn't see what had happened, but every laugh that exited their mouths felt like it was at my expense.

"Oh m-my God," the boy stuttered, his eyes searching for a way around me and this situation. "I didn't see you. I-I am really sorry." He knelt down, trying to recover his paperwork, which was now covered in coffee.

"Clearly." I sat my mug down and grabbed some napkins to pat myself dry. The boy shook off the liquid from his papers and stuffed them back into a yellow manila folder, drying his palms on his khakis.

"Hey, listen," I used the sweetest voice I could muster up. "Why don't you let me take those." I cut him off with a wave of my hand when he tried to resist. My thumb left a coffee print in the folder, a perfect maze of intricate circles as I grabbed them from his hands. "I mean look at them. There is coffee all over them. I can get them cleaned up and filed for you. I was a paper pusher once too, you know?" I forced out a smile. The boy looked uneasy but agreed as he made a beeline for any direction that wasn't mine.

Straightening the files against my arm, I waited until the boy was out of sight before rounding the corner of the wall blocking the girls from my view. I forcefully cleared my throat, causing Francine's friend to jump. She tried to quickly regain her composure by straightening out her blouse and picking off invisible lint. I walked closer to them, looking down as I towered over the table they were sitting around. Unease crept onto their faces, making me feel powerful. They should be worried.

I let the stack of files fall from my grasp, making a loud smacking noise against the wood of their table as they stayed centered. This time they both jumped as if I had personally attacked them. They moved deeper into their chairs as I slowly reached toward them, not breaking eye contact to even blink. I grabbed one of the doughnuts they were snacking on, still positioned between them, and popped it into my mouth, licking the powdered sugar off my lips as I chewed.

"These are for you two." I drew back slightly, my words coming out muffled but discernible as I finished chewing the dessert. "Complete them by the end of your shift, or work into the night. I'd be more than *happy* to escort you home since it would be past curfew. They need to be cleaned and filed appropriately."

"What? No! Those are not ours!" the redhead spoke up, gaining confidence.

"Hmm…" I posed as if I was thinking, tapping my finger against my chin. "That's weird. They are sitting right in-between you. I have told you to complete them. It seems like that would make them yours." I reach forward, grabbing another doughnut. "Hurry on now. Todd's orders," I added just in case they wanted to argue more, knowing they didn't know I was lying and that my power over them really was limited for a couple more years.

"Come on, Lindsey." Francine insisted, grabbing the files and motioning for her friend to follow.

"Yeah, you're right. If we stick around any longer, we'd probably end up like Alec too," she muttered under her breath before following, but I heard every word. "Oh, and by the way, looks like you had a spill."

I KNOCKED ROUGHLY on Todd's office door, taking my frustration out on the heavy wood rather than pummeling either of those girls' faces, which I'd much rather do. I knocked again with force that stung my knuckles and when I didn't hear a response, I entered without waiting. I wasn't in the mood to be put on hold. Voices quickly stopped talking as I walked into the room.

"Samantha, I was in a meeting." Todd was clearly not impressed that I barged in.

"Sammy." I corrected, not bothering to apologize for interrupting. I rubbed the sting out of my hand.

"This is Gray. As we discussed he will be working alongside you for your upcoming assignments. He has just graduated from our facility in Arizona."

I rolled my eyes at Todd's attempt at avoiding the word partner.

Gray stood up, turning to face me. He was a tall man with dark brown hair that was cut and styled short. He didn't appear to be overly muscular but didn't look out of shape either as his grid styled button-up hugged the curve of his arms. His features were sharp, but big hazel eyes softened his face and accompanied a smile that gave him a much gentler look. Gray offered his hand out to me, but I made no move to take it. This man wouldn't last a second in the field and I just needed the chance to tell Todd that.

"I'm Gray." He lowered his hand and flashed a bigger smile instead. "I feel sorry for that door." He nodded to the hand I was still rubbing. I stopped, pulling my hand down, not returning his smile.

"Yeah, that was established," I spoke stiffly. I wanted to discourage him as much as I was going to try to convince Todd this was a bad idea. Something seemed to click in my brain. "Weren't you standing out front of this place yesterday?"

"You're the girl from yesterday?" Gray chuckled softly.

"Should have taken my advice and turned around," I said, causing him to stop laughing. His thick eyebrows pulled together, studying me, hopefully to rethink working together. I'm sure I was more than he wanted to handle, and I planned to keep it that way. If no one wanted to work with me, Todd would have to let me go out alone, right?

Todd cleared his throat at the tension, and it was all I could do to not roll my eyes at him. I wanted to be back in the field. I needed to be so I could muffle the emotions that became harder and harder to suppress with nothing else to take my mind off them. However, doing that with someone else around made it harder because I would have to focus on them not getting hurt the whole time too.

"You might have spilled something on your shirt," Gray suggested.

The heat returned to my face because I knew the whole front of the very white shirt, which I should have known not to wear being that it wasn't my normal black wardrobe, was covered in an obvious coffee stain. I needed to make it a point to start doing laundry more often.

"Oh, well, would you look at that." I shot him a look, not trying in the least to be friendly.

"Sam, how about you get suited up and I will send you the coordinates for a tagged. You can get Gray some supplies as well, maybe show him around and get acquainted," he said.

"*A tagged?*" I asked, annoyed that he was still limiting my jobs. I was much better than one vampire. I wanted more.

He shot me his parental look and as much as I wanted to push it, he was probably right. I decided that trying to convince Todd not to make me go through with this right now probably was not going to help my case. I would go along with this for today because I was sure that after this assignment Gray would be running out the door if his hesitation yesterday was any indication of his willingness to be here. I didn't say anything more to Todd as I motioned to Gray on my way out of the office, assuming, unfortunately, that he would follow me regardless. I made my way to the elevator with him at my heels.

"So, everyone says you're one of the best hunters here. I'm truly honored to be working with you." As he spoke his words hit every nerve in my body, sending painful shocks up my spine. If I was the best Alec would be alive and I wouldn't be alone. I pummeled the elevator key until I was sure whoever tried to call it next would find it broken. Finally, the doors silently slid open. As we stepped in Gray tried at conversation again. "You know, with you as my partner—"

"Whoa, wait a second." I turned, stopping him from following me into the elevator, the doors closing slightly then banging back open, sensing that people were still in the way. "I don't know who you have been talking to, but I'm not the best and let's get something straight, we're not partners." My voice was cold even to me. "I'm only here to make sure you don't get killed out there as you learn the ropes. These things are not pets, they are *real* monsters, ones that kill every day. So, while you are doing whatever it is you're supposed to be doing, I'll be doing the real service and taking out as many as possible to save what's left of the human race."

Gray didn't miss a beat and pushed past me. I followed, hitting the basement key, allowing the doors to finally shut. "Well, who knows when you might need some help then." Out of the corner of my eye I saw him smiling.

I laughed a fake laugh out loud as the elevator started moving to a lower floor.

"Listen, you look a little too pretty to know anything about fighting, let alone vampire hunting," I said. "There's more that goes into this than you think. I don't know what they taught you over there, but this is real. It's the big leagues now and there is no going back. Once you're out there, that's it."

He lifted his eyebrow, ignoring most of what I said. "You think I'm pretty?"

The elevator doors chimed, then opened, saving me from showing the heat that refused to leave my face today. I counted my breaths; it was going to be extremely difficult to not purposely let him get eaten.

The walls of the basement were painted a dull gray, resembling concrete, with no accents or decor. There were no doors other than the elevator and one that led to an emergency staircase. The high shelves could put a library to shame, though these shelves didn't house books. I walked up to a rack that had over a hundred different utility belts and grabbed one similar to the one I wore and tossed it at Gray. He was examining the room and startled when the belt hit him in the chest, barely grabbing it before it fell to the ground.

"What was that for?" He hugged it closely, faking a hurt look.

"You're going to need something to put weapons in. I can't babysit you the whole time and I would hate to have to kill you for turning into one of them," I said, moving on to find him something he could change into because the slacks and button-up shirt he was wearing would not cut it.

He didn't have a smart retort and I decided to count my blessings as I grabbed a stake off the wall and handed it to him. He eyeballed the weapon like a foreign object, rolling it awkwardly in his hand before placing it and the belt on the table next to him. I went back to work, grabbing everything I could imagine he'd need, wondering what exactly he had learned when it came to hunting. I was definitely going to have to talk to Todd about it. I deposited a handful of items onto the table next to his belt; he was slowly becoming a mule with everything I grabbed for him, but I wanted to make sure he would have a fighting chance in case I couldn't get to him in time.

"This is a basic issue phone," I said, holding it up to him. "Keep it on you at all times, and do you see this button?" I pointed to a little raised section on the side. "Press this repeatedly, at least three times to send a distress signal."

He shook his head and took it from me.

I started building his belt, adding a gun with some silver bullets already loaded in it. The silver wouldn't kill a vampire, but it would stun it enough for me to jump in if he needed saving. Gray was watching me intently, and I didn't like it. It made me feel like he was taking some of those research notes on me. I moved uneasily through the aisles of weapons, making my way to a table map that would have the location of our next targets—I inwardly groaned and corrected myself—target. The green grid flickered slightly, but I could clearly see the vampire was located in a sewage drain just southeast of an old elementary school.

"Hey?" Gray tapped me on my shoulder, which almost made me jump out of my skin. I was not used to having anyone around me.

"What the hell are you doing?" I yelled. "Don't you know it's not okay to sneak up on people like that?"

"Sorry, I called for you a few times, but you were really focused." He seemed amused, but it faded slightly. "Do I really need to carry this thing?" He displayed the belt.

"Have you ever dealt with one of these things?" I let the words drip from my mouth like poison. "These abominations won't give two shits about the fact that you're new. They're not going to go easy on you. They will kill you. So yes, I would recommend having all you can carry."

He seemed to consider this. "They used to be human, just like you, ya know?"

The idea made me sick, more than aware of the fact, but it didn't change that I had seen exactly what they could do on more than one occasion. This wasn't some undomesticated pet we could bring inside and nurture until it loved us, these were heartless creatures that only knew they needed to feed. I didn't know a single real human who looked like one of these things and decided blood was more nutritious than food.

"Listen, if you want to be a blood sucking monster be my guest, go talk to them, but don't be surprised when it's me driving a stake through your heart next," I snapped, forcing myself not to feel guilty overreacting so sharply toward the new guy. I couldn't afford to rose-color this for him.

Gray flinched, his lightly tanned skin wrinkling around his eyes, but decided against responding, which I thought was the best thing he had done all day. I grabbed a strap that I clicked around my thigh, sliding a small .380 into the holster. I didn't normally use guns but always had one on me. I preferred the close combat a stake allowed. I wanted to be near every time I took one of these things out.

"Take it easy on the newbie." Alana's husky voice carried from the door.

"Just being realistic." I defended myself. Alana walked to us, introducing herself to Gray with a strong handshake.

"She's normally not this cranky. Has she had her coffee yet?" She laughed when she turned and saw the coffee spill on my shirt. "Well there, that explains it!"

"Oh, laugh it up!" I said, not truly angry.

"Only one tagged, huh?" Alana asked, looking at the grid. "Did you let Todd hear it? Who am I kidding, of course you did." She laughed, knowing me well. "Maybe you'll get lucky and it'll be some tagless." She encouraged me. Alana had the same resolve I did and was her happiest after a big hunt night.

"No, not really." Her brows rose with the admittance, but she let me continue. "Figured it made sense having a recruit with me to accept a small job."

"A recruit by choice?"

I shot her a look that said *of course not.*

"Well, it's a quiet night, so he will probably be fine." She winked at him, earning her a big smile in return.

"All right." I cut the conversation off, not needing to see the flirting Alana was known for today. "We're gonna get changed and head out. Happy hunting!"

I led Gray back toward the elevator and watched as he clipped the belt around his waist. As we waited for the doors to open, I wondered if I was too harsh to him. I thought about apologizing, knowing it was the right thing to do, but decided against it. I pressed the button as we stepped inside and prayed he was smart enough to stay out of the way so he wouldn't get hurt like everyone else did, especially around me.

Chapter 5

NIGHT WAS MOVING IN QUICKLY, giving the city an eerie feel. We broke through into the Deserted in record time. The yellow streetlamps still shone bright, illuminating the trash that littered the pothole filled street. I looked up at the sky. The stars were impossible to see with the thick clouds and the little light that still tickled the horizon. Gray was in newly issued combat boots and the same black cargo pants most of the men wore. I opted for my trusty black jeans matched with a tank and boot of the same color. I fought better in comfortable clothes.

We needed to get a move on before the sky fully darkened, and the tagged vampire decided to go out for a meal, or we would be chasing it all over the Deserted. Wind whipped my ponytail back and forth. I tried to flatten the stray hairs being pulled from the elastic with my palm, but they only came undone again with the breeze. Gray stepped closer to me, sending goose bumps up the back of my arms. It was difficult getting used to having someone with me again, my body acutely aware of his presence.

I lifted the heavy, rusted sewage drain cover in the middle of what I imagined used to be a nice, quiet neighborhood. I frequently daydreamed of how it was before the vampires, absorbing any story someone would share of the time like a child listening to their grandparent reminisce. How nice it must have been to live with such blissful ignorance, not having to worry about being mauled and drained by a beast that may have been your neighbor a week prior.

"All right, I am going to drop down into the drain and make sure everything is clear. *Do not* drop down until you hear me alert you, are we understood?" I used my serious voice on Gray as he tried to hide the smile that played at the corners of his lips.

"Aye, aye, captain!" Gray stood straight and saluted me, forcing me to grit my teeth so I wouldn't tear into him and alert the vampire of our presence before we wanted it to know.

The ladder down was rusted, pieces of the metal missing and other parts not looking remotely durable, so I quietly lowered myself into the sewer by my arms, only letting go after straightening out my body, hovering just above the ground. You could barely hear my feet splash in the inch of rainwater that drained from the city's recent storm. I glanced around, trying to make out my surroundings. The tunnel was long and narrow. I couldn't see anything besides yellow emergency lights that illuminated a small area every ten feet or so. The humidity down here was heavier, weaving into the sulfurous stench of the stagnant water and clinging to my skin.

I went to walk forward, but the audible splash behind me stopped me in my tracks. I whipped around, pulling my stake out simultaneously, and grabbed the intruder, shoving them to the side into the cold brick so their face was pressed up against the scratchy stone. I pulled their arm behind their back and twisted it into a breaking position, then shoved the point of my weapon against the center of their back.

"Owe, hey, quit that!" Gray yelled and squirmed until I released him. He straightened out his shirt as he backed up from me. "Are you crazy?"

"*Am I crazy?*" I scoffed at him. "You could have just got us killed!" I was whispering, but it still came out more like a yell. I started walking toward him, my feet splashing in the water. "I told you to *wait!*"

He put his hands up in a protective gesture. "Hey, listen, I'm sorry, okay? I'll listen next time, cross my heart." By this time his back was pressed against the dirty tunnel wall and I was in his face as he drew an imaginary line across his chest.

"If you want to die, that's on you, but don't get me killed in the process!" I turned around and slowly made my way down the tunnel, not beckoning him to follow, knowing he would regardless. Gray was beyond frustrating, seeming to know how to *irk* every nerve I had, but secretly I was petrified of having to worry about someone else again. I didn't want him to get hurt. I really didn't want anyone to.

"You know," he started, as he quietly caught back up to me, only hesitating for a moment before falling into step with my stride. "You're kind of scary when you're mad."

I decided not to reply and instead checked around corners that turned into dead ends with iron bars that allowed the water to continue flowing through them. The tunnel seemed to go on forever, but I still couldn't find a place the vampire would choose to hide. There was no way we missed it on its way out, especially not with the amount of noise Gray seemed to make naturally.

I pulled a pocket-sized beacon out of my belt and checked for the red dot indicating the location of the vampire. The screen only showed a green grid that flashed, no indication the tagged even existed although I was sure being underground was distorting the signal. I ran my hand along the wall to guide my way to each light. I only wanted to use my flashlight if it was necessary, not wanting to draw more attention than needed to our arrival. I checked my fingers for any sign of blood under each lamp. Vampires were messy eaters and would definitely leave a trail.

"It doesn't look like anything is here." Gray sounded like he was trying to convince me so we could get out of this hell hole. "Maybe they moved?"

"There's only supposed to be one. When they're tagged, we watch them for at least a few days, seeing where they travel and how long they stay in certain areas. We make sure this is where they spend their days and pinpoint when they start to leave. It's not that this tunnel is empty; it's that we don't know it. It's not mapped out. If we are unlucky this place could come to life quicker than we want it to. Let's just hope we get to it before it figures out that we're here."

"What if they are intelligent and know how to evade all your tactics?"

I couldn't tell if Gray was being serious or if he was just being a smartass. After tossing it over, I was considering the latter, but I was also surprised that nothing was standing out like normal nests. The sewer was dirty considering what it was, but it didn't look used from the perspective of a hunter.

"Intelligent? Don't make me laugh! We have a whole department dedicated to finding stuff like that out and I have been doing this long enough to know how they behave. They are vicious killers, but they're no different than a rabid animal. They have a desire that they want filled and that's all they're looking to get done. When it comes to their intelligence, they have none—" Just as the words left my mouth my hand hit something in the wall. It was a little abnormal dent, small enough that it would have easily been missed unless someone knew it was there. I tried to look closer, but the next emergency lamp was still a few feet away. "There's something here, but I can't see anything."

Suddenly light illuminated a hidden door. My finger had trailed across a superficial lump where the door pressed into the wall. I looked back toward the light source to find a very happy Gray. The crack was almost impossible to see even with the extra help, so I ran my finger over it a few more times to get a better feel for its exact location.

"Seems like you needed me after all." He beamed.

I took a deep, steadying breath and reached down to feel my belt, quickly realizing the flashlight I had was now gone from my waist and pointed toward the hidden door. I hadn't even felt him remove it from my belt.

"You couldn't have used yours?" I asked incredulously, shooting a look over my shoulder, trying to not be blinded by the incandescent bulb.

"Yours was closer."

I couldn't see his face but imagined he was wiggling his eyebrows suggestively just to annoy me.

I briefly envisioned strangling him but reminded myself I needed to keep him safe, otherwise I would add to my already guilty conscience. I took a few more breaths to force my annoyance down then pressed against the wall and heard a small exhale of air. Slowly the door clicked and popped open, startling me back into Gray. He used one hand to steady me and leaned in, depositing my flashlight back into its rightful place. Even through the rancid sewer smell I could catch a hint of mint from his shirt.

"This doesn't mean they are smart," I snapped, pulling quickly from his grasp. "Clearly this was used as some type of bunker. Probably another government lie."

Gray snickered behind me and I had to refrain myself from shoving him through the door so he could encounter whatever it was on the other side first. I pushed on what I had originally thought was a wall and it opened farther. Carefully I stepped through, holding my hand back to Gray, motioning for him to stay put as I walked in. The door closed behind me with the same sound as when it opened.

"You have got to be freaking kidding me!" I turned to see Gray standing right behind me looking extremely guilty, already putting his hands up defensively like I was going to attack him.

Lights flickered once, and then twice before brightening the space we stood in. The room was large and looked relatively clean despite having the same dirty brick walls that lined the tunnel outside. It was packed with furniture that looked at least fifty years old. Everything was covered in cobwebs and dust. A desk was catty-cornered with a wall, a matching chair lazily pushed into it. The grime appeared to be disturbed there, but it was hard to know if it was human, vampire, or just the vermin that frequented the area.

There was another door at the back. It was metal, with a rectangular peeking window positioned vertically. I walked toward it and tried the knob. Locked. I didn't have a pick for the lock on me, so I used my forearms to brush through the dirt to see if there was anything on the other side.

"What is this place?" I said rhetorically.

"Looks to be a room. Look, there is even a door!" Gray said flatly. I turned back to him; this time fully intent on punching him as I stomped his way. I had enough of his sarcasm. If he didn't want to be here, he could have helped me plead a case to Todd. Where was his voice then?

The sound of a deadbolt clicking stopped me.

Gray launched at me.

I stepped back, prepared to fight him but something else grabbed a hold of my arm, squeezing it until the blood stopped flowing. Gray crashed into whoever had a grip on me, ripping me back. We all fell into a heap on the floor and I was the first to catch my bearings. I jumped up and looked down, my mind quickly calculating my next move. I could see Gray struggling to roll on top of the vampire that held him down. I needed to intervene before Gray ended up dead.

Using my right foot, I kicked the vampire in the ribs as hard as I could. He grunted as a crack rang out and rolled off of Gray, who maneuvered to the side, trying to get up.

"Are you all right?" I called to him.

I tried to regroup, noticing his lack of an answer, but just as quickly as the vampire was off Gray, he was coming at me. I reached for my stake, but the bloodsucker was faster. He grabbed my hand and shoved it back into my utility belt, hard. It easily ripped through the holster, the tip of the stake sliding into my thigh as I cried out in pain.

My natural reflexes disobeyed my strict training as I reached for the stake that was now lodged in the tender flesh of my leg. The vampire's hand shot out and connected with my cheek hard enough to push me backward into the door we had just come through. I lost sight of him, seeing stars as my head bounced off the door. I faintly heard a gun being cocked before it was fired, the loud echo making my teeth rattle.

The vampire cried out and turned from me. I tried to move forward, but I couldn't seem to get my feet to work the way my brain was thinking and swayed, sprawling back into the door. The latch triggered, sending the door flying open, and without the support my body tumbled out of the room and back into the cold, dirty sewer water. The freezing liquid seeped into my clothes, the smell burning my nostrils. I struggled to catch my bearings enough to stand back up, falling once, then twice until my world stopped shifting. Finally, I stood on shaky legs to see Gray standing there, by himself.

"Are you okay?" he asked, racing toward me. He tried to reach for me, but adrenaline still had me in fight mode.

I pushed him forcefully, wanting everyone and everything to keep their distance from me as I surveyed the scene. He stumbled back but kept his balance. He didn't approach me again as a worried look plastered across his face. I looked down at my leg. Beautifully carved wood protruded from my skin. I reached down and grasped the handle, biting my lip in anticipation.

Breathe. One. Two...

"Wait!" Gray yelled, panicked. "Don't you think we should go to a doctor?"

I ignored him and pulled. Pain rippled through my leg, but I kept my face blank. Once it was out, I took it out of the now ripped holster, placing it handle first into my back pocket for easy access and safekeeping.

"We should wrap that." Gray tried again. "So you don't lose too much blood." A weird look crept up his face as he stared at my injury, unable to peel his eyes away.

"It's just water," I lied. He was probably right, but at the moment I wasn't overly concerned with that. "I didn't know you had it in you. I'm impressed."

"Had what in me?" Gray asked.

"The vampire. I can't believe you actually killed it. I thought for sure you were a goner." I laughed a little to mask the pain I was in.

"I didn't kill it," he said.

I froze. If he didn't kill it where was it? And why wasn't it coming for us?

"What do you mean you didn't kill it? Where is it then?" I was going back into defense mode, checking our surroundings to see if we were being stalked.

"When I shot it, it took off," he said.

"No—no, no, no. That's not how it works. They don't run because they're wounded. That never stops them," I said.

"Well, when you let him hit you—" Gray began. The blood drained from my face and anger clouded my features.

"Let's get something straight, I didn't allow it to get close to me. *You*"—I poked him in the chest—"this is *your* fault! You are a distraction and it caught me off guard. This never would have happened if you weren't here!"

Something was definitely off here. This had never happened before, but he was right, the sewer was quiet and even as I pressed the door to check the room again the only sign that our vampire was even there to begin with was the foot marks in the dirt and the single shell casing still smoking on the floor.

"Well, you're supposed to be the best." He followed behind me as I searched. Gray was seconds away from me drowning him in the foot of water we stood in.

"That still doesn't explain why you're standing here, *alive*." Vampires didn't just stop.

Gray considered what I said and shrugged. "He didn't attack me after I shot him."

"*It.*" I corrected through my teeth. "Why the hell did it attack me then?"

"Maybe it didn't like your tone?" This was not the time for him to be sarcastic. I couldn't come back with a rebuttal; my adrenaline was dying down, making my leg pulse with pain.

"None of this makes sense," I said more for me than to Gray as I started limping back into the room. First thing tomorrow I was going to be riding solo again, but right now I was more curious about what had just happened.

I went back to the door, which was now unlocked. He had definitely come through here. I pushed it open and peered into an even darker corridor. I stepped one leg through into the abyss and my world swayed. I reached out to grab onto anything but came up short. My body seemed so heavy, gravity taking advantage and pulling me down quicker than I could shove my hands out. I prepared for the ground, but it never came.

"Whoa!" Gray shouted as he gripped my waist, stopping my fall. "Come here."

He pulled me back, letting the door crash closed. I sat on the ground, it being the only thing that was reassuring me I wasn't actually spinning. I shivered and knew I needed to get out of here and into clean clothes before I ended up sick, giving Todd another reason to sideline me. My eyes settled, so I tried to stand back up but was met with Gray's hand.

"I don't think that's a good idea," he said.

"I'm fine," I argued, pushing against him and standing up. My world was still wobbling, but I looked him dead in the face anyway.

"You almost fainted, but you're *fine?*" he asked, obviously not believing me.

"Fainted?" The word made me draw back. "I do not faint. I am not a damsel, nor am I weak."

"That's not what I meant. I just mean you could have a concussion or something. Plus, I know for a fact that isn't just water on your pants. You're bleeding badly," he said, genuinely concerned as he lost the sarcastic look that usually resided on his face. I couldn't help but admire Gray with his thick, furrowed eyebrows, admittedly making him look cute even in the limited light.

Wow.

Maybe I was losing too much blood. I looked down at my wound but couldn't see much. My black jeans were soaked, but the warmth coursing down my thigh confirmed he was right. I didn't really think it was bad, but it still needed a good cleaning and to be closed so it didn't get infected. Gray pulled a blade out from his pocket and stalked toward me, his features serious as he concentrated.

"What do you think you're doing?" I grabbed his hand as he went to steady my leg, freezing his motion.

"We need to see how bad it is." He tried again.

"Listen." I stopped him and moved away, heading back in the direction we came in from. "Thanks, but no thanks. I agree I need to get out of here, and I'll get it checked out but please don't touch me."

My blood pulsed with the desire to keep going, to chase after the vampire and finish what we had started, but I knew I needed to get my injury looked at, even if admitting it soured my mouth. I couldn't risk an infection taking me out of the field, forcing me to be alone with my thoughts without distraction.

"Well, suit yourself then." I heard him mutter under his

breath as my feet splashed heavily in the water. With every step the pain radiated up my thigh, spreading throughout my hip. I did my best not to limp, but it was difficult as the throbbing increased and my leg began to feel heavier.

We reached the opening that led up to the now very cold, dark street. I looked around for something we could use to hoist ourselves up but came up empty-handed. What little bit of the ladder that was left now lay in the water at our feet, probably falling as Gray entered without permission before.

"Lift me up." I didn't ask Gray, just waited for him to follow my directions. "Then I'll pull you up." I was surprised when he didn't argue, though he still used the opportunity to sigh, drawing a glance from me.

He intertwined his hands together and motioned for me to step on them so he could push me. I used my uninjured leg to step into his palms, ignoring the pulsing as the other leg tried to hold my weight, and reached for the road. My arms were weak as I pulled myself up and I lost my grip. I yelped as I went back down, expecting to kiss the hard ground once again, but Gray's arms caught me easily. Somehow my stomach rested against his chest, which was much harder than I had expected it to be with his grip at my legs. The ache in my thigh was hardly noticeable with the embarrassment rapidly growing in my belly.

"You okay?" he asked in a throaty voice.

"Y-yeah." I had rested my hands at the tops of his shoulders and upon noticing ripped them back like I had been burned. "Let's go again." I cleared my voice.

He heaved me up once more and I dug my fingers into the asphalt, not willing to repeat what had just happened, and pulled myself out. I took a moment to lie on the gravel and catch my breath. Everything was immediately a little better as I inhaled fresh air, calming me.

"All right," I shouted down even though I was sure he could hear me if I talked at a normal octave, "take my hand!"

"Are you sure you can pull me up?" I could only see the part of his face that was illuminated by the moonlight. The blue hue turned his eyes black with no light to bounce off the flecks of color I knew were there, but that same expression curled the corners of his lips.

"Well, I could always just leave you there and pretend I tried." The idea was oddly intriguing as I thought it over before he cleared his voice to remind me he was still there waiting.

I reached my hand down and waited until I felt his fingertips brush mine as he jumped. With my stomach flat on the asphalt, I used my left hand to brace myself against his weight. We locked hands and I pulled as much as I could. He reached his hand out and gripped the street, pulling himself up the rest of the way.

"Thanks," he said, sitting on the street with his legs still hanging through the opening.

"Did you hit it?" I asked, not being able to get the thought out of my mind.

"The vampire?" he questioned, but I was sure he already knew what I meant. "Yeah, in the back. I was just trying to make sure it didn't kill you." Gray explained it like I was questioning why he would shoot at all.

"They don't flee." I pressed again, but all I got was a shrug.

He seemed to be looking off into the distance, taking in the surrounding area, which was exactly what hunters were trained to do. I got up and started toward the Protected after waiting for Gray to get up and follow me. I made sure to keep my back to him so he couldn't see the way my face contorted with each step. As soon as we reached the line, I could see taggers scouting the rooftops and knew hunters were near. By how relaxed they looked, it had definitely been a much less eventful night for them. I threw a wave up, not knowing who was waving back but smiling when they did. I wasn't close to any of the field workers anymore, but I knew they would still have my back if I ever needed them.

"You can make it home from here, right?" I asked Gray.

"But don't we need—" He began.

I didn't let him finish, already walking away, heading for home. It took everything out of me to not limp. Every step was fire, burning my limb from the inside out, but I didn't want to show how weak I knew I was. The very thought of it taunted me, reminding me why I didn't have my partner...why I didn't have my Alec.

I definitely didn't want to go back to work tomorrow. Being responsible for someone else brought me to a place I never wanted to be again. Even coupled with his sarcasm, immaturity and the fact that I occasionally felt like pummeling him, I didn't want him to get hurt because of me.

I hurried through the empty streets. The temperature had dropped significantly, freezing my nose and making it run as I crossed my arms to try and retain the heat that escaped through my wet clothes. I kept replaying the night's events in my mind. Where did the vampire go? I had never seen them run, always opting to fight to the death. They had never shown mercy in a fight, never returned someone once they decided they were their meal...

I forced my mind away from the poisonous thoughts of

the past—of my past—and back to the present. My apartment building loomed over me as I walked up the steps and punched in the code to open the door. The long journey up the staircase to the second floor, one-bedroom apartment felt like a walk through the Sahara, every step making you wish it were your last.

I unlocked the door and walked in, releasing my belt with a *click* and placing it and my keys on the small table next to the door. A bottle of a clear alcohol I could never get used to was on top of the fridge. I reached for it, ignoring the way the movement pulled at my injury, and cursed to no one for being shorter than I needed to be. With one last jump I caught the neck and pulled it down. Limping to the bathroom, I watched as droplets of blood soaked into my carpet. The light was brighter than I anticipated. It illuminated the dreary white walls, making me squint while my eyes adjusted. I caught my reflection in the mirror. I looked tired and worn down. Little pieces of blond hair were pulled loose from my ponytail, framing my face in ringlet curls that only occurred after a long day of work. I looked hard, trying to find any part of who I used to be in my reflection, but like always, I came up short.

I turned from the mirror and slowly peeled my jeans off, clenching my teeth when they became snagged on the dried blood around the hole in my thigh. Although it was painful it wasn't nearly as deep as it could have been. Nothing some stitches couldn't fix. I grabbed the first-aid kit from under the crowded sink, preparing to practice my sewing skills once again.

I opened the bottle and took a painful chug before pouring the rest onto the open wound. It ignited a fire in my leg than slowly grew steadily before it succumbed to a deep throbbing. I used a nearby washcloth to put pressure on the cut, sinking to the floor and pressing my back against the shower door. Blood seeped through the cheap cotton, spreading like disease on a map, pulling me into a place I didn't want to ever see again. My mind drifted away like a dream, leaving a familiar image.

My mother's beautiful, laughing face as she watched my dad fan away the flames from a stir-fry she had attempted to make. She was an awful cook, really. If my dad hadn't taken up most of the cooking, we would have probably starved. I remembered he laughed a deep belly chuckle as she hid her face like she was embarrassed. When they embraced each other all you saw was true love. That was the last happy memory I had of them. After that every memory was covered in blood.

I shook my head like it would change the fact that my stomach was in my throat and I might vomit. I cleaned off my wound and pulled the needle and small forceps from the kit. Threading the needle and holding it with the surgical tool, I shoved the clean end of the cloth into my mouth and pushed the needle down into my skin, biting down into the cotton to keep from screaming. Each suture seemed harder than the last, but I followed through, sweat dripping from my face when I finally finished. I wrapped the area with gauze and set my bloody tools on the floor next to me. The slow, steady ache of my heart became a soft rhythm that dragged my eyes back down. Before long I found my head resting against the wall, giving up and letting sleep take over.

Chapter 6

"HE IS IRRESPONSIBLE, disobedient, and completely untrained." I was out of breath and starting to wheeze by the time I had gotten all my complaints about Gray out. "I can't pull his weight."

I had spent the better part of the afternoon in Todd's office going through the list of reasons why Gray was unfit to be a partner and why it was better for me to work alone. Todd stared at me, not interrupting as I yelled about all the reasons I had meticulously rehearsed on my walk here. He patiently intertwined his fingers and kept perfectly still, listening. I even resorted to limping at times for dramatic effect. I mean, yeah, my leg still hurt, but I had been through much worse than that and normally wouldn't have showcased the discomfort.

"So," Todd began once I had slammed my hands on his desk, the sound echoing throughout the office, "it sounds like you let him catch you off guard, and with consequence, you were not prepared for the attack."

"Have you been listening to anything I've said?" I growled.

Todd seemed to have his 'I don't want to hear it' attitude in full effect today, being grumpier than normal. He probably thought this was my whole plan from the beginning, which I mean, I wasn't thrilled about having a partner, and it was my plan to fly solo, but I didn't plan on getting stabbed in the leg or have a vampire ghost me.

"He disobeyed direct orders that would have kept us both a lot safer and kept the enemy from fleeing." I added the part about the vampire fleeing with purpose. I wanted to see if Todd thought that was as strange as I did. I studied his face for a change, but it didn't look like he gave it another thought.

"It sounds like you guys are just out of sync. This is brand-new for both of you. Plus, from what I understand about Gray, he is renowned for being one of the best in his class. Just like you, he may have an issue submitting to orders after so much success," he said.

"What are they teaching in that state if he's considered the top of his class? And what about my leg?" I gestured toward the wound that was hidden under my pants.

"You and I both know you have endured much worse than that," he said blandly, and I couldn't be sure, but I thought he added an eye roll.

"Okay, what about the vampire fleeing? Have you ever heard of that?" I tried again, pressing him.

He seemed to think this over before letting out a long breath to answer. "No, it is strange. You did say it was group less, right? Maybe they're adapting. They are just like wild animals and wild animals without a pack tend to flee when the odds aren't in their favor," he explained casually.

"What fracking documentary did you watch that gave you that information?"

Todd shot me another look, so I mouthed out a sorry.

I had to admit he made a good point. Maybe I was forgetting that any species had the ability to evolve and even if I thought they were nothing more than monsters it didn't mean they couldn't become smarter to try to preserve themselves. The problem was we weren't training field agents to expect them to do anything other than attack. D.O.V.E. was established just after they crawled out of that government hole where they were hiding. All of our information was based off of what we could gather from confiscated government reports and field experience.

"Still you have to agree that it is dangerous taking him back out into the field after yesterday." I pressed on. "He needs more training, more experience, otherwise we might not get so lucky."

"That is something I agree with, but I have the solution." He threw up his index finger in an *"aha!"* moment. "I think a visit to our training site together would be extremely beneficial. Maybe you could teach him a few things. Take a week or so and piece together the things he's missing and get back to work. We need you and everyone we can get out there." I knew Todd well enough to know he was just trying to stroke my ego.

It worked.

"Fine. But let's be clear, I do not like this." I pointed an aggravated finger at him before turning on my heel to leave his office, knowing it was either do this or don't hunt at all for only 'Todd' knew how long.

As luck would have it, I found my nose pressed painfully into a steel chest. A chest that smelled slightly like mint and...pine? That same chest rumbled out the most annoying chuckle I had ever heard. A chest I wanted to drive my fist through. Gray's chest.

"In a hurry to leave with me?" he joked.

I wasn't laughing, even less now that I was the last to find out about this little escapade. Clearly, I had been conspired against and I took the bait without hesitation.

"Don't flatter yourself," I barked, squinting my eyes at him.

"Someone woke up on the wrong side of the bed. I am assuming that your clean shirt means you haven't had your coffee yet."

Todd laughed behind me as I conjured up the meanest look I could to shoot back in his direction too. Somehow, I had ended up between aggravating Gray and bothersome Todd, neither seeming to be on my side about anything.

"How's your leg?" Gray asked, getting serious.

"Just fine. No thanks to you." I pushed through my teeth and caught the raised eyebrow of Todd. "Okay! Fine, so it's not as bad as I said." I threw my arms up in defeat and stalked past Gray and into the lobby, almost sure steam was coming from my ears like a train, wishing I hadn't heard Todd yell out that we were leaving today.

I opted for the stairs instead of the elevator, taking the steps two at a time to try and work out some of my frustration. I wasn't happy about having to spend another minute with Gray let alone having to train together. I don't know what I was supposed to teach him that he shouldn't already know. I figured the best I could do was show him how to stay out of my way so I could do my job.

I found myself thinking back to when Alec had to train me. I wondered if he felt similar. I knew in the beginning he looked at me like his little sister, never wanting me in the field and feeling like it was his job to protect me. I would often sneak out and watch him train from a distance, running to hide every time he busted me spying as if I was a child. After what felt like months, I didn't know if I had convinced him it was more protection if I could fully protect myself or if he was just worried that I would hurt myself trying to learn it the wrong way. I was annoying and rebellious, but if it bugged him, he never showed it.

"Sam," he'd say in his no nonsense voice, looking at me under dark lashes that matched messy midnight hair. He'd complain about the gray hair I was surely giving him, but I never saw one strand of silver. I used to get lost in his eyes, loving how they'd be a rich brown one second and turn blacker than the night as soon as they locked onto me. Now that I looked back, I think it was a sign that his feelings for me were present then too. I was just too naïve to see it.

We shared everything together. Rarely leaving each other's side after we became partners, but I could never tell if I'd ever be more than a friend to him. Not then anyway. I don't know what changed. That day in the break room, I suppose. I was caught off guard when he placed his hand on mine and it lingered, seeming to test the waters. My skin ignited under his touch, heart racing. I hoped the heat didn't reach my face, but I knew it did. He looked at me differently that day, more than a mere girl, but like I was a woman.

I felt alive. Wild even.

I didn't make a fuss about it and for the first time I looked back, mustering all the emotion I could, trying to send him my feelings through my eyes, and when his pupils widened and those straight teeth appeared, I knew that he knew. For how long I didn't know but, in that moment, there wasn't any doubt about my feelings and for some reason there was no doubt in my mind about his either.

He walked me home from work that night, like he always did. The air was hot, making my shirt stick to my skin in the humidity, rich and salty with the scent of the ocean wafting in from the west, bringing a much-needed wind to combat the summer swelter. We stopped at my door, the same door I stop at now, but he didn't let me punch in the number. Instead he took my hand in his and placed it on his chest.

"Tell me if I'm wrong—" He started to say, uncertainty heavy in his voice. Alec was never unsure.

His heart beat heavily under the thin cotton of his shirt, and mine quickly matched pace. It was getting dark, but I could easily make out the sharpness of his jaw and the bend of his nose, which had been broken more times than my own. His lips were parted slightly, dry but swollen. Instead of answering I took a chance and stood up on my tiptoes to match his height. My palm shook lightly as I brushed my fingertips to his face. His breath caught as I caressed my lips against his. The touch was gentle, mixed with inexperience and fear, but if he minded, he never said. He reached up, deepening the kiss, his tongue teasing the tip of mine, the sensation ending all too soon as we parted out of breath. Alec rested his forehead on mine, his eyes gazing at me bewildered. I remembered in that moment I felt whole, a broken girl getting some of her pieces back. If only I knew that it would never last.

"Sammy?" Alana's voice pierced through the memory, saving me from myself. "What are you doing in here?"

I looked up. I had somehow found my way into an empty huddle room. The lights were off, but the sun shining through the window still illuminated the space.

"Hey! I had to sit for a second. My leg got messed up last night." It wasn't a complete lie, but it saved me from having to admit that my past haunted every moment of the present. "What's up?"

"Are you busy?" she asked.

"Not right this second." I admitted.

"Good, I brought you coffee." She pushed a drink out to me.

"Well—" I stammered for an excuse.

"I don't want to hear it." She set the drink right in front of me, forming a coffee ring on impact, and sat down. "You have been avoiding me for weeks, avoiding everyone. People are worried and listen"—she stopped anything I was going to say—"I know you're going to give me some flimsy excuse about being busy and lie straight to my face as if I don't know you, but it's not doing you any good. I don't even recognize you anymore."

I tried to force words to come out, but only guttural sounds made it past my lips.

"I know what happened...to—well, I know everything you have been through has been a lot. It would be a lot for anyone, but you can't just shut down and try and handle it all on your own. You need to talk about it and figure out how to heal. I feel like shit for even saying it, but life has moved on, and it's not waiting for anyone. This is our world now." She smiled, brushing her hand over mine.

"Was that your attempt at a pep talk?" I asked.

"You know I'm no good at this stuff." She chuckled, leaning back in her chair. It was true, she had always been the *roll with the punches*, and *rub some dirt on it* type of girl.

"Listen, I get you're concerned and trying to help, but I *am* coping," I said, pulling away.

She raised her brows, so I continued.

"I'm heading out to the training center in a bit to help with the new guy. Everything Todd is having me do I am doing. I'm taking on less work, and honestly I am feeling better." *Liar, Liar, pants on fire.* "Point is, I'm fine. I will be fine, and you don't have to worry about me."

"I don't believe you," she said matter-of-factly and I had to suppress a grimace, knowing I wasn't getting one over on her.

"I didn't think you would, but honestly, don't worry about me. I have everything under control." I grabbed the drink and walked around her chair, giving her a rare pat on the shoulder. "Trust me," I added.

"You know," she said to my back, "when all of this is said and done, when you have worked yourself to the bone and have nothing left to give, when you realize none of that is going to bring Alec back or change the pain you feel, I will still be there. If you don't die first."

I paused slightly, my spine straightening as her words rang true.

I knew that was the path I was on, though nothing made me feel better than hunting did and the fear of death didn't even reside in the deepest depths of my subconscious. It was only the fear of others dying that rocked me to my core and drove me on. I cocked my head to peer over my shoulder at her and tried to display my best fake smile, hoping it appeared genuine. The light cut across her face, framing tearful eyes.

"It won't come to that." I promised, not believing a single word.

Chapter 7

I OPENED the building's glass doors that led out to the city, immediately seeing the full-sized SUV parked directly in front of me, one wheel up on the curb with a man in a black suit standing by the back door. I wasn't completely surprised. I knew Todd would make sure we left right away, rather than let me come up with an excuse or ghost them for a few days.

The driver, who I didn't recognize, opened my door and moved to the side, which I took as a silent *don't even think about running*. I sighed, walking up, and thanked him as I stepped up on the nerf bar, sliding into my seat, the black leather cool against my skin. I stopped mid-click of my seat belt as the other door swung open. Gray, being taller than me, got into the SUV much easier than I did. He quickly settled into his seat, not bothering with his own safety belt. I bit my lip. Of course we would have to share vehicles too. I could just imagine Todd in his office looking down on us, smiling, keenly aware of my fury.

"Don't look so happy to see me." He smirked, and I had

to admit, if you took away the fact that he was the most frustrating person I had ever had the displeasure of working with, his smile wasn't horrible. A headache erupted behind my eyes, so I rubbed the bridge of my nose, trying to coax it away. I couldn't believe I just thought that.

"I'm not." My tone was rough as I tried to not look embarrassed about the silent compliment I had given him. "Stop smiling, you look dumb."

Smooth, Sam.

"Where's your stuff?" Gray asked me.

"Where's yours?" I retorted, scrunching my face when he pointed a thumb to the bags already in the back. I sighed before answering his question. "I already have stuff there. I go to train a few times a year…normally."

The car started rolling forward and I was already preparing myself for this being a long ride. I settled back into my seat and leaned an elbow against the door. I could feel Gray staring at me, but I looked out the window, pretending to be interested in the dreary scenery of our deteriorating city.

"You know what?" Gray's voice no longer sounded light and happy.

"What?" I asked, turning back to him, making my best *I don't want to talk to you* face.

"You're a bitch," he said.

"What. Did. You. Just. Say." I clenched my teeth so hard I thought they would shatter after having to pick my jaw off the floorboard. I shot daggers at him, but he didn't shrivel away from me like everyone else did. Our driver looked up into the rearview mirror, but quickly looked away, minding his own business.

"Oh, I did not stutter. You have been impossible from the beginning. Do you think I chose to work with you? No.

Forced is a more accurate description. You're rude, stuck-up, egotistical, and like I just said, a *bitch*." His voice was cold enough to make me shiver.

"I—" Anything I wanted to say got lodged in my throat. I couldn't defend myself. I knew I had been nasty to Gray, but working with someone else felt wrong. It burned the open wound of my heart like alcohol on a fresh cut. Alec died because of me, and the girls at work were right, anyone else who was around me for too long would die too. I couldn't protect him, and I couldn't get Todd to change his mind, so my next best option was to get him to refuse to work with me, forcing Todd's hand to let me be alone... how I belonged.

"Sammy?" Gray's voice pulled me from my thoughts.

"I don't want a partner," I stated simply as emptiness filled my core, not feeling nearly as angry about the name he called me, knowing I'd been acting as such.

"You think I don't know that? Look, I get you wanna be all Rambo on your own, but can't we just make nice? Just for now until a team opens up for me? I promise to stay out of your way, unless you don't want me to." Gray wiggled his eyebrows and that old smirk was back. I rolled my eyes at his innuendo and nodded in agreement. It wasn't like I had much of a choice.

"Fine?" he asked, seeking verbal confirmation.

"Yes, fine." I agreed again.

"And I'm sorry. I shouldn't have said that," he said.

"It's not wrong." I gave a small smile before looking back out the window.

For the first time the silence between us didn't feel heavy. We had broken the city limits and were venturing out toward a looming tree line. I watched the clouds gather closer together, pregnant with the rain that would wash over the city like a baptism, and tried to forget the storm that had been brewing in my chest for years. I leaned back into my seat and settled in for the couple hour long car ride.

"WHAT'S UP, CHIPMUNK?" *Alec's smile made my heart skip.*

"I don't know." My brows furrowed as I tried to decide what I was thinking. Something was scratching at the surface, begging for me to have that "aha" moment. I felt like I was looking at a puzzle, but without the last piece I couldn't tell what the image was. "Something just seems wrong."

Alec waited as I gathered my thoughts. I sat hunched over at the desk in his apartment, my index finger digging into my temple, eyes burning as I sat too closely to his computer screen, unblinking. I had been trying to clear my mind with a meaningless game of Solitaire but couldn't get out of my head. Just as I had moved my card to the place I wanted it in the game, I was moving, swiveling around in the chair to face a kneeling Alec. His hands braced against my knees, drawing soft circles with his fingers into my skin.

"I don't understand why Todd was so short with me. I am ready for more. I am ready to kill more vampires." I felt heavy. Todd was my dad's best friend, of course he wanted revenge too...right? Wouldn't me being in the field more make him happy?

"You know, he has been dealing with a lot, trying to fill in the big shoes your dad left. He probably just shows his hurt a different way than you." I loved how positive Alec was, a complete optimist. "You don't exactly make it easy on him." He chuckled softly. "I couldn't imagine having a daughter that was so quick to throw herself into danger."

"He's not my dad! My dad is dead, and those things did it. I want to find every last one of them!" I choked as the words left my

mouth, my throat burning as I tried to keep my stupid tears from falling to no avail.

Alec made a sound in the back of his throat, and for a brief moment I thought I saw tears in his own eyes, but before I could tell him it was okay, he pulled me in close. I wrapped my arms around him, nuzzling my nose into his shirt to breathe him in. I didn't think I could get through this without him.

"I just miss them so much." I whimpered.

"I know." Alec leaned his head down and whispered in my ear. His breath kissed my nerves and sent goose bumps up my spine. "I don't know what I would have done if something happened to you too. I love you, Samantha."

I knew Alec loved me, and I loved him, but I couldn't say it. The words were stuck in my chest, so instead I answered with my actions. I leaned in and kissed him softly. Sinking in as close as I could get, pushing through the blackness that had darkened my soul. Trying my best to drown out every painful memory that played itself in my head. Trying my best to forget the look on my parents' faces as they died.

A BUMP JARRED ME AWAKE. Something hard was under my cheek, turning that half of my face numb. I opened my eyes slowly to see I had fallen asleep and leaned on Gray's shoulder unintentionally. I quickly pulled over to my side of the SUV, trying to put as much space in between us as I could. Gray's head was resting against the glass with his fist propped under his chin, keeping him upright. He looked peaceful, a small smile pulling at his lips as each breath he took fogged the window. He stirred and I looked away, feeling like I had gotten a glimpse of something I wasn't supposed to see.

"You can lean against me. You're not that heavy." And

just like that, I was judging the distance between us to see if I had to move over to hit him or not.

"Yeah. I'm okay." I rattled my brain for something better to say but nothing surfaced.

"We're here," our driver spoke without turning back to look at us.

We approached the gated D.O.V.E. training facility. The lush trees populating the property hid it from view of the main road. The driver stopped to talk to security, waiting for them to check his credentials and wave us through. The dirt road stretched on for a few miles before revealing the large, renovated home stationed on a once abandoned estate. The sun was starting to descend in the sky, but training was still in full swing. Groups of prospective field agents were actively practicing offensive and defensive fighting tactics outside with coaches monitoring their every move, critiquing and adjusting where needed.

The SUV pulled to a stop in front of the old mansion. As I stepped out, I motioned for Gray to follow me down the gray and blue pebble stone walkway that led to the wooden French doors. He hovered behind me, close enough to feel his presence, but far enough that suggested he was uncomfortable with his surroundings. I couldn't blame him; the first time I came here to train I was overwhelmed too. Between the size of the estate and the talented people who worked here, I never thought I'd survive. I reached out for the handle but before I could open it, the door flew open and I was engulfed by a rose-scented perfume I knew very well while small arms encircled me and squeezed tight.

"Sammy! They told me you were coming!" a small voice chimed, barely recognizable due to a thick Spanish accent.

"Momma Maria." I gave Gray a quick glance to see him smiling, before returning the embrace. "I missed you."

Smack. A newspaper I didn't even see her holding swatted me in the shoulder.

"Ouch." I rubbed the target spot, pretending to be hurt.

"What was that for?"

"Oh, so *now* you miss me? *Mentirosa.*" She scoffed.

"I'm not lying!" I knew she wasn't being serious.

"Ay, I must have just not heard the phone ring anytime you called. Silly me." She placed a hand on her forehead for dramatics. "I *am* getting older."

"Oh shush!" I walked past her through the door.

"Umm." Gray's voice sounded uneasy.

I turned around to see Maria stationed right in front of him, staring intently. He shifted from foot to foot, probably trying to decide if he should force his way around her. The sight was hilarious since Gray towered over her by a few feet. Slowly he stepped by, but she stayed close enough that he had to brush Maria to squeeze through. She squinted at him, as if she was trying to see something more but couldn't get a clear picture. I enjoyed seeing Gray so uncomfortable and figured if nothing else came out from this trip, this made it worth it.

"I'll show him to his quarters then." I would save him...for now.

"Be careful," Maria responded and she walked off toward the east wing of the mansion, I assumed to start dinner. Before she rounded the corner, I heard her mutter something that I didn't understand. From the looks of it, though, Gray knew exactly what was said.

"Be careful?" I laughed. "She thinks if you tried something, I couldn't take you? Please! I mean, look at you!"

"Hey!" Gray looked offended. "I am stronger than you think."

"Sure." I was still laughing as I motioned for him to follow me up a winding staircase, turning toward where the boys stayed in the house. The walls were a rustic orange with pictures of past hunters hung on them. On a small bronze plaque under the images was their name, how long they served, and who they were survived by. They were put up like gravestones, a way to mourn losses. I paused, forgetting I wasn't alone as we passed by Alec's. Most hunters didn't smile in their photos, thinking it was the tougher look to stay neutral, but Alec smiled big. He never cared what anyone else thought and it showed that even here, he walked to the beat of his own drum.

"Sam?" Gray asked, startling me.

"Sorry." I cleared my throat and looked forward. "It's this way."

I hated these, just another reminder that we were losing this war. My parents' pictures were the biggest, located right as you entered the foyer, but I refused to look at them. Acknowledging them hurt too much. They were together in the picture, like they were in life, the same bronze plate positioned carefully under the portrait. Samuel and Rachel Cordova, founders of D.O.V.E., survived by their daughter, Samantha Cordova.

We walked down another hallway with intricate paintings of wars before the vampires came out. People I did not recognize held weapons while posing with cigars in their mouths for the camera. I silently wondered if we would have still fought so passionately with each other had we known we would need to come together to survive now. Positioned right above each painting was a small light that illuminated the art. It was the only lighting in the hallway, which allowed you to see well but still kept things dimmer than the rest of the house.

We arrived at a set of white French doors with two matching lights on both sides. I reached forward and shoved them open, revealing a bedroom that was well thought out. A large bed was pushed against the back wall with dark wood nightstands on each side. To the right was another set of French windowed doors, which opened up to the balcony looking over the training field. The sunlight lit up the room, magnifying the delicate cream paint. The room looked bright and cheery rather than ominous like the hallway.

"Well, here you are." I stepped to the side. "Dinner is normally around six, but there is always food. We aren't training tonight, but be ready bright and early tomorrow. If you need anything call for Maria, she'll take care of you."

Gray still looked slightly uncomfortable but walked past me anyway. He faced me, looking like he wanted to say something, but I turned on my heel quickly. If he was uncomfortable that was his problem. I wasn't here to hold his hand. I was here to brush up on my own skills, so I could get back to doing what I did best. Killing blood-suckers.

I started the long walk to the other side of the house. The girls and boys were separated by sides. It was old-fashioned, but it didn't bug me that much. The only person I ever wanted to be close to was Alec. I suppose it bugged me then, but Alec and I were resourceful when it came to finding extra time for each other. We explored every inch of this property, making it that much harder to be here without him, but it also made me feel a little closer to his memory.

In the beginning my trips here were always rough,

knowing it was the same place my parents founded and trained at, but Maria helped to make me feel as at home as she could. She was like the second mother I needed. Alec came to train with me too. By then our friendship was blossoming into something more. At that time, I wasn't sure what was happening, but I did know I loved him more than a friend. I was so frustrated because I wasn't learning fast enough. I wanted to get out into the field. I wanted to kill as many of those monsters as I could. The more discouraged I got the more Alec insisted that it was something that was learned, it was not always a natural instinct to fight and I would get better. He was right, I did get better, but not good enough.

Warmth trailed down my cheeks, startling me as I opened the door to my room. Rarely did I let my emotions sneak to the surface, but being here blurred the line I had perpetually drawn. The room was always reserved for me just in case I ever needed to come back. I spent months here training and before I lived on my own it was my second home when I wasn't bumming it on Todd's couch in his high-rise apartment. The room had been kept tidy in case of my arrival, but nothing moved from the spot I had left it in. The same cream walls and king bed greeted me. The neutral plush comforter tucked tightly under the mattress with a thick throw blanket lazily tossed on top of it.

Alec would always walk me to this room, convincing Maria he was saying good night, and wait for her to slip down the hall. I shut the door teasingly, but he'd always stop it with his hand, sliding through my halfhearted attempt to keep him from entering. I'd feel giddy as we tried our best to be quiet, getting lost in each other and the sheets. He'd always sneak out before sunrise but never left without placing a kiss on my forehead. I'd keep my eyes closed but always woke at his touch. If Maria knew, she never said anything.

The ache in my chest grew, increasing the more I let myself remember. I didn't think it would ever go away. I sat on the bed and yanked off my shoes, lazily tossing them in different directions with a thud. I ran frustrated fingers through my hair, gripping tightly at the roots. There was so much anger balled up inside, wanting an escape but with no true way out. I was angry at myself, no matter how many times I was told it wasn't my fault. I knew if I had trained harder, I could have saved him.

After a brief moment I got up. "Suck it up, Samantha." I urged myself out loud.

I sighed deeply and headed for the remodeled bathroom. The walls were a deep burgundy that stood out against the marble tile. It was cold on my feet, so I tiptoed to the tub that was adjacent to a standalone shower. I turned the knob to hot and began to peel my clothes off of tender skin. I had become careless. A glance in a long mirror confirmed that. Bruises still speckled my skin, some accompanied by tears in tissue that just could not take the pressure. I was still healing. Todd was right, but I didn't want to admit that my body couldn't take the way I was working this job.

I slowly lowered myself into the scalding water. It stung my skin, but I continued, rejoicing in something that could distract me from my thoughts. I reached up to pull the elastic holding my hair back so it could fall around my shoulders. The tips floated in the water, turning my blond hair into a dark color. A dull ache started in my head, the throbbing growing with every passing minute. All I did was feel. I just wanted a moment to not feel.

I pressed my eyelids shut and sucked air into my lungs

before lowering myself in the tub, letting the hot water cover me completely. Under the water I felt a little bit better. Everything became muffled and supported by liquid, my body felt weightless, making the ache in my limbs more bearable. I let the air out of my chest, slowly floating all the way down, stopping only as my back rested against the heated porcelain of the bathtub. If it was possible, I would have stayed like this forever.

A fire sparked in my chest as I ignored my lungs' plea for oxygen and stayed underwater. The steady beat under my ribcage increased slowly at first, then faster with every passing second. My body begged me to quench our need for air, but the haze that was encasing my brain, like that of a little devil residing on my shoulder, whispered, saying we could last a little longer. I focused on my heartbeat. The steady thump, thump was soothing.

Something muffled interrupted the rhythm. I tried to ignore the sound, but it came again. Suddenly, hands gripped my shoulders, ripping me up from my liquid cocoon. Water splashed over the top of the bathtub, spilling across the floor, as I gulped in a hungry breath. I tried to fend off the intruder with one hand and cover myself with a nearby towel with the other.

"Are you crazy?" I thought I said, but quickly realized that accented voice was not my own. Maria, hands on her hips, giving me a look of complete disappointment repeated herself. "Are you crazy?"

I tightened the towel around myself and carefully stepped out of the tub. Trying my best to not slip on the pool of water that scattered all over the tile.

"Don't you knock?" I asked. I was annoyed, but I immediately felt bad for the harshness of my voice.

"Ay, you better watch your voice with me, little girl."

She used a tone I had only heard a few times in my life. Mostly when I was doing something really bad.

"You scared me, is all." I lowered my head, walking into the bedroom to find my robe. I heard Maria clicking her tongue, but she followed behind me anyway.

"What were you doing in there?" she questioned.

"Thinking," I said.

"Underwater?" she asked.

"It's…" I paused; my entire body slouched with no real good excuse for what I was doing. "Quiet." I lifted my shoulders and straightened my posture, turning to force a smile, but when my eyes met hers, they were filled with tears.

"You are not okay," she stated simply.

"The bruises will heal, you know that." I assumed she was talking about my painted skin.

"No, no, no. Right here, *mija*." She pointed to her heart. "You're broken. But you have to be strong. Your parents would want you to be strong."

I didn't want to admit she was right.

"I can't do this right now," I said, shutting her out.

"I don't have to be okay with this." Maria was stubborn and I prepared for a long talk but was surprised when she shook her head and disappeared out of the room.

The door shut with a click behind her. Exhaustion drew my eyelids down, making me sit back on the bed. I was so tired of being questioned, I didn't want to talk about what happened. I just wanted to focus on my job. I lay back into the soft comforter, deciding I was done with today. Tomorrow I would try to really train Gray because even if I didn't want him around, I wanted to make sure I was out in the field, killing those monsters even more.

Chapter 8

"YOU CAN'T EXPECT a fox to stay in the hen house and not eat the chickens," Alec said, easily stepping back from my jab.

"Are you calling me a chicken?" I huffed out, circling him, trying to find an opening.

"Never." He laughed as I almost tripped trying to tackle him.

"So, I'm a dog?" I raised an eyebrow.

"What? No, of course not!" He stopped, laughing. "You're missing the point here."

There was my chance.

I kicked my leg out, sweeping it under his. Alec started to fall back, and I began to celebrate my victory. I hadn't been able to pin him one time and this was my chance. Alec went down with his shoulders bouncing off the mat as I approached him fast, trying to throw my weight on him to keep him down, but I celebrated way too soon. Alec adjusted his weight, pushing his arms back behind his head, and shoved himself back up in a move I had never been able to replicate. Unnaturally fast, he had me turned around with my arms pinned behind my back. He nestled in close, his nose tickling my ear, and he let *out a victorious chuckle. His breath was warm against my skin, sending goose bumps down my back.*

"I meant that you're a predator, not prey. You will never be prey," he said softly.

I could feel his heart beat strongly against my back, a slow, steady rhythm that didn't match the unsteady racing happening in my own chest. I smiled despite myself. He thought I lost, but I felt like I had won this match. There was a prize much better than proving I was better than him. It was getting him this close to me, even if just for a moment. His grip on me loosened, but he didn't back away as I turned my head into him, breathing him in.

"Then why have I been caught?"

BUZZING WAS SURROUNDING the contents of my dream, slowly dragging me back to the reality I was hibernating from. I opened my eyes, trying to blink through the hair that was netted around my face. Using my hands to push it aside, I rolled over to the alarm clock, slapping it forcefully when I realized it was six in the morning.

"This should be illegal." I groaned loudly, trying to convince my body to lift the microfiber comforter that was keeping me warm. I didn't even remember setting an alarm. Part of me wondered if Maria came in and did it. Probably in revenge, I decided.

As my toes hit the cold floor, I almost gave up and went back to sleep but dragged myself into the bathroom, running the shower water as hot as I could withstand, urging my mind to wake up and leave the memories back in bed. The water soaked into my hair, running down my body like little snakes, slithering the sleep down the drain.

I turned the handle to the off position and left the warmth the water was providing. I wiped my hand along the mirror, exposing my reflection. Damp hair clung to my collarbone, woven around faint scars scattered across my skin. My eyes were cloudy, telling a story of all the darkness I had encountered in the last few years. I couldn't recognize myself. Anything good about me, anything happy had appeared to have been buried alongside every loved one that was now gone.

I quickly dried off and threw on a pair of comfortable yoga capris with a tight black tank top and a light jacket I could easily take on and off. As I tied my running shoes, there was a knock at my door. I tried to ignore it, but the person knocked again. I rolled my eyes, wondering why Maria had to be so persistent, especially this early. I turned the knob, pulling the door open, meeting the eyes of someone who was most definitely a morning person.

"Good morning!" Gray sang.

"Didn't Maria tell you to meet me at the mats?" I figured she would tell him that's where I was heading.

"Yes, but she also mentioned that you are much happier after a cup of joe," he said. The smell reached my nose right as he said it. My nostrils tingled as my eyes sank to his hand seeing the Styrofoam cup I hadn't noticed before. I wanted to be angry, but I also really wanted that coffee. "And since we're sparring today, I thought it would be best to keep you as happy as possible." Gray held out his hand to show his offering like I hadn't already been eyeing it.

"You should have just met me there." I pushed past him, making sure to grip the coffee out of his hand on my way.

"And miss the look you just gave that cup? Hell no.

That might have been the only time you have ever looked that happy." He laughed and I let myself chuckle with him. "And a laugh?" he asked. "If I had known coffee gets that response from you, I would have tried this a lot sooner."

"We should hurry." I took a sip of the drink to silence anything that I would have said back. Part of me was still reeling from having to train him and the other part of me, a very small part, was enjoying having some playful banter with someone. I took another sip. The coffee was black, my favorite.

Gray followed me as we headed outside to a large building behind the house. The gym was added as an additional building to allow for indoor training to combat the weather. The architecture was modern compared to the aged house out front. We walked through two large doors that opened into a roomy space with blue mats distributed evenly throughout the room, separated only by a few inches. Even with it being so early, there were already people sparring, the sounds of grunts and yells echoing off the walls. I recognized a few people from D.O.V.E., but mostly it looked like new recruits.

We navigated the room while people used combative sticks and rubber stakes to learn how to maneuver around and find a kill spot for vampires. I found an open mat in the back corner, still sipping my coffee, and ushered Gray to the spot. I took one more long swig of my liquid energy and set the cup off to the side.

"Grab your kali sticks." I instructed Gray, pointing to the set of hollowed oak sticks cut to regulation size.

He reached down, fumbling the wooden training tools in his hands awkwardly as I grabbed my own. I returned to the mat, swinging the sticks smoothly through the air at nothing, wanting to work out the kinks in my muscles and re-familiarize myself with the weapons. I braced myself on the mat with my knees slightly bent, holding one kali out in front of me defensively and pulling the other behind my head, readying it for an attack.

"You ready?" I asked.

Gray stood stiff with both instruments held at his waist. He made no move to attack me and I had to refrain from rolling my eyes at how uncomfortable he looked. I straightened back up, dropping my weapons to mirror his own.

"You can't fight like that," I said. "Didn't they spar while you were in training?"

"Of course they did, it's just that…" Gray answered, uneasy. "Are you sure you want to do this?"

"You're not gonna hurt me." I laughed at his hesitancy. "Actually, your stance makes me feel like I should hold back a little, so I don't hurt you. It's all wrong."

He shot me a look, which I returned in full force.

He looked at me a moment longer and then got into a stance similar to the one I was in before. It looked unnatural for him, but I quickly followed suit and waited for him to throw his first move. Gray stepped forward, swinging the stick at me sloppily. I matched the movement, easily throwing my arm up and blocking his attack. The wood clashed together, making a hollow but loud *crack* as they connected. I maneuvered to his left, using the free kali to strike the back of his knee, hard. Gray's leg buckled under him, sending him down to the floor, only to be stopped when he threw out his hand to catch himself.

"I'm also not going to go easy on you. You have to be able to defend yourself," I said before swinging my kali again.

This time the clash of the wood startled me. Gray had pivoted on his knee, blocking my attack and issuing one of his own that I barely had time to jump back from. The tip of the stick grazed my stomach as it passed. He rose from the ground, allowing me time to plant my feet and get back into a fighting stance.

"Neither will I, and don't worry, I can," Gray said plainly, but with more confidence than before.

He moved at me again. He was fast, faster than I thought he could be as he advanced on me, forcing me to the end of the mat, my heel brushing the hard concrete, making me unbalanced. I readjusted and mirrored his movements, countering each attack as he threw them, blow after blow ending with opposite wood clashing together. We danced around the mat, swinging and blocking as quickly as we could. Sweat dripped from my brow as I focused on trying to find Gray's weak spot.

"I thought you couldn't fight that well," I questioned Gray as he swung at me, forcing me to block the hit as the words left my mouth. "Were you trying to hustle me?"

"The objective word is 'thought'." Gray still focused on my movements. "The word you should have used was assumed. Maybe I learned different from you, but I still know more than a few tricks."

"Okay, maybe I did assume, but it's not like you were much help the other night." My words were breathy as my breathing became more unsteady with the increased cardio.

Gray became annoyed and swung harder, throwing too much of his weight at me. I sidestepped him and swung around, bringing my kali around fast, smacking into his back with a stinging *thud*.

"You're rusty then," I taunted.

Gray didn't pause, trying to swing again only to be blocked.

"No, not rusty, just calculating." An evil grin grew across his face.

He faked an attack, which I tried to block. I lurched at him, but he spun to my right, catching me off guard. I lost my footing and tried to regain my balance too late because I was pushed forward by Gray's kali against my back, the sound hurting more than the actual contact, just as I had attacked him only a moment before. I fell forward, instinctively dropping the combative sticks and catching myself with my hands. I threw myself onto my back, trying to get some momentum, but stopped short when Gray jabbed me in the stomach with his kali.

"You are too distracted when you're being cocky." He smiled as I lay in defeat at his feet. "Check."

"You are too." I felt for my weapon, my fingers twitching against the texture.

"Wha—" He started as I swung my kali around, sweeping it under his feet, sending him sprawling to the ground next to me.

"Checkmate," I said, resting my head back against the mat.

Gray laughed out loud. The sound echoed through the room contagiously, drawing us looks. I laughed with him. Well, I tried to laugh. It came out more like repeating coughs as I tried to catch my breath. I thought about a similar time with Alec. I wanted to be better than him so badly, but Alec was born to hunt. I would lie in wait, trying to attack him, get him off guard because I knew that was my best chance, however he always saw me coming. He never let me win, but as I got better at fighting, I realized that letting me win, stroking my ego and building a false sense of skill would have hindered me more than anything. My laugh dried up in my throat. I was betraying Alec by letting myself be happy. He would never get the opportunity to be happy again. I got up from the mat, wiping the sweat from my face.

"You okay?" Gray sat up but didn't stand.

The question always tugged at my heart. My brain screamed NO! I was not okay, but my mouth never formed those words.

"I have a couple of things to do," I lied. "I am going to set you up with one of the instructors to continue your training today. You know more than I thought, but when you're actually out in the field you might not see the attacks coming like you saw with me during this lesson. I think it will help having someone who's been out there recently, even if it's stuff you think you already know."

"I can wait until you're done, then you can train me," Gray suggested, but I waved my hand at him.

"No, I really have some stuff that needs to be completed while I'm here. I'll send someone along and see you later today."

Gray's eyes burned into my back, but I didn't offer anything more.

I exited quickly, only stopping long enough to ask one of the male instructors to go through simulations with Gray. I may have even personally asked for him to not go easy on Gray because I knew 'he could take it.'

I had to get out of that building. It was like the walls were closing in on me, threatening to steal my breath away. I shouldn't have agreed to come here. It felt so wrong to enjoy a moment, even worse to enjoy a moment with someone else.

I made it into the fresh air. It entered my lungs,

relieving some of the anxiety building in my chest. I
decided to stroll along the outskirts of the property, trailing
the tree lines but not entering the forest. The summer had
all but left us, the brown leaves prominent as they floated to
the ground in the wind. The chilled air dried the sweat that
still coated my body from training with Gray. I was really
surprised at how well he did, still convinced that smooth
skin and lack of bruises meant he hadn't trained hard like
the recruits you would normally see, but then again in
today's world you had to be tougher, stronger, and smarter
if you wanted to survive.

The path I took was not new to me. Alec and I would
stroll here, talking about what the world would be like
without the vampires around. I would talk about how much
I missed my parents, how unfair it was that they were gone.
So many times, I would come out here to cry. I didn't want
anyone training to see me, the daughter of the founder of
D.O.V.E. weak and defenseless. The last time I was here,
before I was deemed capable of transferring to the field,
trying to swallow my emotions by myself, I had felt Alec
before I heard him…

*"Sammy." It wasn't a question. Alec knew it was me out here
whimpering in the dark, trying to hold back the tears that came every
time I thought of that night.*

*"Go away!" I yelled, not wanting to be seen like that, especially in
front of him.*

*"Being alone isn't going to help. Training isn't going to help. Hell,
even killing as many of those bloodsuckers as you can won't help!"
Alec never raised his voice, never at me, which caused me to quiet and
look up at him.*

*I squinted in the dark, the moon lighting up his features but also
casting shadows across his face. It didn't matter. I knew exactly how*

Alec looked. I had memorized each scar on his chin, the way the sun brightened his eyes, making the yellow specks hidden in them sparkle in spite of Alec promising his eyes were nothing but brown. His raven hair was neatly combed back tonight, but a section always managed to break free and dance in his face. I didn't need the light to know how Alec, my Alec, looked and I certainly didn't need it to tell me how we felt about each other.

"When will it stop hurting?" I whispered to no one in particular.

"Never." He was blunt, but honest. The answered question broke my heart, but I knew that him lying to me was not going to resolve the emptiness I felt.

He stepped closer to me, his cologne wrapping around me in a familiar embrace. He pulled me in close, breathing me in before pushing me back slightly. Alec's index finger trailed the length of my jaw before resting on my chin, ushering my face up to look at him.

"Time will dull it, Sammy. But even though you will never stop missing them, you won't ever have to miss me." Alec crushed our lips together in a frantic but gentle need. I wrapped my arms around his neck, kissing him back, letting the pain and burden I felt be shared between us, if even for a moment. I clung on to Alec as if I were dangling from a cliff and my very life depended on neither of us letting go. He pulled back from me, resting his hand on my cheek and using his thumb to wipe away the tear I hadn't felt myself shed. He led me back to the house and I caught myself praying that when he said I would never have to miss him, that it would always be true.

The lunch bell rang, stopping me from traveling further into my mind. I hadn't realized the distance I walked or how long I had been reminiscing. When I looked back everything appeared miniature, but I could still see the recruits leaving the gym and heading back to the house for their food. I knew I should go too, but my appetite had long gone.

"You said I would never have to miss you," I whispered to no one. "You lied."

"WHERE HAVE YOU BEEN?" Gray questioned me right as I walked through the door as if I were a teenager returning from sneaking out my bedroom window. He walked down the stairs as I closed the door behind me. His hair looked wet and I wasn't sure if it was from sweat or a shower.

"Keeping tabs on me?" I asked jokingly.

"No, I was coming down for food and you just happened to be walking in." He paused and laughed softly. "And now it sounds like I am making excuses and stalking you, so that's great."

I smiled but didn't respond as I made my way to the dining hall. I heard Gray fall into step behind me as I rounded the corner and walked in. The room was an over-sized dining area. Three elongated tables sat parallel to each other, each sitting twelve people a piece. Trainers and recruits were still piling in, the space becoming scarce, which was normal around lunch and dinner time even as most had to eat in shifts. I sat at an open seat toward the end of the table farthest from the door we had entered through and was not surprised at all when Gray picked the seat next to mine.

"I meant it, you know?" he said.

"Meant what?" I asked while pouring myself a glass of water. I offered him the pitcher, but he declined with a slight wave of his hand.

"I wasn't stalking you," he said.

"Yeah, I'm sure. You just so happened to come down as I came in, huh?" My tone was playful.

"Where did you go?" Gray asked.

"I told you I had some things to take care of," I said bluntly, trying to encourage him to mind his own business.

He raised his brow but let the conversation drop. I hoped he hadn't seen me strolling around alone. Maria and the kitchen staff came out, lining everyone's plates with grilled chicken and vegetables. A few people bowed their heads to say grace while others dug right in. The smell was intoxicating. My meals at home mostly consisted of microwavable dinners and snacks. I didn't know if it was the lack of time I had that kept me from cooking, or my inability to conjure up anything remotely edible.

"Not religious?" I asked Gray as he cut into his food.

"Not particularly. You?" he answered.

"I don't know. I guess not. I mean my family—well, when they were around, we never went to church. I always wanted to believe in something, that there was someone out there watching over us," I said.

"But you don't?" Gray asked.

"I don't know what I believe in anymore." I meant it. Gray stared at me intently, waiting for me to say more, but I didn't want to dive into why my faith had been rocked time and time again, so I changed the subject. "How'd training go after I left?"

"Well." He ran a fast hand through his hair and laughed, looking away shyly. "Would you believe they wanted to recruit me for training?"

Water flew from my mouth in an audible mess, soaking my food and drawing nervous glances from the people around us. "You're lying!" I said.

"Scout's honor!" His fingers made a cross at his chest before Gray leaned into me, dropping his voice so I would have to close the short distance to hear what he would say. "My trainer said I might even be as good as you."

I straightened when he wiggled his eyebrows at me, albeit cutely, much more annoyingly than anything.

"They were probably just trying to not hurt your feelings. Though I have to admit you have potential, you're too slow and stiff." I offered, ripping into the bread I pulled from a basket stationed in the middle of the table. "You have a lot to learn still before you are able to teach others."

"Well, I am the lucky recipient of guard duty too, so I guess my training wasn't half bad." He reached over and snatched the piece of bread I had planned on eating from my hand before I could place it into my mouth and popped it into his own. He smirked, making a big show of chewing. Some of the girl recruits around us snickered, seeming to find his actions cute, which...*annoyed me?*

Big bay windows let natural light shine through the dining room, allowing the electricity to remain off for the time being. I focused on the glass, the sun burning my pupils, forcing them to water in defense. Silverware clattered against glass as people finished their meals and quickly dispersed, some going up to their rooms while others went on guard duty or back out to train. I pushed my chair back from the table, setting a napkin over my plate and getting up from my spot. I caught Maria staring at me through the rotating kitchen doors and gave her a small wave as I stood. I knew she was worried about me, but I couldn't focus on that right now. Instead I was trying to understand why all of a sudden seeing the way people looked at Gray, or the way he sent smiles so freely back, got under my skin. Was I *jealous?*

No. No way.

"Where are you going?" Gray asked as I started to walk away.

"I thought you weren't stalking me?" I said. Gray made a face and I laughed. "I am going to relax. Might as well catch up on some Zs if I'm not working."

"Wait—" He seemed confused. "You don't have guard duty too?"

I choked on a laugh. I wanted to tell him to not stress about it since vampires never got close to the facility, but I refrained. If he was anxious, it would be a great real-world experience for him, and I would have the added bonus of knowing he was in no danger.

"No, I guess it was the luck of the draw." I tried to hide my smile. "Good thing they have you now."

"Somehow I don't believe that for a second," he said and I shrugged, feigning innocence, not knowing which part he didn't believe, and opting to stay quiet altogether.

I made my way up to the women's quarters. I took my time and tried to not feel a little guilty about leaving Gray to fend for himself. The unexpected jealousy that spouted still crawled all over my skin, making me extremely uncomfortable. I didn't understand where it came from when just a day ago, I was actively plotting Gray's murder.

"Sam?" a small voice called out.

I turned, half expecting for no one to be there. A girl, shorter than me, stood behind me. Her hair flowed down in soft curls past her shoulders, almost looking auburn against the soft light being emitted throughout the hallway. Her eyes shined bright, pure of the pain and suffering most of us here had already experienced.

"It is Sam, right?" she asked.

"Yeah, umm, do I know you?" I felt like I had seen her face before, but no name surfaced in my mind.

"Yeah, well, I mean I guess not, but we have met once!" she said. "You helped me while training."

It took a moment before it came to me.

"It's Cindy, right?" I remembered her from my training days. She became my shadow and as much as I wanted to be annoyed, Alec reminded me that it should be flattering to be a role model. He said she reminded him a lot of me, which I groaned about.

"Yeah! I just saw that you were back and wanted to say hi, let you know I have been practicing really hard! They might even let me go on watch duty!" Her excitement made me smile. I felt that same way when I was training, even if my excitement was based on revenge and not moral obligation.

"You must be getting good then." I gave Cindy my most genuine smile. "Maybe you should train with us tomorrow?"

"You came with that guy, right? Gray?" she asked.

"Yup, but I am sure he wouldn't mind. Bet you could even teach him some things!" Redness crept up her neck as she wrung her hands out.

"Oh, I dunno." The corners of her lips lifted to her ears. "But he is cute!"

I laughed. I didn't want to admit that he had his features, but she was right. There was a softness about him when he laughed, and the way his lips curved up when he found something funny. If only I could get his mouth sewn shut.

"What do you say then? Meet me out back tomorrow morning?" I asked.

"Okay!" She practically yelled, turning to walk back but stopping briefly. "Don't tell him I called him cute, okay?"

I promised I wouldn't before she left and returned to my

room. I shut the door behind me, feeling lighter than I had in months. Not happy, yet not as miserable. I had closed myself off to everyone, shutting out anyone who tried to help out. My pain was unbearable, but I now realized the loneliness was worse. I missed my parents, and I missed Alec more than I could ever imagine, but I also missed feeling okay.

Chapter 9

"I WENT to your room this morning, and I have to say I am surprised you're here before me." Gray laughed and handed me what was seeming to become his *please be nice to me* morning coffee. "I get the sneaking suspicion you're not a morning person."

I couldn't help but smile back while simultaneously inhaling the daily liquid energy. "What makes you say that?" He was right.

"Well—umm, hi?" Gray said confused and I assumed his eyes just landed on Cindy, who was decked out in black hunting gear with her game face on. I guessed I should have let him in on our little secret.

"Gray, meet Cindy. Cindy, this is Gray."

She threw her hand out forcefully, grabbing Gray's own hand from his side, and shook it a few too many times, his arm resembling a limp noodle.

"Cindy is about to graduate to the field, so I thought what better to do than have her help with training considering you just went through this." I watched Gray look her up and down, taking in her small stature. "Don't let her size fool you, she is fast and agile." I assured him.

He still didn't seem convinced, but I ushered them to the middle of the mat anyway.

"We are gonna start out with some basic grappling." I moved off the mat. "First one to pin the other person three times will be considered the winner."

"Are you sure this is fair?" I could barely hear Gray's question over the scoff that came from Cindy.

"For who?" Her eyebrow rose with the question. Her confidence seemed to entice Gray and I could see the competitive side of him had awakened.

"Okay, just don't say I didn't warn you," Gray teased.

They got into position, arms out in front of them, slowly circling each other, each matching the other's pace. Cindy moved forward, locking arms with Gray, who was caught off guard by her assertive advance. He looked at me for reassurance and immediately regretted it when she side-stepped him, the movement sending him back to trip over her waiting leg. Once on the ground she easily spun around and pinned his shoulders down.

"That's one!" I called out.

"Wait, what?" Gray got up, looking around as if another person had jumped in to help.

"That's one," I repeated. "She pinned you fair and square."

A sound escaped his throat somewhere between disagreement and bewilderment.

"Shouldn't underestimate me just because I'm a girl— or small." Cindy cut him off before he could deny it.

"Okay!" I slapped my hands together, rubbing them in excitement. "Let's go again!"

Gray got back on the mat, looking more determined.

Cindy assumed her same form while Gray seemed to take her more seriously and give thought to her movements. They locked arms again, struggling a little more against each other's counter movements this time. Gray spun her around, locking his arm around her neck and linking it with his other to keep her in a hold. I could tell he still held back, ensuring she had plenty of room to easily take her breaths. She struggled against his embrace, but his strength was harder to break.

Cindy stomped her heel down on his toe, forcing him to break the hold immediately. Gray shouted out a curse and reached for her again. Cindy dropped to her knees and scurried herself in between his legs, jumping up to face his back. The movement was fast. One second Gray was trying to understand where she was going, the next he was tripped up before he could turn around to face her. As soon as I saw both shoulders hit the mat, I called it.

"That's two!" I yelled.

"Oh, you have got to be kidding me!" Gray didn't look mad, more like dumbfound that such a small girl could maneuver around him like she was doing. "That's cheating. My toes are still throbbing!" He limped slightly to showcase it. I had to hold back a chuckle since it reminded me of what I was just doing to Todd to try and get Gray reassigned.

"All is fair in love and war." I repeated what my mom used to tell me anytime I complained about fairness in the world. She reminded me war will never be fair, but love would be plentiful. "Plus, vampires don't play by the rules, so sometimes to win, you have to get a little dirty."

Gray stayed silent, but Cindy offered up a high five that I gladly accepted. The sound adding insult to injury.

"All right." Gray's face said he meant business. "Let's go again."

"Sam!" My name was called across the gym floor. I looked up and saw a familiar face from D.O.V.E. standing in the doorway. She gestured for me to follow with a head movement and disappeared through the door.

"Wait! What about my rematch?" Gray asked as I started toward the exit.

"We will have to call it best two out of three," I hollered over my shoulder. "Looks like you lost!"

Cindy broke out into a laugh and Gray muttered under his breath. I smiled and followed the tagger. The air was fresh against my face. It reminded me how muggy and sweaty that room could get. I rubbed my brow on my arm to wipe some of the moisture away. I paned to the left then right, searching for the girl. A throaty sound came from the wall to my left, so I followed it. As I rounded the corner, she was leaning against the structure looking bored. Her ginger hair was pulled tight in an elastic, but somehow her pony-tail still looked professionally styled. She stood taller than me, having at least a foot on my height.

"Special delivery," Leah said, unimpressed. She was one of our best sharp shooters, rarely missing her target. I hadn't worked with her much in the field, but I knew of her and her abilities.

"For me?" I asked anxiously. She looked at me sideways, casting a *who else could it be for* type of look before handing me a medium-sized yellow, sealed manila envelope with the name *Sam* written in the middle in black marker. "Who's it from?" I asked.

"I owed Ruby a favor and she said that you seemed to really want this." She looked over her shoulder at the tree line, thinking before turning back to me. "I don't know what it is so don't ask, and I don't want to know what it is if you already do so don't tell. Knowing you, it can't be good." Her lips stayed in a thin, taut line as she spoke to me. "By the way, the grids are down. It shouldn't affect you out here, but I don't think they will be back up soon so keep an eye out anyways."

"Thanks for the heads-up." I pursed my lips. The trackers had been installed to limit herd movements so what happened to my parents wouldn't happen to other unsuspecting souls, but the problem was they never actually seemed to work.

I wasn't exactly liked around work, so her stiffness toward me didn't completely come as a surprise. Besides carrying the Cordova name, there wasn't much more I had given people to like about me, especially after Alec. He seemed to know everyone, getting along with the meanest hunters, everyone only having good things to say, and I was accepted because I was always around him. I knew people blamed me and my rash decisions for his death. I couldn't fault them for that because even I blamed me.

"Listen—" I began, but was cut off.

"Everything okay?" Gray asked. Cindy trailed closely behind him. By the looks of it, I guessed he wasn't overly annoyed at being bested by a girl. Leah sighed, probably feeling like she'd been saved, and gave a curt nod, using the opportunity to leave before I could guilt her into helping me more.

"Yeah, just work stuff," I lied, waving my hand like it was no big deal.

"Take a walk with me?" he asked, catching me off guard.

Cindy excused herself with a heavy throat clear, muttering something about needing to shower, and after a brief pause I nodded to Gray, still feeling weird about the unwanted jealousy yesterday.

"So, what's the issue?" Gray asked me as we started on an invisible path around the courtyard. "Don't say nothing, because I can see it all over your face. Is it whatever's in that package?" He finished before I could deny it.

"Oh, this?" I held it up. "No, no, this is nothing. She was telling me the grids are down again. Trackers were meant to make everything so much easier, but we didn't plan for them to have so many problems," I said, tucking the package securely under my arm. He eyed me once more and then relaxed, content with my answer.

"With relaying?" Gray asked.

"No, they relay fine. It's the system we use. It crashes frequently and we lose them. Sometimes it's just for a minute, sometimes a day. It just depends, but it's danger-ous," I said.

"Can't you fix it?" Gray suggested.

"Well, no, not me." I laughed and he gave me a look that said I knew what he really meant. "But we could. However, money is not going into that stuff. It doesn't seem like it's going into anything important." I sighed. "I'm gonna change all of it, though."

"Change it?" he asked. Gray reached out for my hand to steer me out of the way of a hole I hadn't noticed. His touch sent warmth up my arm, which quickly spread to my cheeks as I pulled my hand away gently, adding some distance between us.

"Well, I will inherit the company and when I do, I want to restructure everything," I said confidently. "Start putting the money into the things that matter. Our employees, research. If we can make a better vaccine, eventually there will be no one left to infect and then all we will need to do is kill off the vampires. Right now it seems like the only things being funded are buildings and marketing scams to get more hunters to join the cause, not anything that will be able to protect those very hunters."

"Wait, what?" Gray stopped walking, so I turned to him.

"Yeah, the company is mine when I turn twenty-one," I said. "It was my parents' and that's how they wrote it in the event of their death. I honestly didn't know they could, but I guess it's a thing. Todd is essentially sitting in until I am of age." I used finger quotations for the 'of age' part. "I know it sounds ambitious."

Gray stared at me like he was seeing me for the first time. I must have been rambling on, so I waved my hand in front of his face. His eyes focused on mine, but if he was going to say something the words never came out. The moment seemed to stretch on forever before he cleared his throat and turned away. He ran his hand through his hair purposelessly because it fell back to the same place it had just been lying.

"It makes so much sense now," Gray said so quietly I almost didn't hear him. I didn't understand what he meant and before I could ask, he moved on. "You said vaccine, not cure. You don't believe there is one?"

I blew air through my nose, trying to quiet the sigh. I wanted to believe something like that was possible, but I knew in my heart there was no going back. The vampires were no more than a shell of who they were before, and I didn't believe a cure was going to bring back their humanity.

"It's not that I don't, I just think we're further away than before with everything that happened." I looked toward him, waiting for him to confirm he knew about the *accident*. He nodded. I didn't think there was anyone who hadn't heard how close we'd been to being able to treat this. "I can't lie to you and say I think there is any going back once you have changed, but if we had a cure and could catch it in time, before people transitioned, there could be a real shot to change our future. I'm going to make sure it happens."

Gray smiled at me, making me look away.

"You don't believe me, do you?"

"No, it's not that. I have just never seen you so passionate about something before. I do believe you, that's the thing. It's hard not to with that type of drive." His eyes bore into mine and I knew he meant it.

I knew I had a lot to learn, but I was determined to change everything, even if that meant D.O.V.E. eventually wouldn't be needed anymore. I wanted to see a world where the things that went 'bump in the night' only happened around campfire stories.

"Cindy's seemed to take a liking to you." I changed the subject as we turned and started making our way back to the house.

"She's a tough little girl," he said with a sad smile.

"Don't let her hear you say that," I teased back, knowing if she was anything like me, calling her little would light a fire under her to prove she was no such thing.

"I just mean, I can't believe she will be out there fighting soon." He clenched his fists, but quickly shoved them into his pockets like he didn't want me to see. I understood what he meant. Seeing people who should be enjoying their childhood having to grow up and protect those who couldn't protect themselves. Cindy should be prepping for prom, not learning how to kill.

"I get it, trust me. I don't like it any more than you, but

the problem is we just don't have the numbers anymore. We are spread so thin as it is, plus there are much easier jobs than this one out there. How can we compete with places that ensure you come home to your family every night? Without people like Cindy, the small population that's left would only be around as a food source." I wanted to say how it wouldn't be like this forever, but like a jinx, the front of my shoe caught part of the pathway that had rose with the soil, sending my top half toppling over the lower. Just as I thought I would hit the ground, Gray's hand snatched out at lightning speed and caught my arm, stopping me from embarrassing myself more.

My face burned bright, while his eyes sparkled in the light. I could see him trying hard not to laugh at me, adding salt to my already gaping ego. I stood up straight, but he didn't release my arm, his fingertips pressing softly into my skin. My heart picked up as I looked back at him, his hazel eyes a mixture of yellow and green in the sun. I sucked in a sharp breath as those eyes dipped down to my lips, Gray's long eyelashes hiding what he was thinking. Like a trance had been broken, he let me go and stepped back, running his hand back through his hair like a habit he couldn't kick.

"I should go," I said, but for some reason didn't want to.

"Yeah." Gray laughed nervously. "Me too."

The seconds seemed to drag on with neither us moving. Finally, Gray let out an audible breath, pulling his lips into a small smile before he turned away from me, offering an awkward wave, and left me on the porch to watch his back.

I MANAGED to make my way to the library without being

stopped. The room had vaulted ceilings with the walls painted a velvet red. All the trimming was original, stained a natural dark brown, which lined the floors and doors. Matching bookshelves were custom made to fit against the walls. They didn't reach the roof like the libraries I had seen in the movies, but they still looked large in the comfy space.

Tucked away in the corner was a lengthy desk with three monitors sitting on the sturdy wood. I sat in the middle and wiggled the mouse, bringing the screen to life with the picture of the open ocean kissing a pastel-colored sunset as its background. I used my index finger to tear through the seal on the package, jamming it into the corner and pulling it across, ripping the envelope. I tilted it to the side, dumping its contents onto the desk in front of me.

Out came a CD in a clear case. It lacked any writing or description, but I knew what it was. Ruby had come through on my favor. I shook again, a little folded note toppling out on top of the disk. I opened it, smoothing it against the edge of the desk to get the crinkles out. Ruby's handwriting was small and sloppy, the kind I would expect from someone who had to jot notes down quickly, not having the time to take care with the letters on a page.

Don't ask me for anything again. -R

It was a pity because she was useful, but I agreed even if she wouldn't know that. There was no way I could have gotten Elias to hand this over and if I had gone to Todd about it, he would say that I was phishing and needed to take the time off to deal with my grief. No one seemed to believe that it was off how close we were to a possible cure and in the next breath the only person who had the answers wasn't alive.

I opened the flimsy disk case and plopped out the CD

before sliding it into the reading drive. The cursor took a moment, displaying a rotating circle before launching a media viewer in a small window. I pressed the blue arrow to press play, noting it seemed like a day's worth of feed rather than just the moments leading up to it. I used the mouse to fast forward through most of the video, not wanting to miss anything but also knowing that the event happened toward the end of the day. As I reached the end, I pressed play again, letting it run at normal speed.

The view was split into four different windows, showing people coming and going from the lab, the hallway, inside around the tables and a side view of the cage. The vampire was tucked back from the lights, trying to stick to the shadows. It didn't look overly agitated, but it didn't appear anyone was in its direct line of sight that would have looked like a meal either. Zoe, the lead scientist, stood next to the computer holding a pipet over a test tube up toward the light. The contents just looked like liquid on the screen, the video too blurry to make out colors or amounts.

She turned to the door, pressing goggles up on her face, which tangled what I remembered as being champagne-colored hair in the straps. I looked down to see someone enter. From their clothes I could tell it was a hunter. They sported the basic issue wardrobe of someone in the field. Zoe smiled and put her test tubes down in a holder, facing the visitor. I couldn't see who it was with their back to the camera, so I pressed rewind on the video, trying to get a glimpse of their face as they walked through the hallway.

A lab tech I hadn't noticed went to leave just as Alana walked up. They exchanged words that couldn't be heard since there was no audio, but it seemed friendly enough as Alana passed, catching the door before it closed, and walked in. My eyes darted back up to the lab screen. Zoe walked to her like she was expecting she'd show up. She moved her hands animatedly, passionately discussing her topic. I wished I could hear what they were saying, but if I had to guess she was talking about her discovery.

Suddenly, the smile left her face and Alana turned her back to Zoe, pressing her palm against her forehead. Zoe reached out for her, brushing her fingers against her shoulder, but she pulled away, distressed. A look of confusion passed over Zoe's face before the camera clicked off, all screens going gray with fuzz.

My eyebrows pulled together tightly, a tension headache forming between them as I tapped the screen with the tip of my finger like I was trying to wake a fish in a tank. Was there something wrong with the computer? I pressed play again with zero luck, the cameras had stopped working…or they were turned off.

I didn't understand. I had spoken with Alana briefly over what happened and she never disclosed that she had seen Zoe right before the accident. I didn't even remember her being overly beat up over the whole incident. Actually she was one of the main people to tell me I was overreacting thinking it was anything but what the report said. Why didn't she say anything?

And more importantly, what happened to the video?

Chapter 10

THE NEXT TWO days passed in a blur.

I couldn't stop thinking about what I had seen on the video, or more like what I hadn't seen on it. I definitely didn't want to see Zoe die, but I was prepared to stomach it to see exactly what had gone down. Furthermore, I found it curious that the report declared it was an accident despite omitting information about what I was really hoping was faulty cameras. There was no way that Alana could...

No, of course not.

We had gotten word back from Todd that he would need us back by the end of the week and that he *really hoped* we were on the same page. I told Maria to tell him we were, but I really wasn't sure. Each day we trained together with Cindy tagging along. The conversation was always light and fun with her, but once Gray and I had to interact it became awkward and tense. I often ended our sessions early, letting him finish training with others and Cindy so I could sneak away and get some distance or turn in for the night. I was sure Todd would be furious when we got back, and we were not only not on the same page but ended up in different books completely.

A cold breeze blew through the window, making my arms prickle. The sensation drew me out of a deep, dreamless sleep I barely remembered falling into. I crept from bed, sliding into a soft robe. I tiptoed over to the French doors that led to the balcony, trying to keep my skin from the icy floor. A metal lever locked the doors open, keeping them from slamming against the breeze. The lock was cold, and my fingers struggled to pull it down. Finally, the thing clicked and allowed me to move the door closed. I worked the other side but stopped. A dark shadow hovered under my balcony.

I quietly stepped out, pressing up against the stone rails to get a closer look. Gray was pacing on a walkway that mazed through a large garden. Every other turn he would get too close to a flower, brushing it with his arm, causing it to sway back and forth before coming to a stop. I squinted my eyes, trying to make out what was going on. I knew he was on watch but instead it looked like he was hiding away, trying to keep from being seen too easily.

He seemed stressed, occasionally running his hand through his hair aggressively. He sat on a nearby bench, but his posture looked all wrong as he stared into the distance. I pulled back from the ledge, closing the door softly behind me. I found some slippers that I pushed my feet into before making my way out of the room and down the stairs. I went through the back door, bumping into a few patrolmen. They looked at me but didn't ask why I was outside. If my reputation had left me with anything other than being a bitch, it was that I was helpful in a fight, so there was no concern about me out on the grounds after dark. Even dressed like I was.

The slippers slapped the bottoms of my feet as I came up to the garden. The air made me fold my arms across my body to stop the shivering. I worked my way along the same path Gray was pacing, but he was nowhere to be found. I walked farther, wondering if maybe he had already made his way back. The lavender fabric of my robe brushed the same rose as I strolled too close to the side of the walkway, forcing it in motion again. I turned to it, steadying it with my hand, the petals like silk against the calluses of my fingertips.

"Couldn't sleep?" The voice made me jump back. I caught my finger on a thorn, tearing the skin slightly, drawing a pinprick of blood. "You okay?" Gray asked as I hissed, putting my finger in my mouth, licking the coppery warmth away. When I turned, Gray's eyes were dark, watching me.

"You scared me!" I snapped back at him. I hated being caught off guard and that seemed to be Gray's specialty.

"Does it hurt?"

I shot him a look that said it obviously didn't.

"Figures if it did you wouldn't admit it. What are you doing out here—in that?" His dark gaze flashed, trailing my robe, which felt way thinner than when I left my room. I crossed my arms over my chest, even more aware of the chill as I tried to hide the evidence he shamelessly stared at. I didn't need a mirror to know crimson had crept up my neck and coated my cheeks.

"I was coming out here to check on you." I stared back, trying to ignore the way my heart had picked up its pace.

"It's just guard duty," he said.

"So, guard duty is stressful enough to make you pace?"
I questioned. "You looked upset." Gray's mouth opened
and shut like a fish out of water. His eyes burned into mine,
challenging me to look away, but I refused.
"I don't think I have seen you in anything but black," he
replied.

Something about the way Gray said it, slow and calculating, and the way he stole another glance made my body
shiver for reasons other than the temperature. "Don't
change the subject. You can tell me, you know?" I didn't
recognize my own voice and suddenly I wasn't comfortable
out here by myself.

"Oh, right, because you're so forthcoming?" His tone
took on an edge that forced me back a step. I didn't know
why, but it hurt. I pressed my lips together as anger built in
my chest. "Are you going to tell me why you have been
weird the last two days?" he asked, waiting as the silence
rained down around us.

I couldn't respond. I didn't want to admit that being
around him made me remember feelings I reserved only for
Alec.

He turned to walk from me, and I fought the urge to
flip him off when that same anger left me so fast, I ended
up breathless. I could see it in his shoulders. He was hurting, and he wanted to push me away. He was doing the
same thing I had been doing to every single person in my
life who tried to be nice to me.

"Wait!" I hollered even though he would have been able
to hear me regardless. "I lost someone recently."

He stopped, turning his head toward me to see if I
would continue.

"His name was Alec. I am sure Todd gave you a high-level overview of it, but he was more than my partner in the field." I paused. The words struggling up my throat, regurgitating something I hadn't said since Alec died. "I loved him."

Gray faced me, eyes filled with understanding and pity that I didn't think I deserved. My own eyes stung with unshed tears, threatening to release the dam of emotions I had been fighting off for months.

"I lost someone too," Gray spoke softly, my ears straining to hear him.

"Recently? Is that why you were upset?" I asked.

He hesitated like he was considering his answer. Gray rubbed at his forehead, like he was trying to massage away a headache. "Kind of. My family," he said. I wanted to share my empathy, but he continued, cutting off my chance. "My father, my mother, and my two sisters." He swatted his hand, motioning to nowhere in particular. "This world ate them up and left me here alone." He laughed like it was funny, however I knew that sound. I'd heard that brokenness.

"I'm sorry." I meant it. I wanted to ask what happened but pushed the curiosity down and gave him a sad smile.

"Me too." It was a mere whisper, but the response felt heavy as it reached me. It felt deeper than this conversation, like maybe he was sorry for more than just my loss.

"Are you on patrol tomorrow?" I asked.

"Yes, unless you tell Jackson to take it easy on me and let me off." His smile told me I was caught.

"Yeah, sorry about that." I laughed, pushing my next words out quickly, before I could change my mind. "Did you wanna get out of here? Tomorrow night? I figure since you're being worked extra hard because of me the least I can do is show you a good time. You know, my way of saying I'm sorry." The words sounded ridiculous out loud and I found myself nervous for his answer.

I could see Gray's eyebrows rise in the moonlight, that light smirk tugging at his lips. "That's an awfully nice way to say sorry."

"Umm—that came out weird. Not like that! I just mean that, well, if you want, there is a bar about twenty minutes away or so and we could get a drink. I mean, or not." I was rambling and prayed he couldn't see the heat I felt on my cheeks.

"Can we do that?" he asked, surprised.

"Can is kind of the operative word here. We can, but that doesn't exactly mean we should." I chuckled. Technically the rules were clear. Without clearance no one was to enter or leave the facility. That way every person was accounted for constantly. I personally thought it was outdated thinking, but it stemmed from a time when no one was sure how to track the vampires and their whereabouts. No one had ever pressed the issue, but it didn't stop the occasional rebel from breaking the rule and it never stopped me.

"Why does this not surprise me with you?" he asked rhetorically.

An evil grin spread across my face as an answer.

"Tomorrow?" he asked, like he might be busy. "All right." He finished with a smirk.

"You better get back to your post. Don't forget we have training bright and early." I started to head back to the house.

"You don't cut anybody any breaks, do you?" Gray called to my back, but I could tell he was joking.

"Never!" I yelled back, laughing, well aware it was true. I didn't.

I snuck back into the house, the heater making my still flushed cheeks burn hotter. I didn't know what I was thinking. Sneaking out was seriously frowned upon, recruit or not, but it seemed worth the risk if it meant clearing the air. The stairs creaked under the weight of my feet as I tried to make my way back to my room quietly.

"A little cold outside, is it?" I didn't have to turn to know Maria was standing there. Her presence was of a mother's who had just waited up all night for her teenager to return, spanning out like a physical touch and instantly making you feel guilty.

"What are you doing up?" I questioned her without looking into her eyes, feeling like a child getting caught stealing from the cookie jar.

"I was about to ask you the same thing." Maria wore a light pink nightgown that stopped modestly at her ankles, the end trimmed with delicate lace. She had one hand on her hip, crinkling the fabric as she stared up at me from the foyer.

"Todd would want me to play nice with Gray. I have to make the best out of this situation, otherwise we'll both be miserable," I said, shrugging to show that it wasn't a big deal.

"Since when have you given a toot about what Todd wants, Sammy?" she asked, but I couldn't answer because I never had.

"I am not a recruit, Maria. I didn't think I had a curfew." I turned, crossing my arms in front of me.

"Is there something going on between you two?" she asked bluntly. The question angered me. No way there was. I was just playing nice, trying to make something good out of a bad situation. At least, that's what I was telling myself.

"No, it's not like that. I am just being his friend. If we

have to work together then I need to make sure we are gonna be successful," I said, seeing the disapproval in her eyes. Gray made me excited. There was something about him I couldn't put my finger on, and I realized that maybe I was starting to want his company. It hurt knowing that something that was making me happy was making Maria so unhappy.

"It's not that. There is just something about him. I have a bad feeling," she said. I was taken aback. Maria liked pretty much everyone. I knew she missed Alec too, but I didn't think she was being fair.

"You're just being overprotective." I turned to go back up the stairs.

"Sam, it's not—" She tried to explain, but I hollered good night over my shoulder and continued up.

I didn't want to hear it. We all missed Alec; she should know that I missed him more than anybody. I knew how she felt because I felt the same way just yesterday. I didn't want to replace him in any sense. I was closed off and tender over the idea that I would have to work alongside anyone when it wasn't Alec. My heart broke every time I thought of his name, but for a few moments I started to understand. Gray wasn't replacing anyone. He could never, even if he tried. No one could. But blaming him for not being someone else wasn't going to take the hurt away.

I only had a few options. I could not work with him and be taken out of the field completely. I could work with him without training and get both of us killed in the process, or I could try to get on the same page with him, help him train and get better so I could get back to work and he could be placed with the next open team. I could be given bigger assignments, kill more vampires, and help to avenge the death of so many good people. I could make sure the death of three of the best people I knew wasn't in vain.

I made it back to my room, feeling wound up and stressed. Was it wrong to enjoy the little bits of laughter I had stolen today? Was this me forgetting Alec? Was this what Todd wanted me to do? Was this healing? The lightness that had visited me leaked from my body, leaving me cold and empty. I wondered if Alec would be disappointed in me for smiling, if he would have felt like I was betraying him.

No. I shook the thought from my mind. Alec only ever wanted me to be happy. He wouldn't want me wallowing in my own self-pity. He'd want me to get stronger, better, and to take out as many of those bloodsuckers as I could. I knew his death was my fault. I should have gone for him, should have made sure we waited for backup, but instead I was reckless and rushed in knowing he'd come after me. He wouldn't let me do anything on my own. I was his Achilles' heel and he was mine but not in the way of weakness, in the way of strength. I couldn't push Gray away because I needed to be out there and if that meant training him and having a partner again so be it. I was bound and determined to make this work.

I wasn't leaving the field just yet. I had unfinished business. I knew I was on to something. Every day I spent on this earth, I was going to try and make it a better and safer place for the people who couldn't do it for themselves. I was going to earn my title as the president of D.O.V.E. I was going to go down in history as one of the best hunters, as the daughter of the founders of the best protection agency in the world.

I lay down with a sense of purpose I hadn't felt in a long time. For the first time in months I wasn't sad to be waking up the next morning, I wasn't disappointed that the sun had risen but rather motivated to make a real difference. I finally felt like I could breathe. I knew what I was going to do, and I was going to start as soon as I made it back to the city. I was going to make them proud.

Chapter 11

"YOU'RE DISTRACTED!" I yelled at Gray, pushing my hand out aggressively so I could help him up. His shoulders were against the mat, having taken a nice kick to the gut from me. Cindy had left, not able to stand and watch how we were training anymore. I had hoped a break and lunch would do the trick, but we were back at the mats, and nothing had changed. Most people had already called it quits for the day, but it hadn't even seemed like we started.

"You're just as angry as usual!" Gray snapped back, refusing my offered hand and getting back to his feet.

He was right. We only had a few more days and I wanted to make sure he was as prepared as possible, but all morning Gray had been holding back. His answers were short and his actions lacking motivation. His head wasn't here and if it was like this on a job, it could get one or both of us killed. He approached me lazily, as I easily maneuvered around him, opting to flick him in the back rather than take him down again.

"You're not even trying." I picked up my rubber stake,

holding it like I would in the field. His eyes flashed as I lunged at him, zeroing in on me. I faked an attack to the right, before spinning the opposite way, swinging my fake stake to hit him in the middle of his chest.

Gray came to life, his hand moving faster than I could see, snatching my wrist before I could make contact. He yanked painfully, pulling me forward, and spun, somehow sending me sprawling to the ground. I landed on my hands and knees heavily, the impact burning up my thighs and into my hips. I flipped around to see Gray standing over me, a surprised look plastered across his face.

"Are you okay?" He quickly bent down, but I swatted his hand away.

"What the hell was that?" I barked, my knees still aching.

"I guess your training has been paying off." He tried to laugh, but it sounded forced, his eyes scanning me like I had been broken.

"Don't look at me like that!" I said, staring him down. "I'm fine. I can take care of myself." I brushed myself off and stood up, trying to prove it to him. Last thing I wanted was someone feeling bad about training with me. Sure, my ego was bruised right now, but I had learned my mistake and I wouldn't be letting Gray catch me off guard like that again. "Let's go again." I ordered.

"No," he replied.

"What?" I choked out, confused.

"I just, I think I am done for the day." He looked away from me, jaw working. "Probably just tired." He rubbed the back of his neck like he had slept wrong and it was kinked.

I wanted to push him, but he just seemed so...off.

"Okay." I agreed. I hoped he wasn't getting sick or something. He had had guard duty every night and while that was uneventful, having to get up and train again was probably exhausting. I wondered if going out today was the right decision when it would be his first chance to really rest. I followed him outside, the air between us heavy.

"We are still on for tonight, right?" Gray said to the wind as the door shut behind us.

"Are you sure you're okay? We don't have to—" He nodded before the words had even left my mouth, sensing the question. I sighed, not believing him but knowing it was less helpful to pry. "Yeah, meet me out front at exactly ten. Be very quiet," I said. We most certainly did not have permission to leave, but I also happened to know there was a shift change and someone was indebted to me. That would be our opening. "Better to ask for forgiveness rather than permission, right?"

"Right." Gray laughed, but it lacked the usual depth it normally had as we headed back toward the house.

We parted in the foyer to go up to our rooms to rest. I only stopped to ask Jack, a student on duty tonight, for a long overdue favor. When he tried to resist, I reminded him of the time I covered for him during his rendezvous through the forest to impress some girl. He hesitantly agreed and I let myself get excited over doing something so mischievous. I was sure Todd didn't think I was going to have any fun out here.

I spent some extra time getting ready, soaking my sore muscles under hot water and using some perfumed wash that was probably expired instead of my normal bar of soap. I didn't have much here in terms of 'going out' clothes, so I went for basic black jeans and a loose rocker tee from a band that was around well before I was born. My parents handed these shirts down to me from their younger days, telling me stories of going to concerts and seeing rock bands—no *hair bands* they called them. I would listen and wonder what it was like to live so carefree. I tugged on my trusty boots, tying them tight. They were a little bit worn down but never failed me in comfort. Hair and makeup weren't really my thing, so I pulled my hair into a high ponytail, patting my cheeks to give them some much needed color.

Should be good enough, right?

I left my room with a leather jacket draped on my arm, closing the door gently to make that *click* as silent as I could. The floorboards squeaked under my weight, sending my nerves into overdrive. They never squeaked before; it was like they were ratting me out before I could even get caught. I shouldn't feel so anxious. I had done this before with Alec. We never got caught, never got into trouble, but tonight felt different. Leaving the training grounds was a serious no—no, even if most of the students attempted it.

I passed a grandfather clock just as it chimed on the hour. The noise sent my heart into my throat, gluing my feet to the ground as it chimed twice more. When I didn't hear anyone stir, I moved forward, quickly descending the stairs. The door was already cracked, so I peered outside.

"Jack?" I whispered to the singing crickets.

"No, it's Gray. You invited another boy?" Gray pouted.

"No, well, yes, well, no, not like that. Where's Jack?" I asked, flustered.

"Right here." His voice rang from the same place as Gray's.

"If you were there why didn't you answer?" I asked, stepping out onto the porch, the light illuminating them both.

"I was going to but, uh…" He looked from Gray to me.

"I jumped in first, he means." Gray finished the

sentence laughing, draping an arm around Jack's shoulder and fisting his hair like he was his little brother.

"Just a real comedian, aren't you?" I frowned at Gray, who then returned with a smile.

"Jack, are we in the clear?" I asked.

"Yup, all set. Take the car and go now. Everyone's at the east wing checking out a...disturbance." He smiled and handed me the keys, palming down the tangled mess that his normally sandy and long hair now was.

"Do I even want to know?" I asked.

"Probably not." A frightening gleam entered his eyes, reminding me he was a slight pyromaniac.

"Just don't burn down the place," I said.

"I am offended." He covered his heart like I had stabbed him. "You don't think I know what I'm doing?"

"We better go," I said to Gray, who was doing the mental math. His eyes opened wide as the light bulb in his brain went off. I grabbed his arm and steered him down the porch before he could ask more questions. We were going to lose our window.

An old BMW was waiting for us. It was a luxury car before, but lack of care showed in chipping paint and sun-rotted leather seats. We jumped in and I started the engine. It roared at first but came down to a soft hum as I put it in gear and rolled forward. I kept the lights off to try to keep the attention away from us. We might get caught on our way back, but I was determined to make it out and enjoy one night for the first time in what seemed like forever.

"Do you know how to drive?" Gray asked, eyeing me carefully as I over adjusted mirrors and jerked the wheel too hard to the left, sending us off the gravel path slightly before correcting the car.

"Define 'know'." I gripped the wheel a little tighter as I got a feel for it.

"You're joking, right?" Gray asked while pulling his seat belt tightly across his body and clicking it into place.

"We don't really have driving courses anymore, you know. Honestly, I never really had the extra time to get a driver's license, anyway. Mostly I just walk or take public transportation like most people nowadays." I shot him a toothy grin.

"But you at least have basic experience." It sounded more like a pleading question rather than a fact as he looked from me to the road I hadn't looked back at and then back to me. "The road's that way!" He encouraged with a frantic jab of his finger.

"Alec showed me a time or two." I shrugged, taking the wheel with me. Gray's eyes opened wide, but he kept his mouth sealed tight.

I flipped the lights on as we made our way onto the pavement with a gentle bump. The sound became soothing as we switched from the rocky path to a mostly upkept street, only running over the occasional pothole.

Gray took a breath and I finished where I left off. "Plus, it's not far, there's a town that is protected by a D.O.V.E. sister company so we can easily get supplies to the training facility. Not as big as the city, but they still know how to have a good time. It's guarded twenty-four seven, so the bar will still be open for a while longer," I said. "We'll be fine." Gray didn't look assured but nodded anyway.

I carefully navigated the road based solely off of memory. Normally Alec would drive us, though he drove with much more ease. He'd have the radio up with only one hand on the wheel. The first time we came out here he paid the bouncer to let me in. The smell of smoke gave me a headache, but I played it off because I didn't want to look like a baby in front of Alec. I begged him for a shot even when he said no, but he finally gave in considering I had gone through all the effort to get the fake I.D. and convincing him to let me keep it. It was my first drink of alcohol. When it hit my tongue, I spat it out, choking on the bitter burning that was still lingering in my mouth. Alec laughed so hard I tried to leave, embarrassed, but he gently gripped my elbow and guided me back to the barstool. He said it happened to him his first time too, but I knew he was lying.

I had never been to LIV without Alec and as we were approaching the turn, the yearning made my heart skip. I swallowed the emotions down. I was going to enjoy tonight no matter what. I wanted to be happy. I needed to be happy and just for a single moment I wanted to pretend like I wasn't the reason he was gone. Plus, I wanted Gray to have a good time. I had started to realize he was just as stuck in this whole situation as I was.

Gravel crunched under the tires of the beamer as we pulled into a tight parking spot. I looked at Gray, who was simultaneously clutching his heart and the 'oh shit' handle on the ceiling. "We made it!" I beamed, sounding a little bit surprised myself.

A strange sound escaped his mouth as he failed to tip his lips upward and still gripped the bottom of his seat with white knuckled hands. "Yup." It came out as a choke. "We did," Gray said, removing his seat belt and all but darting from the parked car. I followed him out, slamming the door behind me.

"Don't go kissing the ground on me. It wasn't *that* bad." I scoffed at Gray as he side-eyed me from across the vehicle. I returned his look with an eye roll and motioned for him to follow me. I was secretly pleased to enact some type of revenge on him for all the times he'd been purposefully annoying but kept the thought to myself.

The building was connected to a small strip mall. The other stores had long shut down for the night, not risking being open the same time vampires hunted. It was worn down but active, the parking lot full of cars. Moths bounced off of exposed lights above the sidewalk, their bodies making audible clinks against the glass. Security was stationed outside the door. The guard to the right recognized me right away.

"Sam?" he asked, pulling dark sunglasses down his nose. The look was purely for intimidation, unless the buzzing neon sign that hung crookedly in the window was too bright for him.

"In the flesh," I said and smiled. "How are you, Nick?"

"Good, good. Hell, I haven't seen you since—" He stopped, realizing what he was about to say.

"I know it's been a while. Working." I slammed my hands into the pockets of my pants and shrugged my shoulders to play it off. It killed me that everyone knew about what happened, but Alec's death was a major loss to D.O.V.E.

"Well, it's good to see you." He looked toward Gray. "And who might this be?"

"Fresh meat." We laughed together, leaving Gray out of the joke.

"Well, come on in!" He slapped my shoulder as I passed him.

We walked into a dense cloud of smoke, the mixture rich of cigarettes and cigars with the lack of ventilation. It stung my eyes in a nostalgic kind of way, instantly clinging to my clothes the way smoke seems to do. I led Gray through a throng of people to the bar, having to yell over music that was two octaves too loud.

"A beer?" I asked.

"Sure!" he said. "I'm gonna hit the little boys' room."

I gave him a thumbs-up as he left and waved down the bartender. Loui was in his late forties and overweight. His tank was an off-white color from dirt rather than design. Last time I saw him, his beard was black, but now it was sprinkled with gray, giving him a salt and peppered look. He still wore a gold wedding band even though his wife had left him for someone else years ago. I was pretty sure he told the suitors that she died to better his chances.

"Long time no see," he said as he walked up to me. "The regular?"

"No, can you make it two long necks?" I asked. He raised his brow but didn't question me as he reached below the bar and twisted the lid off of two domestic beers. I tended to lean toward the liquor, so such a request probably seemed lite.

"You here with someone?" he asked, looking around.

"I was reassigned. I have to train someone for D.O.V.E."

He clicked his tongue at me, knowing I would have never asked to have someone working alongside me after Alec.

"How's your daughter?"

"Married now. Even got a little one on the way." He smiled big. "Scary world out there, but at least there's still love, right?"

Someone called for him, saving me from having to respond. After losing Alec, I wasn't so sure about the whole concept of love. Love made things complicated, and time and time again it seemed like love got more people killed than it made them happy. I leaned against the bar, taking a long swig of my drink. It was ice-cold but would have been better if it wasn't a lite beer. I knew beggars couldn't be choosers, so I drank again. I never paid for drinks here, but the toss-up was that I rarely asked for anything specific. I just took whatever was in abundance since shipments took much longer to arrive now as the streets became more dangerous.

"Hey, sweetheart!" a voice screeched over my shoulder. I clutched my beer and prayed whoever yelled it wasn't talking to me, but I knew I didn't get so lucky when I felt two hard taps to my shoulder.

I turned in my seat, bringing my drink with me, and leaned back against the bar, propping my shoulders up casually. I stared down a man, clearly two sheets to the wind, who was smiling from ear to ear. If I doubted it before, the rich alcohol smell lingered around him like he bathed in it.

"I'm—" He tried to introduce himself, but I put my hand out to stop him.

"Please don't, I'm not interested, but thanks," I said, intent on ending the encounter.

He scratched at the five o'clock shadow on his chin as I turned back in my seat to face the bar. *Mr. Didn't Get the Hint* took the empty seat next to me and offered his name again.

"I'm Mason." He leaned in close to be sure I heard him clearly. "Like the jar."

"And I'm not interested," I said again, this time with more venom in my words.

"Can't I just buy you a drink?" he asked.

I took a long swig from my beer, looking forward to giving him an answer in a nonverbal cue. He seemed to think it over, but undeterred and with a false sense of confidence he got closer, close enough his hot breath bounced off my cheek.

"Come on, baby." The moisture from his sweaty palm could be felt through my shirt as he placed his hand on the small of my back. "You should be lucky I'm even giving you the attention you're getting." His breath hot against my ear.

I slammed my beer down, hard. Liquid swam up the neck of the bottle, spilling out in a foamy mess and onto the counter of the bar. In the same motion I reached back, grabbing his wrist, and yanked his hand from my body in a tight hold. I quickly swung under his arm, reaching with my free hand for the back of his neck while kicking my barstool away to grant me more room. I dug my fingernails into his neck as his drunk mind failed to catch up with my motions and slammed his head down into the bar. I yanked the arm I was still holding into a painful bend, getting close to his face as he screamed out in agony.

"You should learn to take a hint." I growled, tightening my grip. His face slid easily through my spilled drink, but I didn't loosen my hold. "I think you've had enough and it's time for you to leave, don't you?"

He did his best to nod, agreeing, so I let go. His eyes were wide but didn't hold my gaze for more than a second before he turned on his heel and stumbled to the exit, knocking into Gray's shoulder as he returned from the restroom. Gray looked at me, astonished. Other patrons in the bar had backed up and formed a small circle to see the commotion but quickly returned to their own business now that the excitement was over. Gray walked to me as I readjusted my stool and gave Loui the 'okay' sign with my thumb and index finger, letting him know it was over. Gray sat in the seat that was just vacated and reached over for the full beer, handing it to me when he saw me try to drink from my practically empty one.

"I think you deserve this more than me." He smiled. I thanked him and took it. "I would have jumped in, but you didn't exactly look like a damsel."

"Hopefully that doesn't chop down your ego. I'm sure there's a pretty girl here who wouldn't mind being saved." I laughed.

"No, I don't think so." He disagreed with a soft smile.

"You don't think someone would be into you, or are you just not into girls?" I asked jokingly. Gray's face distorted, and I was sure that if it wasn't so dark in the bar it would even look beet red. He turned to Loui, grabbing my wasted beer and lifting it up, signaling for another.

"I'm just not looking for a relationship," he finally said after getting his drink and taking a deep chug.

"What *are* you looking for?" I asked, having to lean in slightly so he could hear me better.

"Are you flirting with me, or asking about work?" He took pride in being able to turn the tables, making me just as uncomfortable. I wanted to smack him, but I kept my hands to myself and tried to breathe the crimson that had blossomed in my cheeks back down.

"Definitely work," I bit out, pretending to be angrier than I was. "It takes a certain type of crazy to want to be a hunter, so which one are you? The hero? Maybe you have a vendetta? A death wish perhaps…?" I pried.

"Which one are you exactly?" he asked and I straightened my back on the barstool.

"A little bit of them all," I spoke loudly, trying to extend my voice over the deafening music. "So now that I answered, no more stalling. What's yours?"

Gray seemed to toss the question over in his head before

answering.

"None of them," Gray stated, glancing away before trailing his eyes steadily back to mine. "Mine is just because I don't have a choice."

"Everyone has a choice," I said, knowing that D.O.V.E. wasn't drafting recruits like the government used to do for their armies.

"Not everyone, Sam." His voice seemed to crack with pain, but as soon as it was there it was pushed aside, masked by his normal grin that spread from one side of his face to the other.

My heart thudded awkwardly in my chest as I stared at him. There was much more to Gray than what he displayed on the surface. A tale of the same pain that weaved its way under my own skin, its claws hooking into the soft fabric of my soul, never letting me go. When I looked at him, I saw someone who tried much harder to hide their despair, but as it seeped through the cracks his eyes resembled mine. Lost.

"You don't seem surprised," he said, misunderstanding my look.

"I'm not." I took another drink, trying to moisten my suddenly parched lips. "I guess everyone has to do what they think is right." I wanted to ask why he felt like he had no choice, but I realized that's probably how so many people thought. Hunting was where the money was and if you could stomach the lost and handle the danger it was one of the best ways for the lower class to move farther into the city, closer to safety.

"You said you're all three." Gray's voice brought me back. "Is that because of Alec?"

I tried not to flinch at hearing his name, though I wasn't sure how successful I was.

"Partly," I answered honestly, still uncomfortable talking about him. "And my parents. As you probably know, they weren't lucky either." I pursed my lips, the cynicism coating my words. I couldn't look at him when I talked about them, afraid he could see through the strength I was struggling to demonstrate.

"You know it wasn't your—" He tried.

"Please." My voice broke, my weakness shining through the facade I exhaustingly kept up against my attempts. "Please, don't say it."

"I get it." He took another drink. "My family—they were infected."

I couldn't control the sharp breath I sucked in. I couldn't fathom what he was dealing with inside. Out of everything, I could always fall back on the fact that the people I loved experienced the true death and didn't have to walk this earth as a monstrous bloodsucker. I could find a sense of peace in that. It was something that was grounding as I floated aimlessly through a sea of misery.

"I'm so sorry." I drifted closer, my knee brushing his. Him not having a choice to be a hunter made more sense. "The cure, it will change everything." I tried to be positive. "People won't have to lose their family ever again."

"It's too late for them," he said so softly I almost missed it. Gray leaned in, the distance between us shrinking. He reached out, brushing a fallen strand of hair behind my ear, his soft touch lingering against my skin. My breath hitched in my chest, but I didn't move back. "I'm sorry too." He finally pulled away, leaving the space between us chilly.

"F-for what?" I sat back awkwardly, trying to stifle the fluttering in my chest.

After a moment, like he had to decide what his answer was going to be, he said vaguely, "Everything."

"Thanks," I said simply. "It's okay."

"It's really not." His look seemed far away, but I shrugged anyway.

"It's why I want to keep hunting. Why I want to make the changes to the company." I looked down, not understanding why I felt embarrassed. "Why I'm fighting so hard to find out why we don't have a cure."

"You don't think it was an accident? What happened?" he asked, surprised.

"I—uh." The words tumbled from my lips. "It's just that—I mean, doesn't it seem strange?" I asked, finally. Gray didn't blink, his gaze boring into mine uncomfortably. His grip on the bottle tightened and he used the short nail of his thumb to scratch at the label, tearing it.

"Who would want the world to stay the way it is?" he asked, not looking at me.

"No one, I guess." My answer was automatic, my thoughts not keeping up with the movement of my lips. I paused for a moment. "Vampires." I shook my head, trying to rid my mind of the murky thoughts swirling there.

"Now that I believe." He chuckled, bringing the bottle to his lips again. I joined in like it was a joke. I thought back to Alana and how she looked on the video. She was definitely distressed. I didn't share the rest of my thoughts on it with Gray. I needed them to be more coherent first. I did, however, silently decide that we would be leaving first thing tomorrow with or without Todd's permission, and I was going to ask Alana myself.

"I don't know what I'm doing," I spoke honestly, to everyone and to no one in particular. Gray raised a brow, so I elaborated. "I don't know anything about taking over D.O.V.E. and it terrifies me. I have brought it up to Todd, but he is either unwilling or doesn't have the time to show me the ropes. People around me don't particularly like me, not that I have given them a very good reason to lately but still. Sometimes..." I trailed off before returning. "Sometimes I think about just going rogue and—"

Gray reached for my hand before I could continue.

"That is the last thing you should ever do," he spoke firmly, but still managed a gentle undertone that made it clear his words were out of concern and not malice. "I know you will figure it out. I don't know if I have ever met someone more motivated than you." He gave my hand a quick squeeze, which I felt in my chest.

"Yeah," I said, not sure if I meant it. "I guess so."

The bar was already starting to clear out. The music had been turned down to a dull roar as people trickled out, leaving their trash behind. Glass bottles clanked against each other as the bussers cleared tables to wipe them down and stack the stools on top. The bouncers came inside to start clearing the stragglers out so they could go home too. Nick walked toward us and I knew we were about to get the same eviction notice as the others.

"I know, I know," I said. "We will get a move on. I didn't know you started closing earlier than before." I smiled at him, but he didn't smile back.

"Something strange is happening," he said in a hushed but urgent tone. "The system is back on."

"I mean that's good, isn't it?" I asked. Businesses had limited access to D.O.V.E.'s system, only able to see tagged and their locations so they could close shop if anything got too close. It was most important for any place that was willing to stay open past nightfall, when people became vulnerable.

"I don't think so," he said, voice shaky. "Sam, you're gonna want to see this."

Chapter 12

NICK LED us to the back room, where Loui was hunched over a screen, whispering to himself. I rounded him, glancing at the screen to see what had them so stressed. It took a moment to register the red dots moving together. Fifteen or more tagged were moving in unison up the grid just to the east of us. I looked at Gray, his eyes wide and body rigid as Nick tapped the screen, right in front of the moving dots.

"Where are they going?" he asked. My eyes followed their trajectory, trying to recognize which direction they were moving. It wasn't toward the strip mall, it was…*oh no.*

My heart free-fell from my chest with the blood that had drained from my face, leaving me cold and sickly. The training facility. They were heading right to the facility, where we were supposed to be, where we would have been able to help. They were well equipped, but I didn't know if their system was on or how never having to deal with a herd would affect their response time.

"We need to go now," I yelled, racing out of the door back into the bar, with Gray closing in behind me.

"What should I do?" Nick called out after us.

"Stay here, stay safe," I hollered back. It would be better for him to watch out for whoever was left around here. He was trained but not the way the hunters were, and I feared he'd be more of a burden than help.

"Loui, where's the phone?" I needed to get back, but I also needed to warn them, and I didn't get cell service out here. He grabbed the handset from under the bar and handed it to me. I dialed the number I had been forced to memorize years ago, listening to the ringing on the other end, praying someone would pick up.

Nothing. I tried again.

"They aren't answering!" I was panicking. "Gray, we've got to go. Loui, lock up tight tonight until I can make sure there are extra hunters here."

I ran to the car, swinging the door open and jamming the key into the ignition. Gray was barely in his seat before I had the car in reverse, the tires taking a moment before they could catch traction and catapult us backward. He slammed the door shut as I stomped on the gas, heading back the way we came to the facility. I drove better speeding and scared than I did calm.

"Sam, slow down!" Gray begged.

"I can't, people could die!" I snapped back, trying my best to focus.

"You could die!" he yelled back at me.

"You'll be fine." I tried to calm him, positive he omitted the 'we' to seem tough. I thought he'd argue more, but when I casted a glance his way, he averted his eyes, trying to keep the stress that was etched across his face hidden.

We came to a skidding halt in front of the gate, sending rocks flying, ricocheting off of the objects around us. I barely heard Gray ask me to wait before I had opened the door, running straight for the gate. No guards were at the front and even though the gates were open when we left now they were sealed shut. The light shined across the grounds, reminding me of the lights that plagued my nightmares, electrically buzzing all around us.

"It's locked," I said, hearing Gray get out of the car and walk up behind me. "I don't hear anything."

Bang. Bang. Bang.

Shots were fired in rapid succession followed immediately by a scream that pierced its way right through me. I grabbed the gate, pushing it forward and then yanking it back to try to get the lock to budge. The metal moved back and forth clanking, but holding firm not matter how hard I pulled. I needed to get over there.

"What are you doing?" Gray yelled, but I had already heaved my body halfway up the gate. I threw my leg over the top and shifted my weight to the other side. I searched for a piece of iron to rest my foot on but came up short. I lost my grip and fell, tumbling to the ground in a painful heap. Rocks cut into my palms, the sting barely fazing me as I took off on foot toward the mansion. Gray called out for me, but I didn't stop. Instead I pushed my legs to move faster, taking me closer to the gunfire.

I'd never run so fast in my life, making the half a mile stretch seem like yards instead. I passed the house, heading to the back where shouts and monstrous howls were still ringing out. I hadn't even made it halfway before I saw the first rattled body. He was just a kid, his hair soaked in what I could only guess was blood, eyes wide-open in a never-ending stare. I slowed slightly, looking around, trying to gauge the area. To my right was a headless vampire lying unnaturally in its death. Next to it was another recruit. Hair flowed over her face; her arms positioned awkwardly next to her. I pushed forward, but it seemed everywhere I looked there were bodies, both ours and theirs. Quiet showered down around me. I couldn't hear anything but the crickets hiding away in the trees.

Where are the rest?

Suddenly, I was knocked off my feet. The impact sent me flying, landing hard, flat on my back. The wind rushed out of my lungs with such ferocity I thought I would suffocate. Before I could get up, I was straddled. I threw my hand up instinctively to stop the fangs from coming down on my neck, managing to get my forearm lodged into its neck. The vampire sank its claws into my side, digging into my flesh. I screamed out, agony rippling through my nerves, making my arm buckle, bringing its face closer to mine. Saliva leaked from its mouth, burning my skin as it dripped down my cheek. I bucked until I could wiggle my leg up, placing the bottom of my foot flat against his stomach, and kicked as hard as I could.

The vampire stumbled back, eyes like midnight peering back at me as I clutched at my side and looked over at a fallen comrade. His stake was lying just outside of his hand. The creature seemed to understand just as I had decided my next move and lunged. I made myself jump up and leap toward the weapon, feeling the wood touch my fingertips at the same time a sharp grip in my shoulder yanked me back. My elbow crashed to the ground before my back did, getting stuck under me painfully. The vampire lunged forward, mouth wide and ready to feed, unaware I had reached what I needed. I swung my arm as hard as I could, ramming the tip of the stake into its neck, having to push hard to get through the muscle. The bloodsucker let out a piercing cry. I pushed up with the stake still in its neck, managing to shift us and ending up on top of it. Blood splattered across my face as I yanked the stake out and rammed it into its heart.

I kept the weapon as I got up, looking around again. My body seemed slower, but I pushed through, ignoring the increasing pain in my side. Recruits were tending to each other. Trainers were running after the last of the vampires, some trying to drag their prey deep into the forest. The last of the emergency lights had been turned on, painting the ground in bright white, lighting the bodies that lay still and contrasting against the deep crimson of blood coating the land. I heard whimpering in the distance and tried to see past the brightness. I moved closer to it, calling out if anyone was there.

I watched as a vampire pierced its teeth into the neck of a recruit, but from their lack of body movement I could tell it wasn't the first bite. It tried to drag the person to the tree line, away from help, just as the others were doing. For a moment I froze. All I could see was Alec being dragged away from me. I was helpless then, but not this time. I took off after them, ignoring what I thought was my name being shouted. The vampire didn't see me coming as I tackled them both, knocking it off of her neck. She fell to the ground unmoving and I rolled with the creature to the side through the fallen leaves and sticks, landing with my knees on both sides of its body. I raised the stake high and stabbed, over and over again, ignoring the cries, the blood, not even realizing when it was gone. I stabbed for Alec, for the pain I still felt, for all the lives lost, for everything I would never have back. I tried to bring the stake down again, but hands wrapped around my wrist, holding them above my head.

"Let go!" I screamed, trying to pull my arms down again.

"It's gone," Gray said, holding me tight. "It's dead, Sam."

I looked down at the vampire, whose chest now looked like it had gone through a wood-chipper, and dropped my hands. I let the stake fall from my grasp and looked down at hands that didn't feel like my own, covered in color that seemed to paint the story of my life. I turned back to the recruit, standing up on wobbly legs, almost falling over, but Gray held me upright. My heart swelled in my throat, strangling me from the inside out. I tried to cry out, but I couldn't make a sound.

Cindy lay still, un-breathing in front of me.

Fear still laced into her features, freezing it in time with pain and despair. Blood poured from her neck, soaking into her shirt while the excess ran to the ground, pooling around her in the dirt. She was gone. I didn't help her. I couldn't help her. Gray was talking to me, but his words never registered. I tried to read his lips, but I didn't understand. Everyone around me died. I shook his hands off me, looking around at what was left of the facility, trying to count faces and do the math. How many had we lost this time? How many would we continue to lose to these monsters?

"Go make sure Maria is okay," I said, but my voice didn't sound familiar. "She is probably locked down with the newer...with the other recruits." The words felt thick as molasses as I tried to push them from my mouth.

I looked at Gray, but his face was wrong. He seemed to be in a tunnel that kept getting smaller and smaller with every slow blink. My brain felt like it had detached from my body, leaving me to swim in an ocean of nothingness. Gray called out to me, but I was tired. I just needed to sit, just for a second. As I stepped back my legs gave out and I fell, but my eyes closed long before I ever reached the cold, dead ground.

Chapter 13

LIGHTS RAINED DOWN on my face, turning the inside of my eyelids orange. I forced them open just to slam them shut when they burned against the brightness. Slowly I blinked, allowing my pupils to adjust to the light. I immediately knew I was in a D.O.V.E. care center, even without the sounds of the monitors and nurses busying themselves outside of the privacy curtain to my room. It was the equivalent of what used to be called a hospital but much more heavily protected. The room was bare except for the stiff bed I lay on, a rolling table, and the IV rack that had a line hooked into my arm. The smell of bleach was almost overwhelming as I took a big breath in. I scooted up on the bed, pausing when pain shot through my side.

"You shouldn't move around too much." Gray walked through the curtain, the metal scraping as he closed it behind him.

"Maria?" I demanded, the monitor beeping louder.

"She's okay, please calm down." Gray walked over to

the monitor, pressing a button when the alarm went off, alerting the nurses my heart rate was too high. "Unless you want more visitors," he said softly.

"How long have I been out?" I asked, trying to make sense of what had happened.

"Just over a day," he answered, awkwardly picking his hand up to show what he had. "I brought coffee."

Gray sat the cup down on the table for me, but I couldn't even think of taking it. Everything came back to me in one big rush. I closed my eyes to the images, but they transitioned anyway, ending with Cindy's face. I never should have left. I could have been there. I would have saved her, maybe even saved others. I held the tears back, shoving them back down deep, to where I kept everything else.

Dark circles had started to appear under Gray's eyes and blood still stained the bottom of his once white shirt. His arms were sloppily wiped of dirt, leaving clean streaks over his skin. It pulled at my chest knowing that he'd been here the whole time, not even taking the time to change or take care of himself, but even though I didn't say it I was mostly relieved that he was okay. Even if he stayed only out of a feeling of obligation since we were technically partners.

"Why are you here?" I asked Gray, looking nowhere but the ceiling.

"I was worried about you." He scoffed like the question was ridiculous. "You were bleeding badly, and when you passed out, I knew the cuts were pretty deep. The doctor said you got lucky," he explained.

"*Lucky?*" I spat, expelling some of the anger I felt bubbling up in my chest. It was humorous that anyone would refer to me as lucky.

"I was just—" he said, but I cut him off.

"This is your fault!" I yelled, knowing how unfair that was, but needing to throw the blame anywhere before it suffocated me. "We should have never left. We should have been there doing our jobs!"

"Sam," he said simply.

"Get out." My voice was just above a whisper. My heart thudded painfully in my chest. "Just leave."

"You shouldn't be alone." He was hurt, but I pretended not to care. "I know how you feel, but this isn't your fault."

"GET OUT!" I roared, feeling some of the pressure release from my chest, relishing in the tight tug of the stitches I felt hold my skin together. Who else was to blame? This was my fault. I knew we weren't supposed to leave and I did it anyway. I could have saved her...I could have saved Cindy.

Gray went to the curtain, yanking it open. Nurses had stopped, staring back at us, clearly interested in the commotion. He turned like he was going to say something, his mouth opening slightly but thought better of it and left, not bothering to shut the curtain behind him, leaving me open to the looks from the staff. I ripped the I.V. from my arm, daring a nurse with my look to stop me, and ripped the curtain closed. Drops of blood dripped from my arm to the floor, landing in perfect circles.

Tears snuck from my eyes. The constant loss was unbearable. My clothes had been washed, folded, and sat on the table. I grabbed them, tugging the material on quickly, trying not to see the blood stains that didn't come out of the fabric. I refused to acknowledge the agony in my side as the movement pulled at the sutures I didn't have to see to know existed. I left the building, not one person trying to stop me. I was going to kill every last one of those bloodsuckers if it was the last thing I did.

By the time I had reached my apartment I was winded and sore. I stepped into eight hundred square feet of furnished space with no personal touches, nothing making it feel like home. I jumped into the shower, barely rinsing off before getting out and putting on clean pants and a black shirt. I buckled my belt and was back out the door, on a mission, but I needed to stop by D.O.V.E. first.

I was going to need supplies.

The sun was high in the sky, sending its warmth down to the increasingly cold city. I found myself on the bus, making the trek to D.O.V.E since it would be faster and less painful than walking. I needed to conserve my energy. The ride was bumpy and thankfully short. I tried to keep my mind blank as I counted the stops to the one I was going to get off on. When the bus arrived at D.O.V.E. I flew into the building. I didn't have time to waste.

"Sam?" one of the men who worked front desk security questioned, clearly not expecting to see me.

"Hey. I am not working, just grabbing some things." I tried to brush by. I was not going to just lie around and do nothing.

"No, Sam, Todd needs to see you. It's important, but we figured you'd take a little time," he said.

"He's in luck because I need to see him too," I said, leaving him standing at the desk staring after me. I blocked out the hushed voices as I passed by people to catch the elevator. They could say whatever they wanted.

The music didn't play as I rode up alone, or maybe I just couldn't hear it over the scene I kept replaying in my head. The doors chimed as I reached the top floor and headed straight for Todd's office, trying to ignore the gasps and whispers I heard as I passed people by. The door was cracked slightly, so I knocked as I entered the room. Todd glanced up for a moment. He had his phone nestled between his ear and shoulder but quickly cut the conversation short and hung up. I shut the door quietly behind me and turned back to face him, but he had already crossed the room in long strides and pulled me in close, catching me off guard.

"I am so glad you're okay!" He shoved me back roughly, giving me the once-over. "How do you feel? Are you in pain?"

"No…" Todd never acted like this. "I mean, I wasn't until now."

He pulled back farther to lean against his desk and let me sit. The look he gave me was peculiar, as he waited for me to get settled into the chair. He wasn't in his suit today, but rather khaki pants, and a light blue button-up shirt, which was a rare sight. This for him was rolling out of bed. He sucked in a long breath, exhaling just as slowly, and I wondered if he'd been practicing whatever it was that he was about to say.

"What were you thinking?" His voice was pressed through his teeth. This was the Todd I expected.

"I was just trying to—I just wanted to have some fun." I was embarrassed to admit it. I was so ashamed of losing sight of what was important. Why did I think I could relax when my duty was to keep people safe?

"Fun?" His face soured like he had just bitten into a lemon. "People are dead, Samantha, dead. If you want to have fun then read a book, go for a walk, don't sneak away from a guarded compound when you're a valuable asset that can help in situations like this!"

I flinched back like he had hit me. I knew the severity. I

knew what had happened, but hearing it outside of my head made it worse. If I had been there, I could have assisted them. Even if we were unaware of the attack, I would have been able to replace a few of the newer recruits and saved their lives.

"I know," I whispered.

"After everything you have been through, you should know better! Why do you think we have these rules?" he yelled, no longer worried about my feelings.

"I know that, I just——" I tried.

"I don't want to hear it!" He cut me off. "This whole time you wanted to work on your own out of clear hard-headedness and I tried to understand. I tried to understand your feelings against Gray. Hell, I even tried to understand you coming back so soon, but now I know it was just your mere immaturity that has led you here. You were not ready; you should not have been allowed to come back. You need, quite frankly, to grow up." His anger had dissipated, but the words were already said.

"*I need to grow up?*" I asked, perplexed, his words hitting me harder than any curse could have. "I had to grow up! I wasn't allowed to be a kid! I grew up the moment I watched my parents get murdered by those *THINGS!*" I tried to breathe, but I started to see red. "I have dedicated my whole life to D.O.V.E. All I know is how to kill. How dare you try to pretend like you understand. You sit behind a desk! You let us do the dirty work for you so you can line your pockets with money that doesn't belong to you!"

"You are way out of line." He cautioned.

"Oh no. I'm just getting started." I growled, pointing a stiff finger in his direction. "*You.* You are the one out of line. Where were you? You were supposed to be there!" The room went silent, but my heart ached to the point I swore it could be heard from inside my chest. I didn't know why I said that. It had nothing to do with what happened, but it needed to be said. Todd didn't respond. "You were supposed to be there that night. You let them die!" I screamed, letting the emotion rip from me.

"They let themselves die!" Todd spat back. "Your parents were so concerned with you! You should have been training well before then, but no, oh no, they wanted to rose-color this world for you. You would have been able to help; you wouldn't have needed to hide and then we wouldn't be here. You're a spoiled brat who thinks her feelings get to top everyone else's. We have all seen death! Every single day, and that's just the way it is. You're either going to roll with it or end up right where they are!"

His words hit me like bricks, but bricks that I watched someone throw and decided to not move out of the way of. I knew they were coming, and I wanted to feel them hit me. He only confirmed what I already knew. It was expected of me to start my training young. The daughter of the founders was supposed to exceed their already unreachable reputation, but I didn't have a desire to fight then. I begged them to let me do anything else, and they gave in. Maybe it was because of their inability to force this world on me, maybe it was because I was their only child, or maybe it was because it was so easy for me to convince them that my selfish wants were more important than the need to train people and save our race.

"Why don't you just say what you feel, *uncle*. Just tell me how much you hate me. Tell me how much you wish I wasn't here so all of this could just be yours!" I screamed.

"Is that what you truly think?" His laugh was filled with

pain. "I love you, can't you see that? Can't you see that anyone could care about you?"

I knew I was being selfish. I knew we were both saying things we didn't mean. Revenge was eating me from the inside out. It was an insatiable hunger for something to make the hurt I felt fade away.

"Then why aren't you preparing me?" I asked, staring right at him to see if he knew what I meant. When he didn't answer I elaborated. "You and I both know I have to take over soon, and regardless if you don't like that fact, would you rather see me fail, watch everything crumble around us just to hold on to your self-righteous importance?"

"I cannot hunt you down and force you to learn this stuff." He deflected my accusation.

"Then let me make some decisions. Bring me in on where we are and what movements we are making toward change." I crossed my arms. "I want to know everything. I want to hire more people, finish what Zoe started. End this."

"I'd love to let you do that but look at the decisions you make! Do you think that's what a leader does?" His back straightened as he peered down at me.

"I can make this right." It sounded like a question. "Send me on a mission. I will take Gray, just let me find those bloodsuckers, and when I am done teach me every-thing." There was venom in my heart. With every beat it slushed through my veins, finding its way up and out of my mouth like vomit.

"No," he said. I looked up, questioning him with my gaze. "You're done, Sam. I can't send you out into the field. You are too careless, reckless, endangering the lives of everyone else around you. You have run free for too long. I

will not lose any more people because of your irrationality."
Todd's voice carried so much disappointment it made me
sink back. "I know you think you will just inherit everything, but trust me when I say I will not let someone who
cares nothing about others' safety run D.O.V.E."

"You need me. You can't afford to lose any agents. I
know yesterday I made a bad call. I know that——" I had to
pause to keep from choking on the memory.

"You haven't learned a thing." He argued. "You make
the same rash decisions, over and over again, and you take
good people down with you every time. How many more
people need to die? Huh? How long is it going to take for
you to figure out that your feelings cannot come before
those around you?"

The room fell silent, my bones growing heavy in my
body. Anything Todd could have said in that moment
would have been impossible to hear over the sloshing in my
ears. My skin was aflame, burning so hot I wanted to rip it
off. It seemed like my world had started spinning and I
didn't know up from down. I reached out to the armrest to
steady myself, squeezing the material in my hand. Todd
reached for me, but I backhanded him like his touch would
scar me worse than his words had.

"You're so quick to tally the blood on my hands but
forget to look at how sullied yours are. Do you know how
many hunters died keeping people safe? Keeping *you* safe
up here in your tower? I'm starting to think *you* don't know
the first thing about running this place either." I hardened
my jaw so tight I thought it might snap against the pressure,
burning my eyes into his face. I was losing a grip on everything and this time, I didn't care.

"Just stop." He cut off anything I could have added.
"Alec would be here if you had listened. You and I both

know I can't sit here and do this with you anymore. I cannot keep pretending that you're going to magically wake up and start acting like an adult. I am sorry for all you have been through and I am so sorry that you blame me for all the loss in your life, but we won't lose anyone else because of you. See yourself out, Sam, or I will have someone escort you out. I will check on you in a few days, but I have damage control to do now."

If beams could have shot out of my eyes they would have flown through his chest as the fury burned inside of me. I clamped my lips down as tight as I could, locking the words behind them, and shot up from my chair. I threw the door open as Gray tried to enter, almost knocking into him. It ricocheted off of the stopper and flew back as I walked past him without a word.

"Sam?" he called after me, but I pretended not to hear.

I felt everyone's eyes on my back as I entered the elevator, singeing my nerves and making my skin crackle with heat. The doors shut behind me as I slammed my hands down on the safety bar that was secured at waist level in case of an abrupt stop. My fists squeezed the shiny metal tightly, pulling the skin of my knuckles taut against the bone, turning my flesh white as I struggled to not ram them through the wall.

The elevator descended slowly, thankfully not stopping at any of the other floors, allowing me to steam in solitude. I couldn't get out of the building fast enough, pushing the door as hard as I could, hoping it would slam but being disappointed when the hinge didn't allow it. The day was warmer than when I had entered the building, but it could have been linked to the energy crackling under my skin. I used the back of my hand to wipe away the sweat that was accumulating at my hairline before it could fall.

My feet were rooted into the concrete sidewalk, not taking me forward or back despite my brain telling them we needed to move, somewhere, anywhere. What was I supposed to do now? My head ached, flashing images of the people I had lost all displayed behind my eyes like a slideshow. I pushed my fingers into my tear ducts, trying to turn off the painful movie and counter the headache that I wasn't sure would ever go away.

"Move," I barked at myself, ignoring the passersby who looked my way.

Finally, one foot shifted, followed by the other until I was heading in the direction of my apartment. I had no plan. I could go back into D.O.V.E. and say how sorry I was, beg Todd to try to understand that the pain I felt was only manageable by the work I did, but I knew it would be no use. He didn't want to hear it and would not let me go back out under the company name, and I didn't want to force the words out of my mouth and continue to pretend like anyone was safe around me.

She was so close. I knew how hard Cindy was working to finish the academy. We all felt like doing this was our way of saving the world, but someone should have told her there was nothing left to save. We were on the losing end of this no matter how many times we acted like we had gotten ahead. Vampires weren't going away. The population was slowly teetering and with our numbers dwindling. It wouldn't be long until there was nothing left to do but hide and count your lucky days of not finding yourself being sucked dry by what I was sure were creatures of a self-induced apocalypse.

I couldn't swallow my feelings anymore. The pain, the anger I had been pushing down to the deepest parts of my soul were bubbling over like water left to boil carelessly. It felt like black sludge was moving through my veins, turning anything left in me that could be saved into coal that was ready to be lit on fire to burn. I pushed my feet fast with a new resolve. If I didn't get home and off the street, I wasn't sure who would get this darkness I felt unleashed on them first.

Chapter 14

ANGER CLOUDED MY VISION, bubbling up in a gray haze that made it hard to walk straight. Cindy's death, Alec's, even my parents' stacked on my shoulders. I was responsible for them not being here today. Their deaths were on me because if I had been stronger, smarter, and braver they would still be here. The sadness of losing them fueled a rage that burned so deep it seemed my very soul was on fire. I was losing myself to the emotions swirling inside me like a thunderous tornado, but I didn't care anymore.

"You are too careless, reckless, endangering the lives of everyone else around you." I found myself mocking Todd, attempting childish antics to make myself feel better. It didn't work. I was spiraling, and I couldn't get a grip on anything solid to stop. It didn't matter how much I believed he was right, hearing it out loud impacted me more than I would have guessed. The truth hurt, but the lies hurt more. He wasn't being honest with me; he was keeping me in the dark and I was willing to bet it was for a reason.

I ripped open a cabinet in the kitchen, exposing a glass

bottle filled with dark liquid. I wanted to say no to myself, but my world was caving in and I didn't know how to breathe without the numbing haze alcohol could encase my brain in. I tipped my head back and brought the bottle to chapped lips, embracing the heat that was traveling down my chest, pooling into my stomach to fuel the actions I was preparing to take next.

The images of Cindy, of her blood, made me throw my head back and take another long drink from the bottle. It no longer made me choke and gag like a novice. Now I appreciated the release it allowed when my brain would not shut off. I was abusing the substance, but as the rest of my life fell to pieces, I figured adding one more thing to the shards would make no difference.

I took another long swig, feeling the warmth settle in my stomach, numbing my nerves, sending an enticing buzzing sensation throughout my body. My side still twinged with pain, but it was leaving me by the second, faster than any medication would have worked. I was ready. I knew what I was going to do, and without the confines of D.O.V.E. and Todd to stop me I could go as far as I wanted.

I was going to go rogue.

With one last gulp, I grabbed my jacket and headed out to the streets. I was going after every single vampire I could find tonight. No one was going to stop me. I would prove just how viable I was. I was going to prove that I was a protector, not a destroyer.

The cold night air barely fazed me as I walked through the dark streets. The rum I drank kept me warm and the buzz it supplied kept me cocky. I kicked a rusted can, the sound of my shoe hitting the aluminum echoing off of abandoned buildings as I tried to draw attention to myself, walking farther into the Deserted. I kept my hands in my jacket pockets, unclenching and clenching them again to keep them from locking up from the anticipation. I traveled toward the part of the city with the least coverage and the most shadows, knowing they would be lurking for a meal.

I walked for what seemed like forever, but no matter the noise I made, nothing came out to get me. It seemed like when I was sneaking around, I had a target on my back, but now the world was unnaturally silent, the only sounds coming from me. I slowed as the buzz shifted, numbing my mouth and making my ears ring. I rubbed my face roughly with my hand, trying to massage the liquor from my mind so I could keep a clear head, but I could barely feel the motion against my skin.

Suddenly, I heard something off in the distance, down a dimly lit alley. I took half a second to weigh my options before deciding to go check it out and finish what I came here to do. My feet moved sloppily to the alley, aiding me in creating noise. The creature was tucked behind a trash bin, feeding in the comfort of the darkness. The only thing that illuminated it enough to be seen was the flickering lamp positioned above it and its victim, throwing light on them just long enough to catch a glimpse before it was gone again.

"Hey!" I hollered, noting the blood stain on the ground that moved in a slippery line, disappearing into the dark.

I didn't have to yell. As the light flickered again, I could catch the vampire already examining me, trying to figure out if I was worth the struggle or if it should just go back to eating. The latter seemed to win because as the light went out, I could hear the slobbery smacking of it feeding on the corpse again. From what I caught it looked like a homeless man had wandered too far from the shelters. Blood dripped from the wound on his neck and soaked into the claws of the predator that held him. He never had a chance.

"Get away from him!" I shouted again. A deep growl radiated from its core as I took a step forward.

"*Human.*" The vampire hissed in a calculated tone. "Do not test me, for you should be counting your blessings that I found my meal before I found you." It glanced up at me from the corpse, jagged teeth, glistening red in the brief moments of light.

Anything I was planning was stopped dead in its tracks. Blood drained from my face faster than it was being drained from the poor soul in front of me as I tried to pretend the voice I heard was a figment of my imagination and didn't come from the creature who most certainly couldn't talk.

The light above them had a moment of strength and stopped flashing. The alleyway was completely visible, showing the boxes that were set up as a makeshift home for the man. Trash and used clothes scattered the pavement, mixed around, and on rotting food. I didn't know why he was so far from the zone, but knew he never had a chance. The smell mixed with the copper scent wafting from the man's wounds made my stomach churn as unease crept into me.

As I studied my surroundings to gather a plan of action, the vampire studied me. A look of realization registered on its face before he smiled. The light gave out, sending the alley back into darkness. The sound of a motionless body hitting the ground made me step back. My eyes struggled to adjust to the abrupt change of light before it flashed again, making me shield my eyes briefly. The vampire was standing upright, walking toward me with the delicacy of a ballerina despite his build being heavy and tall.

He didn't have a shirt on, the skin of his chest painted red, but you could still make out his body, which seemed far too human the closer he got to me. My eyes traveled back up, focusing on his…face. His hair had all but departed and those familiar blue veins were visible against his pale skin but aside from that he almost looked normal, he almost looked *human*. My eyes bulged as I took another step back, trying to step away from the reality in front of me.

"You're the one who has been hunting us, aren't you?" He laughed so loud I couldn't help but to cringe back. My courage was quickly escaping me like a balloon being deflated. "This must be my lucky night, and you just so happen to be here alone, *and unarmed?*"

Wait, unarmed?

I reached toward my waist to grab my stake and came up empty-handed. I had left it at my apartment. Shit. Unintentionally I looked behind me, thinking about a way out of the mess I had irrationally got myself into. I had just done exactly what Todd said I did, only this time no one was here that I could put in danger. It was just me and this monster. No one was coming for me. No one would even know where to look.

"Why can you talk?" I found my voice. "You're a monster, not human."

"Yes." The vampire let the word linger in the air. "I am definitely not human, but how naïve of you *humans* to assume that we have no sense." He clicked his tongue at me. I stumbled, which brought a wide grin to his face. "Clumsy, aren't we? Tell me, how can the daughter of the great Cordovas be out here by her lonesome, and dare I say"—he sniffed up at the air, drawing in a deep breath —"a little drunk?" He kept creeping toward me, gaining an extra inch on every inch I retreated.

"And yet, I could take you drunk or sober. What does that say about you?" I snapped back with the rage I had almost forgotten about in the moment. I inched to the street, knowing I had made a really bad decision. My ears were ringing, and my vision focused slower than my eyes moved. If I got to the road, I could make a run to a neighboring home and lock myself in until hopefully I could get a message to D.O.V.E. Who was I kidding, I didn't even have my phone. I'd have to pray for daylight. "You're the same as the rest of the pests I have killed. I'm sure you knew some." Trying to keep my tone firm and unwavering.

He advanced on me quickly, not liking my response. "On second thought, they never said you had to be unharmed. Maybe I'll just take a little taste."

I didn't have a chance to ask what he meant about 'they' as he grabbed for me. I evaded his attempt and jumped to the side, almost losing my balance with the quick motion. My world was spinning, but I straightened myself back up in time to put my arms out in front of me in an X and block the hit he had launched at my chest. I kicked out, aiming for his gut, but ended up missing completely. My failed kick pushed me past him and he threw out a jab quicker than I could see, catching me in between my shoulder blades. The force pushed the air from my lungs and sent me staggering forward into the cold steel of a restaurant-sized garbage can farther into the dark of the alley. Farther from escape. The sound that echoed in my ears concerned me if I looked too close there would be an indent of my body in the alloy, but I refused to think about the delayed pain I knew I was about to feel. I squinted down the length of the buildings surrounding me, making out the slightest of light at the end, which I was sure would bring me out to the other side of the street.

This was my chance.

I made a break for the light, pushing off the ground as hard as I could despite my lungs struggling to inhale the oxygen that had escaped me so fast. I suspected I had torn my sutures as warmth tickled my side. My feet slapped the ground twice before the hairs at the nape of my neck stood tall. Long fingers dug into the skin of my ankle, tripping me up and sending me face first into the asphalt. I couldn't get my hands up in time to save my cheek from slamming into the ground. The swelling started immediately, but I had no time to think about it before I was yanked back toward the vampire, the ground tearing into my skin. He flipped me onto my back, straddling me with my arms pinned together above my throbbing head.

He shoved his nose into the curve of my neck, breathing in deep before tracing his tongue up the length of my throat. The smell of saliva burned my nose as I bucked my hips, trying to squirm out from under him with no success. Breathing hard, I stopped struggling to look the creature in the eyes. If I was going to go, it was going to be on my terms, and I'd be damned if I let him know I was scared.

"I can hear your heart pounding," he said, straightening himself up to look down on me, as if he knew of my resolve. His eyes resembled obsidian in the light that had stopped flashing as if to cast a spotlight on my death. I watched his almost human smile turn razor sharp again in a blink. "But don't worry, I'm only going to have a little taste," he said before opening his mouth wide and leaning back down into my throat. "Well, maybe more than a taste."

I closed my eyes, waiting for the bite to come, but it never did. The vampire was wrenched off of me, slashing my arms as he tried to hang on. He flew as if he was hit by a bus, but it wasn't a bus. Hell, it wasn't even a car. My eyes cleared to see a very pissed off looking Gray standing in front of me acting as a shield between me and the vampire who was already back on his feet. My mind's gears were turning. There was something wrong, something that didn't make sense. How could he have the strength to throw that vampire like that?

The vampire crouched down and pounced, but Gray was quicker. He moved to the side, opening up a full view of me. Just as I thought I'd be crushed he shot his hand out, sinking it into the shoulder of my assailant, and yanked him back before releasing the grip, forcing him to crash into the wall. Bits of brick cracked around his body, dusty material raining down around him. The vampire growled, showing off his serrated mouth, but Gray didn't back down. His eyes flashed with rage and I watched as Gray growled back, with a matching set of teeth.

Oh. My. *God*.

I couldn't move. My bones turned into jello as I held my breath, afraid he'd see me there, staring, and decide to share me as a meal. A part of me hoped that somewhere on my way here I had tripped and fallen, and that everything that was playing out before my eyes was some sick joke my brain was playing as a nightmare.

"Move back." Gray growled at the vampire, but I somehow knew he was talking to me. "I said *move!*" he yelled, finally looking my way as he locked arms with the vampire…the *other* vampire.

Something clicked on and I ran like hell, taking off down the street and only stopping long enough to expel the contents of my stomach onto an old bench. I reached my apartment in record time, slamming the door shut behind me and leaning back against it to try and catch my breath. My heart shuddered in my chest as my vision closed in on me. I forced my head down to my knees to try to keep from passing out, but as the blood rushed to my brain, I figured that might make it worse.

Images of Gray, of his teeth, of his strength were flashing themselves in my head like my own personal horror movie. Was everything we knew, that I knew, wrong? Vampires talked? Walked in sunlight? Worked in the very facility that killed their kind? It dawned on me in that moment, I had been showing the very thing I was supposed to be killing how to evade us. How had I not known?

If there was anything left in my stomach, I would have thrown up again. My reflection stared back at me in a decorative mirror that was put up long before I had moved in. I was disgusted with myself, with the things I was too blind to see. My fist shattered the reflection of a little, naïve girl, who couldn't distinguish between the enemy and a human. I didn't feel the glass slice open my fist, allowing crimson to freely drip from the wound onto the floor, leaving a trail of DNA breadcrumbs to the living room. An unopened bottle mocked me from the coffee table. I grabbed it, drinking it in so deep I thought I was going to suffocate. Only then, as my eyes burned like I had been pepper sprayed, did I bring it down from my lips and allow my body to desperately suck in oxygen. The front door creaked as it was opened, and someone entered.

"What the hell is wrong with you?" Gray was yelling before the door had a chance to close behind him. "You almost got us killed!"

"I didn't almost get us killed—" I wasn't sure why I answered, or why I was suddenly unafraid.

Gray cut me off, "Actually, you're right, you almost killed *yourself*! Do you have some type of death wish?"

The question hit home. I went out knowing full well I was searching for trouble. Knowing that I would probably get more than I bargained for when I added liquid courage to the mix. Even then I never expected to see Gray, someone who I thought was a friend, become the enemy.

"I don't have a death wish." It was supposed to come out strong and sarcastic but was more of a whisper. His eyes softened and he reached for my hand and for a moment I wanted to be comforted but as quickly as that moment was there it was gone. I jerked away from his touch like I had been burned, plastering disgust on my face. "But it seems you do. Get out of my house before I stake you like I do the rest of them."

I wasn't positive why I was giving him the option. I was still in disbelief. My heart ached with betrayal, longing for what I saw to not be true. I knew I hadn't admitted to myself that I was developing feelings for Gray, that his presence made my day a bit brighter and now, just like everything else I had ever had it had been sullied, slipping right through my fingers.

"Stake me?" He let the words come out as if they were the most ridiculous thing he had ever heard. "One, I just saved your life! You were almost eaten, so yeah, a vampire saved you! And two, you can't even stand up straight. How are you going to stake me?"

The words ignited a fire in me, and I wanted blood. I wanted blood for my parents. I wanted blood for Alec and Cindy, and I wanted blood to feel anything other than what I felt right now. I threw the bottle of liquor as hard as I could at Gray's face. It slipped from my grasp like I was a pitcher in the major league aimed right at its target, as fast as it could go with its contents sashaying in the bottle. He caught it easily before letting it fall to the ground, shattering into pieces, liquid running down the unleveled pitch of the hardwood floor. I put all my weight into a punch, as I pushed from the spot I had rooted myself in, connecting with his eye. Pain ruptured in my hand, the bones bending at impact as I struggled to keep my balance. Gray pushed me back, causing me to stumble and barely catch my balance against the wall.

I zeroed on my stake; I knew what I had to do.

I tried to bolt past Gray, but he easily captured me, shoving me right back to where I was. My shoulder blades hit the wall before I bent forward to try to escape the sting that burned through my back. Gray reached for my throat and squeezed tight, pressing me back up against the wall behind me. The moon penetrated through the window next to us, lighting up his face as his eyes flashed with anger. My air supply was gone, forcing my body into flight or fight mode. I made a half attempt to claw his hands, trying to get his grip to loosen, but part of me had already given up. I was tired of the ghosts following me, lingering in the shadows. I was tired of the pain. Tired of the memories.

My heart raced, thudding in my chest like the wings of a trapped bat as little black dots danced in my vision, but for the first time, I felt okay. A peace came over me that I hadn't felt since I was a girl. I was numb, number than drinking had ever made me. Than hunting had ever made me. I could feel my eyes start to slip into the back of my head. I was ready.

"You really don't care if you live or die, do you?" Gray's voice easily penetrated my fog as he released my throat.

My body crashed to the floor, disobeying me by sucking in large gulps of air that made my lungs burn. I couldn't help the disappointment I felt. I wanted to give up, I had given up, but now everything was flooding back to me, reminding me of why it was so easy to let go. I let out a single sob, somewhere between relief and despondency.

He ran his fingers through his hair roughly, causing it to stand up in different directions. Pacing back and forth, he muttered quietly, over and over again, seemingly trying to come to some type of conclusion. "You have royally fucked this up, you know that, right?" He didn't sound as angry, but rather his voice conveyed a blossoming concern.

"Y-you're going to kill me…right?" My question came out as if it was a plea.

"Yes…no…dammit, I don't know what to do!" Gray was rubbing his eyes. "You weren't supposed to find out. This was supposed to be easy—no complications, but no one told me all you are is complicated!" He threw his hands up.

"I don't understand how any of this is possible." I motioned toward him from my place on the floor.

"Of course you don't! We survive because you humans think you're smarter than everything. Highest on the food chain. I pity you and your ignorance!" he spat.

I flinched without meaning to and looked away as Gray released a stress filled sigh.

"So, you're a good vampire?" I felt like a child, cowering on the ground, begging Gray to rose-color life for me so I could pretend like everything would be okay.

His joyless laugh bounced off the walls of my apartment, echoing the stupidity of a question that should have never been asked. "No." He silenced the last of his humor. "No, we are all bad."

Chapter 15

SILENCE WEIGHED down on the room, adding to the heaviness that hung between Gray and me. We had somehow moved and now sat on the couch, staring at each other, trying to determine the other's next move. I was trying to breathe softly, almost silently drawing from all my experiences with vampires. I found myself nervous sitting next to Gray. My mind kept having to remind me he was not human, that he wasn't the Gray I had grown to know and lastly, he was just going to kill me just a few moments ago.

His eyes seemed black in the darkness, not resembling the hue of colors they normally showed. An expressionless face observed me, giving me no access to his thoughts or intentions. I wrung my hands together tightly, only stopping when my fingers started to tingle from the blood flow being cut off. I wanted to say something, do something, but I had no idea what, so I just sat there, like a statue waiting for Gray to make the first move.

"I was"—Gray searched for words, seeming to struggle —"ordered to go to D.O.V.E."

"Ordered?" I didn't understand. "Why are you telling me this?"

"Can you just shut up for once?" He didn't sound angry. Instead his words were lathered in fear. Of what I didn't understand since he clearly had the advantage here. "I don't know why I am telling you anything. I just, I know I don't want to kill you. All right?"

That is promising.

"I was ordered," he started again. "To infiltrate the facility. To learn the ups and downs of the operations, of its employees, like you." He gestured to me, but his eyes didn't follow. Instead he seemed to be battling something, but quickly disregarded it and continued on. "There's so much more to the people who were affected by the virus, the *vampires,* than you could even begin to understand. You believe there are only the ferals, and that's the way we wanted to keep it. Humans are in the dark because we have kept them in the dark."

"I don't understand," I whispered to myself, but he heard me.

"The virus, just like any virus, works differently for everyone," he said. "Have you ever been by someone with the flu who seems like they're dying but you walk away with nothing more than a sniffle? It's the same thing. The virus works very similarly. The virus was designed to interact with a person's genetic sequence in particular, latching onto certain chromosomes and mutating them to engineer a better soldier, as you are aware. However, the trials did not have the most promising results. Sometimes it turns people into the ferals you and other hunters kill, eating away at any humanity they have left, leaving only their body and hunger behind, and other times it just takes a part of them. Leaving them pretty much intact."

"What about the vaccine?" I asked, unable to hide the concern in my voice.

"Don't go crazy on me. You aren't just going to sprout fangs. The vaccine does work, but just like everything else it's not one hundred percent. It doesn't work for everyone," Gray said. "And as you already know it needs to be administered routinely, which people are not prone to following."

I subconsciously itched the spot where I had received mine. The vaccine was a breakthrough, a way to ensure hunters could continue to work and ensure if you were going to die at the hands of such a creature that was exactly what would happen. You'd die. Not come back as the very thing you were trained to kill. It was also a way to ensure their numbers stopped growing. If someone became prey, they wouldn't turn into the next predator. No one had ever said that it might not work for everyone, though, that the promise of absolute death might be too good to be true. Every month I'd walk by those white tents, people lining out in front of them for their free vaccine, for their free security.

"How come you can walk in the sun?" The question popped into my head and he laughed, I mean really laughed. "Hey! What!"

"That's just in the movies." He tried to stifle the giggles, but they kept flowing. "The only reason you think vampires can't take sunlight is because that's what you have been told. Sure, the ferals are definitely nocturnal and much more sensitive to the UV rays, but the light doesn't kill them, it just hurts like a really bad sunburn and you can see I have no trouble with it at all. Vampires survive because of all the misinformation that is circling around."

My brain seemed to break, allowing only jumbled sentences to come through my lips. "But we have studied the vampires—the ferals."

"And what has been found?" he pried, but I suspected it wasn't because he didn't know. "You confirm they aren't human, that they have the virus and then what? You know what the things we are fine with humans knowing, they're light sensitive, drink blood. Ignorance is bliss.

"None of that can tell you the things you actually need to know. Vampires have the same hierarchy that humans have," he stated. "I mean, they were human, why would anyone believe that would change? They still want to survive and doing that alongside their food source isn't exactly going to go over well. We have a leader, someone who runs what is considered, at least amongst the infected, The Blood Society." He looked at me intently, probably watching the wheels turn around in my head. "Someone who enforces the rules, who makes sure the ferals stay in line and act as a sort of idealistic defense against the humans. They're our sacrifice."

"But I have never seen a vampire talk." I argued, grasping for anything to make sense.

"We have talked plenty." He snickered.

"You know what I mean!" I snapped back, feeling like my head was going to explode.

"Ferals have gotten the worst part of the virus, Samantha."

I jolted at hearing him say my full name.

"They're trainable, sure, but they are not the same. More of a shell than anything. They're truly gone," he said.

"You talk about this like you know everything. Like you have been around this for a lot longer than I would assume. Like you're—" He cut me off.

"I'm just as much a worker ant as you are, Sammy. I might have my memories and control, but my choices were stripped from me a long time ago."

"That's what you meant at the bar, when you said you didn't have a choice to be a hunter?"

He gave me a small smile at my memory.

"Couldn't we just coincide? If there have been vampires like"—I waved at him—"like you, wouldn't there be a way to live together?" I didn't know why I asked because I didn't believe the words coming out of my mouth either.

Gray's eyes were sad as he confirmed my inner thought. "There are so many people who have lost loved ones to vampires, Sam. Would you want to live next to your parents' murderer?" I opened my mouth and quickly shut it again, so he continued. "It's not different for my people. They're the way they are because of being human, and those same people turned their back on them. They're out for the same blood you are."

"So, you kill people?" I asked, fearful of the answer.

"What would you do if I said yes? Put that stake through my heart?" he asked. I wanted to say yes, but sitting here, having a conversation with the very thing I had dedicated my life to ridding the world of had thrown my beliefs all over the place. He sighed, bending his face into his hands, exasperated. "No," he spoke into his palms before lifting to look at me again. "I don't kill people, but I do steal from the blood banks occasionally. We don't feed like the ferals do. We can still eat 'human' food and can get by without blood for a while. I don't thirst like you would think, but I still need it, especially when I've been injured."

"This is crazy," I mumbled.

"There's something we agree on."

"Why are you doing this?" I asked.

"Because unlike you, I don't have a death wish. I want to survive and to do that I have to answer to people who are a lot stronger than I am," he answered, very matter-of-fact.

"Then where do we go from here?" I asked him, and no one in particular. I looked out the window, at the descending moon, wondering how I had ever gotten myself into this.

"I don't know," he responded truthfully.

I took a second to soak everything in. Sobriety was creeping in and allowing me to feel all the new bumps and bruises populating on my skin. I reached up and kneaded into the muscles of my neck, trying to work out the kinks. The scratches on my arm burned with the movement, so I settled my hands into my lap, linking my fingers to stop them from fidgeting. Gray's eyes trailed my movements, landing on my cut palm. He snatched my hand from me, the movement making me gasp, but I didn't yank back from his touch. He pulled at the hem of his shirt, the fabric giving no resistance as it ripped, and draped the cotton around my hand in tender twists.

"I have to tell Todd about this." I tried to say firmly, but it was laced with the uncertainty I felt about everything.

"You cannot tell anyone that you know what I am. Do you understand?" he spoke more forcefully.

"So, I'm just supposed to let you stay, until when? Until it is time to slaughter us all! You want me to put more of my people at risk while you figure out the best way to hook us to portable phlebotomists?" I snapped at him, praying he'd tell me I was wrong.

"You don't understand! It's not safe, Sam!" he pleaded. "All I have ever known is being hunted. What would you say if it was your parents sitting here and not me?" he asked.

"Don't. You. Dare," I warned. "You don't get to talk about them. If my parents were sitting here it would be because there was no *you*. You and *your* kind killed them. I won't ever forget that no matter how human you look."

"Do you think I would have chosen this?" He turned toward me and yelled. "Do you think I didn't have a family I loved? Did you forget you're not the only person in this world affected by this, that you're not the only person who has lost someone?"

I moved back on the cushion, distancing myself from his revelation. I tried to tell my heart to stop feeling bad, but I couldn't help but be affected by the pain written on his face. He seemed more human than me in that moment, but I couldn't let that get in the way of what I needed to do. I pried, still needing more information before I could decide if he was telling the truth or not.

"I should want to kill you, before you try to kill me." As the words left my mouth my head snapped up. Why had I said that? I knew I needed to kill him, but why did those words feel so true?

"I won't hurt you, Sam." He slumped his shoulders in defeat. "I tried, and I should because that is what I am supposed to do, but I just can't."

I wanted to believe him more than anything and I didn't know why. His words rang with sincerity, but I knew human features or not he was here on a mission. He was here trying to stop us from killing them and finding out about the others. I didn't want to admit I had started to develop feelings for him because that would make what I was about to do next that much harder.

I shot my hand down, grabbing the hunting knife I had hidden under the coffee table, and quickly pressed it to his throat, digging into the soft flesh. Gray didn't move, he only looked into my eyes as a trickle of blood dripped down his neck, soaking into the white of his shirt. I begged my hand to press harder, to end this now, but I was frozen.

"I *should* kill you," I bit out, trying to convince myself while tears I didn't realize had formed streamed down my cheeks, catching at the corners of my lips and tasting of salt.

"Then kill me. I won't stop you," he said.

I stood there. I was at a crossroad. I was supposed to kill him, to avenge my family, but something in me couldn't. Any feelings I had for Gray should have been squashed the moment I found out what he was. I pulled back, throwing the knife. It hit the wall, implanting in the sheetrock as I ran frustrated hands up and down my face, smearing the tears and blood, yelling, trying to rid my mind of its indecisiveness. I sat back down, and he hunched forward, clasping his hands together.

"You have to believe I didn't plan for this."

"I don't buy it," I replied stubbornly.

"Then don't, but it's the truth," he said. "There's a chain of command, Sam. We have to have order the same way humans do and not very many share my sentiments after what they have been through. I've been trying to survive. And honestly what was I supposed to do? Come out as a vampire to the humans and say what? Say that I am one of the good ones? Hell, I don't even believe that."

"But you're helping to kill us off," I spat.

Gray opened his mouth to answer but closed it just as quickly. He looked down, unable to look me in the eye as he thought.

"I want to be able to say otherwise, but I just can't. You have to believe this was nothing more than my need to stay alive," he pleaded. "To not obey, to not follow orders means something worse than death. I would have been locked away until I went crazy, until I turned feral, then it wouldn't have been up to me to not feed. You don't know what prisons used to do to the sanest people, imagine that for someone who's already broken. You can choose to stay in the light, or have it stripped from you, Sam. I need the light. I need the only thing that makes me feel human again," he choked out.

"Are you going to turn over the things you have learned?" I asked.

"I don't think I could even if I wanted to." He leaned back into the couch, staring straight ahead, looking at the knife that stuck out from the wall. "I want to keep you safe, Sam. I just need some time to figure out how that's possible. Akle, our leader…he wants you dead."

"You don't want me safe," I said as a thought slithered its way into my clearing brain. "The act on the facility wasn't random, was it?" Gray's eyes answered before his mouth could. "So, their deaths are on me because I was supposed to die there."

"No!" He gripped at my hand. "You have to understand. I cut through the fence. I allowed them to get in. Those deaths are on me." He looked away, his face haunted. "That's why I encouraged us to leave, even after you second-guessed it. I couldn't tell you the truth and I couldn't just leave you there to die."

"We should have been there," I said, swallowing the anger that bubbled in me, needing to let him explain. "You could have been honest with me. We could have prepared."

"This runs so deep, Sam," he said, pulling back. "You don't understand the position I'm in right now. They're going to know I let you leave. When it gets back, I'll be exiled. When they get through with me, I'll be begging for the true death." He shuddered, not able to hide the torment from his face. "But it was worth it. I would do it all again if it meant you got to live another day."

"This seems like a nightmare," I said mostly to myself.

"Oh, it is. We are all just ants on a hill and someone up there decided burning us with the magnifying glass just wasn't entertainment enough."

"You haven't seen me dancing yet." I tried to break the tension, but it fell flat.

"You know," Gray started, "I haven't felt real, genuine fear in a long time, but when I saw you and that…vampire, when I saw he was going to bite into you, I was so scared. I didn't think I was going to make it over to you in time." He looked away as if he was embarrassed of this fact.

"I went looking for trouble." I admitted. "I think Todd blames me for what happened. I mean, I blame myself too, but he seemed, I don't know." I couldn't figure out what was eating at me over our encounter. I understood him being furious, but it seemed like he was madder that I wasn't there than happy about me being safe.

Gray looked like he wanted to say something but refrained. Instead he slipped his hand under my hair, gripping the back of my neck tightly. "Never do something like that again. I couldn't stand it if something happened to you." And like the end of his sentence was a cue, he kissed me. His lips were warm against mine, unlike what I expected, melting into mine easily. I sucked in a shallow breath before pressing back into him, soaking up the feeling of normalcy, of company. He held tight, his fingertips digging comfortably into my skin as I breathed him in like a moment of bliss that could erase everything in my mind, even if only for a moment.

Vampire.

The word snuck its way into my consciousness and like

a bucket of ice water being thrown on me I jerked back, pressing him away with my palm. My breath was coming in short bursts, just as quickly as my heart was pounding. What was I doing? I was kissing Gray; I was kissing a vampire.

"You need to go." I didn't need to yell, but the sound tore from my chest anyway. Fear seeped its way into my veins like dry ice. I was afraid because I liked the kiss, I liked him. As much as I didn't want to admit that I couldn't deny it.

"Sam, I'm sorry—" I didn't wait for him to finish.

"Please." It was a whisper, but the way his face contorted it could have been a venomous slap. He backed away, hands slightly raised as if I was an escapee from the looney bin considered armed and dangerous. As his foot slid behind the threshold of my apartment, I slammed the door shut, trying to lock out the emotions coursing through me.

I banged my head against the door twice. Stupid. Stupid.

"I'm still right here," Gray called. Crimson rose up my face in a hot wave as I imagined him on the other side, his hand placed against the door as my forehead connected with it.

"Go away!" I yelled back, heading toward the rear of the apartment after turning every lock, as if that would keep him out if he wanted to get in.

I turned the shower on a temperature notch above scorching and peeled my clothes off gingerly. As the water coated my skin, I was hoping for something between washing the day away and my skin melting off. The spray helped to work out the knots built up under the bruises peppering my skin. The base of the tub ran red as the blood rinsed from my body. I tried to not make sudden movements as the alcohol seeped from my bloodstream, leaving me to feel every ache and pain. I knew I should probably make sure nothing was broken, but I didn't want to have to explain to Todd what happened or be forced to lie about the things I now knew.

The shower handle squeaked as I turned it off, but I didn't get out right away. I didn't know what to do, or how to feel. Everything I ever thought I knew had just been ripped out from under me and I had a feeling Gray was still holding something back. I didn't know if I should out him or wait things out and see what his next move was. I worried about him still being employed by D.O.V.E. where I couldn't watch him being that I was suspended and all, but I also worried about his safety. My gut told me Gray could be trusted, or maybe I just wanted to believe that because of the way I felt about him. I mean, my gut also told me to go out and do what I did tonight and look where I ended up after that.

I pressed my fingertips to the bottom of my lip, still swollen from his kiss as if it happened just seconds ago. The corners of my mouth tugged up without my permission. I knew I was in way over my head, and worse I knew that these feelings growing for Gray were not going to be easy to swallow if it ever came down to him or his humanity.

Chapter 16

GRAY HAD TRIED to call the next day, but I needed my space from him. I needed to wrap my mind around everything, and I couldn't do that with him trying to explain himself while I tried to figure out the right thing to do. I did something else instead. I didn't know why I placed the call and by the fourth ring I had almost given up, but then I heard a click. Alana's voice seemed confused on the other end of the line, like maybe I had butt dialed her instead of intentionally reaching out.

"Hey!" I said, feeling a little unsure. "Are you busy?"

"Is everything okay?" Her words were thick with sleep, which made sense. She had more than likely worked last night and on a hunter's schedule ten in the morning was early.

"Yeah, everything's fine, don't worry. I was just wondering if I could take you up on that cup of coffee— I'm buying," I said quickly, hoping she hadn't changed her mind. A hoarse chuckle tickled my ear and then movement.

"All right, I'm up," she said. "Meet me at the shop on the corner. You remember the one, right?"

"Yeah," I said, not liking how close it was to D.O.V.E., but deciding beggars couldn't be choosers considering there were only two in the zone. "Give me like thirty?" I asked.

"More like forty." She laughed again and said her goodbyes.

She was right, it was more like forty. By the time I had found a long-sleeved shirt that could cover my injuries I had eaten up most of my time since I normally wore short sleeves to keep cool while hunting. I had to run to make the bus that had already picked up the bystanders and was on the verge of leaving. The entire ride over my heart pounded painfully in my chest. I didn't know how I was going to bring up what I needed to ask.

The bus pulled up on the opposite side of where I needed to be. I got off and waited for it to pull forward before jaywalking across the street, refraining from giving someone the finger when they honked at me. The smell of coffee and cream washed over me as I opened the door, the bell chiming to alert the workers someone had entered. Alana had already arrived. She was seated near the back, dressed in blue jeans and a simple shirt. I found it weird to not see her in her gear, as she took a long sip of her drink. I saw another was already placed across from her, so I didn't bother ordering.

"More like an hour," she joked, looking up from the rim of her mug. "I thought you were gonna bail." Her smile stretched the length of her face and sent waves of warmth through me. We had grown close being about the same age and training together, and though I had let the relationship dissolve on my end, when I saw her she always looked at me like no time had been lost.

"Thought about it when you recommended this place," I teased back. Alana shot me a knowing look.

"It's been kept quiet. Most just think you're recovering. The only people who know differently would never utter a word." She insisted, looking down at the cup I had sat in front of. "Black, right?"

"As my soul," I replied, clasping the drink in my hands to test the temperature. It seemed cool enough, so I took a sip, letting the caffeine coat my tongue in a bitter film. Alana watched me for a few moments. I could see the questions dance behind her stare and knew I needed to fill the space, try to clear the air, I just wondered if she saw the questions behind mine. "I know I messed up."

"Sammy, what happened, it wasn't your—" I stopped her with a wave of my hand.

"Before you say that is wasn't my fault, don't. I knew the rules, and I broke them anyway. Sure, I couldn't predict what was going to happen, but it doesn't change the fact that if I had been there, I could have helped."

She didn't deny what I had said.

"I agree, you should have been there." She sat back in her chair, placing her cup onto the table. "But we should be so many places that we aren't. You're still young, Sam, it's okay to want to have fun. It's okay to want to feel normal." She let out a breath. "I am not saying I don't agree with the boss man putting you on the bench for a little, I'm just saying I don't want this to eat you up like you have let Alec's death do. You're trying to carry too much responsibility when it's just the cards that have been played."

"I have to be honest, coffee wasn't the only reason for me asking you here," I said, pulling nervously at my earlobe.

"What do you mean?" she questioned.

"I have been digging into Zoe and what—"

Alana cut me off quickly. "Oh, Sam, please don't go down this road again. You know what Todd has said about all of this," she said firmly.

"Just hear me out!" I pleaded, hoping I could ease into what I needed to say. "I talked to Ruby and managed to get a copy of the surveillance tape. You saw Zoe that day, right?"

"What?" She sat straight, her eyes growing. "Yeah, I went and saw her...what exactly are you asking me?"

"I was just wondering if you saw anything unusual. Something worth noting?" I swallowed hard when her look of confusion turned to anger.

"Are you asking me if I had anything to do with the accident?" she asked lowly, the words being forced through her teeth.

"That's not what I'm saying!" I shouted, drawing me annoyed glances from the customers in the shop. I brought my voice lower, leaning forward so she could hear me. "I just meant that maybe you saw..." My explanation dropped off. Angry tears formed in the corners of Alana's eyes, never spilling over as her face turned three shades of red. "Listen, don't get defensive." I tried to control the situation but only made it worse.

"Don't. Get. Defensive?" She snarled. "You're accusing me of the unthinkable."

"No, I—"

She suddenly laughed. "You know this is real rich coming from you. I honestly thought you were my friend. Death follows you everywhere you go and yet you have the audacity to accuse me of killing someone I cared about for what reason? You know what?" She stood, her chair screeching against the floor loudly before bending to look me right in the eyes. "When you stop killing people, then let's talk."

I sucked in a painful breath, the sentence slicing into me and not reflecting anything she had just comforted me about. With those last words she left, the door swinging wildly behind her and the patrons of the shop stared after her and then looked back toward me, curious about the altercation. My heart cracked seeing her hurt, but I also found it strange how upset she got about it. I didn't remember them being super close and she seemed surprised for someone to know that she was there that night.

The idea floated around in my head as I finished my drink. It started to dig at me, making me itch like bugs were crawling under my skin and before I realized it, I was on a bus heading the opposite way of my apartment. Once I got off, I had a way to walk. The home sat on a complex down a long dirt road. It was hidden behind trees that didn't occur there naturally but still flowed easily. I hadn't been here since their death. Refusing to come back and relive it, but as everything seemed to crumble around me, it was the only thing that felt right and steady. I came to a stop and wondered when I thought this was a good idea, or why I hadn't killed the person who had followed me and now stood right behind me.

I felt Gray's eyes piercing into my back, but I didn't turn around, afraid of what emotions were playing on my face. It seemed like a lifetime since I'd been back here, but in the same breath, it felt like mere minutes as I tried to silence the memories ripping themselves through my brain, connecting cords I had tried so hard to sever.

I stood shakily on the rubble that had never been removed. The smell of burnt wood and furniture made me force back a gag, but I wasn't sure if it was real or just imprinted in my nose. My home looked like a skeleton of what it had used to be. Ash painted whatever was left standing, and for a second I was worried that if I moved anything beneath my feet, I'd find red coals still burning. I could imagine Gray opening and closing his mouth, trying to find words to fill the empty space between us, so I saved him from the weight of the silence I was sure we could both feel.

"You followed me?" I asked, already knowing the answer. "How'd you know I'd come here?"

"I think I know you better than you'd like to believe," he replied.

"Guess you're better at your job than I am at mine," I said, realizing how true the words were as they left my mouth. I had barely learned anything true about Gray, but he had been studying me for how long?

"Sammy, that's not fair." He moved forward but stopped as if an invisible force field blocked his path.

"I was only out a minute or two before it went up in flames, you know?" I turned, not looking directly at him as if the scene could be read right from my eyes. "I guess a candle had been knocked over during the struggle with the fleeing vampires. I was told it would be easier to just let it go. Not one person tried to even fend off the flames." My voice cracked. "No one tried to save any of it for me."

"I'm so sorry you went through that," he said quietly. "I didn't mean to make you feel like I was following you. I just wanted to make sure you were okay...after everything."

I gave him a small smile and walked farther in. House remains crunched under my shoes, cracking like bones. He didn't follow, which I appreciated. I didn't understand how being here ripped me open and healed me at the same time. It was like a weight was being lifted off my chest. I had avoided this place for so long, drowning it out like it had never existed.

I stepped down on a section I didn't pretest with light weight. The wood snapped, sending my leg through and bringing me to my knees. I braced myself with my hands, barely noticing the little splinters sticking themselves in my palms. Gray called out to me, but I threw a halting arm out at him, letting him know I was okay. I swore under the soot I saw something reflect against the light, entrapping me in curiosity. I reached down, feeling for what it could be.

My fingers brushed something with smooth ripples. I sat back on my calves as I brought it up and into view. A small box with miniature claw feet had survived the rage of the inferno. I rubbed my arm across the top, transferring some of the soot to my skin. The box was a metallic silver, shining bright even as dirty as it was. I got up, heading back to where Gray was standing, cradling it like a treasure.

"You okay?" he asked.

"Yeah." I fished the heirloom out from under my arm, knowing without ever seeing it before that it was my mother's. She had a love for what she told me was 'antique' style.

"Looks like a jewelry box or something," he said. "Aren't you going to open it?"

I didn't know why I couldn't. It didn't seem right to do it here. It was light, but my hand ached from the weight of having anything that could have been hers. I wanted to open it, but I think part of me was afraid nothing would be inside. Hell, maybe I was more afraid something would be in there.

"I think I am gonna wait," I said. I didn't want to share anything more with him than I already had. "I am not going to reveal your secret if that's why you're following me. I mean, it's either that or you decided to kill me, right?"

"Sam, I wouldn't, I couldn't ever hurt you. I know it's hard to understand, but you have to believe me," he pleaded.

"Because you have been so forthcoming?" I snapped.

"That's not fair!" he shot back.

"How? You've taken everything from me!" I cried.

"Not me." Gray corrected, but it didn't change how I felt.

"Might as well have been." I returned from the ruble to stand by him, knowing in my heart he wasn't here to hurt me. "Right now, we're standing in the place my parents took their last breath. This was planned too, wasn't it?" I asked, already knowing the answer.

"That was before me." He deflected.

"And that makes it what? Better?" I turned to face him, clenching the little box in my hand. "I can still feel her blood on my face, you know that?" I couldn't scrub the memory away. "What about Alec, was that before you?"

"I swear I had nothing to do with that!" He begged me to believe him.

"But you knew about it." I laughed without humor. "I know you think I am a naive little girl and you know what, yesterday you would have been right, but not anymore. How long has there been someone like you at D.O.V.E.? How long have they been feeding our intel to The Blood Society?"

He hesitated before answering. "Since the beginning."

I had suspected, but the admission still unnerved me.

"You're my enemy," I said. "Your people want me dead, just as much as I want the vampires dead. This"—I pointed between us—"can never work."

"What about that kiss? You can't tell me you didn't feel that too!" He was right and it made my stomach churn. When he had kissed me, I felt whole again. Even after finding out about him my body still reacted, outing anything I was trying to lie about.

"I was drunk. I wasn't truly able to understand that you're not my kind. You're not human anymore," I said, trying to look him in the eyes, but faltered, my gaze trailing down from his.

"Liar." He tested, but I couldn't let him know he was right.

"Believe what you want, but it's true. You do what you need to do to stay alive, but I promise you this, if it's at the expense of a single person I know, I will kill you." I meant it.

I left him standing there and knew he wouldn't follow. I had no real clue what I was going to do. I would need to bring this up at some point, but I was worried that I wouldn't be believed. That people would think this was just some sick attempt of me trying to get back in Todd's good graces. Truthfully, the other part of me was worried that they would believe me and use him, make him a science experiment to find out as much as they could about what he had told me. I didn't want to admit I was scared for him, just like I didn't want to admit that despite him being a vampire, I had very real feelings for him.

I HAD SPENT the better part of the night polishing that stupid silver box. As I suspected Gray didn't follow me as I traveled back home. I spent the time tightening my grip on my find like someone was going to jump out and take it

from me before I could figure out what was in it. I now sat
staring at it, unsure of what I was so afraid of. Worst case it
was empty and sat on my shelf as a memento, and on the
other hand maybe it was filled with something that could
bring me closer to the parents I was struggling to remember
at a time before that night.

Screw it.

I pulled it to me, lowering myself to the ground and
crossing my legs over each other. Using my thumb to press
up on the clasp, it made a small pop before opening. Red
velvet lined the inside and I tried to not notice the stray
strand of hair entangled in the fabric. My eyes looked
vacant in the mirror attached to the lid of what looked like
a keepsake box. It was empty besides a piece of paper
neatly folded in half.

I set it down, retrieving the note and carefully opening
it up. Right away I knew it was a picture. I ran my index
finger gently over the black and white faces, tracing the two
I knew resembled me. My dad stood straight looking right
at the camera, looking poised and strong, whereas my
mother let her personality shine. She leaned against him,
mid laugh and radiating love. It took me longer to recognize Todd standing to the right. His thumbs were laced
through belt loops as he faced the camera, but his gaze
didn't follow. He seemed to be staring toward my parents, a
small smirk playing at his lips. A lady I had never seen was
to the left of everyone. Her expressionless face unwavering,
not giving anything away. At the bottom their names were
written in order with fading, black ink.

Becca.

I tested the name out loud, trying to see if it would
spark a memory, but nothing came forward. I studied the
picture, noting the only other thing that looked familiar.

The house they were standing in front of was not the one I grew up in, and it definitely wasn't the fancy loft Todd called home. It wasn't even something I had passed before, but it did have something that gnawed at the back of my brain.

My eyes couldn't stray from the number. Four-eight-eight-four. Where had I seen that before? After a few moments I gave up and placed the picture back into the box and set it up on the coffee table before getting up from the floor. I stretched out as I watched the sunset deepen in the sky, reminding me I wasn't working for another night.

Chapter 17

I STAYED up most of the night, relishing in the old routine, and waited for the clock to strike midnight like Cinderella, only I wasn't leaving a ball. Instead I was dressed in all black, which technically wasn't different from my normal attire, but it felt sneakier under the circumstances. A badge had been left for me in a predisposed location after a quick phone call to a very annoyed Ruby, who reminded me that she didn't want to help me ever again. After some pushing and a verbal promise she obliged and assisted me on my mission, making sure that Elias took the night off so he couldn't ring the bell on my little escapade.

I didn't look anything like Ruby, but I hoped the dreadfully bright pink ballcap that was pulled down on my head looked enough like what Ruby wore and would limit any suspicions if I was stopped by the remaining security. I didn't have an abundance of choices. I couldn't just walk into D.O.V.E. on suspension and even if I could find a way in, people were going to notice me sneaking around and digging through things to find what?

Well…I wasn't sure yet, but I knew I was going to start with Alana's desk.

I held my breath as I walked into the door, casting a quick wave toward the front desk as I lifted the badge to the scanner. The light turned green as I walked with my head down, trying to avoid looking at the cameras. I was a few steps from the elevators before I heard my name called— well, Ruby's name. I turned back, trying to stick to the shadows to hide my face as the guard stood from his chair.

"Your vaccine is due," he said and I tried not to panic.

"Umm, yeah! I already scheduled it, though." I tried to act nonchalant, knowing that there wasn't a lot of wiggle room for vaccines and employees.

"Just make sure it's done tomorrow. I can ask for an escalation if they're booked." His smile turned into a yawn that reached up to the dark bags under his eyes. I was sure if he was well rested, he would have been able to see right through me and I would have been busted.

"I appreciate that! I'm just gonna head up and finish a few things." I backed away.

"Don't work too late," he replied and sat back down, going back to watching the screen and the red dots that populated on it.

I rushed to the elevator, hit the button lightly like the sound could give me away, and waited for the 'up' arrow to light. The cart dinged as it got to the floor, the doors opening to welcome me in. The ride up was uneventful. I don't know if I thought that alarms would go off, or Todd would magically appear and tell me to go home, but my stomach stayed in knots, unease forming as sweat on my brow. The elevator doors opened without incident. I walked through a sparsely decorated lobby, both surprised and not that the building was pretty much empty like I had planned.

No one sat in their chairs or busied about the office and if there were any hunters here, chances were they were below this floor and working on putting their supplies up.

I weaved my way through the cubicles, their walls only at half height to encourage teamwork, looking for Alana's desk. I passed my own on the way with its bare workspace and one pencil lying between the mousepad and monitor. I hadn't used it since Alec and I worked together. He would roll his chair up to mine and try to distract me while I finished up our reports. Finally, I found Alana's name. It was magnetized to the side of the desk with a picture of a fluffy white dog being held up by it.

I sat down in the rickety chair, looking around her desk. It was mostly organized, colorful sticky notes fixed to the bottom of her computer screen and her writing utensils stored in a company cup. I reached down to her filing drawers that made up the legs of her desk. Pulling on the first one, it opened easily, but when I looked inside it was completely empty. I gripped the bottom, expecting it to open just as easily, but I was met with resistance.

I tugged harder, the flimsy metal opening with a *pop!* I rummaged through folders, opening each one to see what was in them. They were full of reports and statistics, everything I would have expected from Alana. I sat back with a huff. I should be happy I wasn't finding anything, right? As the thought crossed my mind, the bottom of an envelope stuffed into the side of the drawer caught my eye.

Leaning forward, I snagged the corner, pulling it from its hiding place. The envelope had been folded three times, the length of it creased by the indents. It tried to forgo my attempt at straightening it, forcing me to rub it against the edge of the desk. I pulled out a letter and opened it while simultaneously rolling the chair I sat on back under the florescent light so I could see it better. It had the small, neat handwriting of someone who took care in what they were about to say.

Where the sea meets the sand, and you first took my hand.

I flipped the page over back and forth, looking for something more with no luck. I had broken into D.O.V.E., into a hunter's desk for a poem? Great. Just another thing to add to my growing list of coaching points. A door opened somewhere in the room, hushed voices speaking. My heart dropped to my toes as I crouched down and tried to slowly close the drawer without a sound.

Tough luck because it was potentially the loudest thing I had ever done.

"Who's there?" a familiar voice called out.

I'm so screwed.

I kept low, creeping through the cubicles, hoping I could make it out without being seen. I quickly ended up on my hands and knees, crawling like an infant to stay invisible. By sheer luck I made it back to the hallway, but as I went to push the elevator button, the light chimed, signaling the doors were about to open.

Sheer luck my ass.

I darted to the left, straight for the lab. I ran Ruby's badge in quickly and prayed for a quick read as I heard the elevator carts come to a stop at the floor.

The lock clicked, the light flashing green.

I grabbed the handle and opened the door, shutting it quietly behind me. The lights were on an automatic func-tion, flicking to life with my movements. A rag was folded up by the door and I quickly grabbed it to hang it on the peephole, hoping no one would notice the fluorescents shining bright when no one was supposed to be in here.

The lab was clean, everything fitting into its space

perfectly. The stainless steel of the lab tables was bold against the harsh white of the walls and tile. Nothing seemed out of place, like it hadn't been touched in years even though I knew an employee had just been in here this morning. I worked my way to the elevator, but the door clicked, sending my heart into my throat. My towel trick clearly didn't work. I dashed to a supply cabinet, closing the door as quickly and quietly as I could manage before the door opened.

"What's the meaning of this?" I had been right it was Todd's voice I heard. It was confirmed further as he stepped deeper into the room, still holding the rag I had used to hide myself in here.

There was another man with him, but I couldn't make out who it was. His back stayed to me as he surveyed the room. He kept tan hands clasped neatly behind his back as he waited. I held my breath, trying to blend into the cabinet. I watched as he shook his head, at what, I wasn't sure. Todd stepped over to a phone sitting on the counter, pulling the headset up and to his ear. He seemed to hit a quick dial button because it was picked up immediately.

"This is Mr. Weathers. Who was the last person who accessed the lab?" His voice was stern, unforgiving. He pulled his eyebrows together as he got his answer at the other end of the line, seeming confused by the answer. "Are you sure? I see." He set the receiver down with a click.

"Is everything...okay?" the man asked Todd, his voice coated with an accent I couldn't pinpoint.

Todd didn't answer, instead turned on his heel, going back through the door. The man stood still, not following right away as he looked around. I knew there was no way they thought anyone was dumb enough to stay hidden in there, but my pulse thumped away anyway, making it hard to breathe quietly.

"Interesting," the man said, my chest seizing like he was speaking directly to me.

Finally, he moved forward, following Todd's footsteps. I wanted to jump at the opportunity to get out of my hiding spot, but I waited until I was sure I was in the clear. I called for the back elevator and stepped in, trying to ignore the smell of death as I rode it down to the parking garage. I snuck out onto the street, not looking back until D.O.V.E. was a small blimp of a building behind me.

Chapter 18

THE NEXT DAY seemed to pass in a drunken blur as I stared at the note I had shoved into my pocket instead of returning, trying to form it into anything that would make me feel like last night wasn't a waste. My phone was off the hook—as in my cell phone was in pieces, scattered around my apartment—and every time the doorbell rang, I ignored it, knowing who it was. Gray had kept trying to check in on me, even though I had asked him to keep his distance. I wasn't sure if he was concerned about me or about my outing his secret to D.O.V.E and ending up with a target on his back. By the end of the second day, and what seemed like the one-hundredth ding from my doorbell, I opened the door, ready to stake the man in the chest due to pure perseverance rather than us being mortal enemies.

"Gray, I swear to—"

Todd stood in front of me, bearing a bag of groceries and some wine.

"I thought we could talk?" He offered and I was too stunned to see him anywhere but his desk to tell him off, so

I stepped to the side and let him in my messy space. Todd looked at me from beneath lowered eyelashes. I knew I must have been a sight to see. I hadn't brushed my hair, sleep was harder to come by, and my shirt was stained with an ominous black spot. I was struggling, and now having him show up to my apartment for the first time I was sure I was busted.

"Sam," was all he could get out as I swept beer bottles off the counter to open up enough space for him to set down his bags. I watched as his fingers tightened around the wine, second-guessing the offering, but I grabbed it and two cups out of the dishwasher before he could change his mind about fulfilling my need for a drink. I was sure I would need it after this anyway.

"You here to fire me for good?" I tried to joke, but it was through gritted teeth. I poured the expensive red into the hand-me-down plastic cups and offered one to him. His pristine hands looked funny around such a cheap item, the gold of his ring contrasting against the bold color.

Todd took a sip as I took a long swallow before placing the cup back down on the distressed countertop. His eyes darted across the apartment, taking in how I was living. He didn't ask about the mess, about the hole in the wall, he didn't even mention the bottles. A defeated look just crossed his face, a sadness I hadn't seen since my parents died.

"The other hunters are asking about you," he stated.

"Did you tell them?" I looked away, ashamed.

"No."

It hadn't always been this awkward between us. We used to get along, joke, and laugh constantly. He was the favorite uncle I never had as my parents were both only children. Now there was something between us. I didn't know if it was my mourning or his, but it felt like nothing would ever be the same.

"I went to the house." I admitted, trying to avoid the inevitable.

Todd's spine went rigid, but his face gave nothing away. "Why would you do that?"

"I didn't know at first, but I think I just needed to feel close to them." I confessed. "Sometimes I miss them so much it feels like I can't breathe." I had to turn away to hide the moisture that formed in the corners of my eyes.

"I know, Sammy," Todd said, and for a second it almost was like he used to say it.

"A box survived the fire, you know? I remember you said there was nothing left but it was tucked beneath the rubble." I turned back to him, excited. "It had a picture of you guys younger, before me, when dad first started D.O.V.E. You all looked—I don't know—happy."

"You all?" he asked. "Your parents and I?"

"And Becca." I corrected him.

"I haven't heard that name in a while." He scratched a cleanly shaven chin and pushed off the counter, gesturing to the groceries. "Do you want to eat?"

"You cook?" I choked.

"There's *a lot* you don't know about me, Sam." He smiled and began searching around the kitchen for anything he could use as a pot. He pulled the food from the brown paper bags and rolled up his cuffed sleeves to keep them clean. "Did you find anything else in the box?"

I pulled out the wobbly stool in front of the kitchen and parked myself on it, resting my head comfortably on my hands while I watched him meticulously cut bell peppers on a makeshift cutting board. The movements were fluid, like he had done it a hundred times, rocking the knife back and forth but still able to move the vegetable over without cutting his fingers.

"No, just the picture, but I don't think I remember Becca. Would I know her? I've never seen her at the office," I said.

"She was only around for a little while you were younger." He shrugged, reaching for a can of tomato sauce. "She went off on her own after a few years and no one has heard from her since."

"Why would she do that?" I asked.

"I always thought it was to start a rival company, but no one really knows. She and I did not see eye to eye, but she was your mother's closest friend then, so I dealt with her and her opinions." A look passed across his face that I couldn't read before his same old neutral expression settled back on it. "She was a hell of a hunter, but no one survives on their own out there, you know that."

I knew he had a hidden meaning meant just for me, even if he didn't look up to confirm it.

"Plates?" Todd asked and I pointed to a little cabinet behind him, laughing at the look he gave me when they were all paper, unlike his imported sets. "So, how was working with Gray? I know having to work alongside someone isn't your favorite even if you have a lot you can teach other hunters."

I tried to keep my face from giving anything away. The urge to protect Gray's secret became overwhelming at the mention of his name. It was hard to understand. All I was sure of is I had to keep him safe for the time being. If D.O.V.E. caught wind of this I didn't think his biggest fear would be the person who sent him.

"Gray is fine." I shrugged, looking away.

"Did anything happen?" he asked seriously.

"Don't go all daddy dearest on me now." I rolled my eyes.

"It's mommy dearest for starters and as much as you don't want to believe it, I want you safe."

I was uncomfortable with him playing a father figure. I wanted my own dad to be here to do that. Todd seemed to get the hint and didn't press further as he placed a plate in front of me that resembled a pasta. It smelled delicious, making my stomach rumble painfully.

"There's nothing else you want to tell me?" I figured I should get it over with now.

"Is there something I should be saying?" he asked, confused.

I shook my head and shrugged. What he didn't know, couldn't fire me…yet.

I dug in, the flavors surprisingly pleasant considering I assumed he'd have cooks and maids. I never thought he'd be a secret chef. Todd made his own plate, but it sat untouched as he watched me eat, his gaze boring into me like I was wearing a dunce hat. I looked up curiously, slurping in the end of a noodle before putting down my fork.

"What?" I asked, not sure what he was looking at.

"I was just thinking about when you were little," he explained. "I should have known then you'd be such a handful when you got older." He laughed, the sound rich as it filled my tiny apartment. "You probably don't remember, but you used to try to hide in the shadows and sneak up on me, pouncing when you thought I wasn't looking. You'd get so mad when I turned and caught you, promising me one day you would scare me." His humor dried up. "I didn't realize how right you'd be."

"I'm not hunting." I promised, hoping I wouldn't have

except for that one time plastered on my forehead with a flashing 'look here' sign.

"Look at you." He gestured my way. "You're a walking miracle. The fact that you have gone through what you have and *survived* astonishes me." He sighed. "Even now, you're safe from the dangers of the job, but you still aren't safe from yourself. You're swimming in your clothes, I can't find a shred of anything edible in your fridge, this place is a mess, and I don't even have to bring up the amount of alcohol you're consuming. I want to know what poor soul you have tricked into fueling such a dangerous addiction, let alone for someone underage!"

I thought about Mr. Becker. I had seen him a lot more often the last couple days, normally stopping by on my way back in. I thought it was because I needed someone to talk to, but I realize now that I was more afraid of being sober at the moment than being alone. I didn't think I was using him, I mean sure, I was lying about my age and only visited because I needed something, but he ran a store. When else was I supposed to see him?

I looked down at myself. He was right. My fitted hoodie, which I was thankfully wearing, looked a good size too big on me and I had started using a belt. I thought I was living my whole life to help people but really, I was just digging myself a grave.

As if he could read my mind Todd said, "I need you, Sammy. I can't lose you too."

I didn't know why the words cut me. I never noticed him mourning. I had never seen him cry. Even after my parents, he went right to work, taking me in and learning the ins and outs of running D.O.V.E. During all that pressure he stood strong.

"I'm not going anywhere." I promised, pushing my

drink away, suddenly its contents turning sour in my mouth, and placing a shaky hand over his. He gave me a squeeze back, letting his touch linger before letting go and cleaning up the kitchen.

"You know that picture I was talking about?" I asked.

"Mhm," he said, scraping the food into Tupperware and tossing the plates away.

"Did anyone search for her?" I asked, drawing my fingers in a figure eight on the counter. "You know, Becca. If she was out there, I think it would be nice to meet her, maybe learn about my mom."

Todd let out an audible sigh.

"She wasn't missing," he explained. "She left of her own accord. I don't even know if she was staying in the state. What's this about?" he pried.

"I was just—" I started, but he cut it.

"What do you not know about your mother that I couldn't tell you? I was around constantly and knew them better than you could. I'd be the best person to ask questions to." He leaned forward, placing his palms against the countertop.

"Real nice," I bit out, pushing away.

"What?" His eyes widened. "What did I say?"

"You just couldn't help but to take the opportunity to remind me I didn't get a chance to know them, huh?" I crossed my arms in front of my chest, hoping the only thing he could see was the anger I felt and not the way those words cracked my heart.

"That is not what I meant, and you know it!" he said defensively." I just meant I'd know them way better than someone who left before you could even walk!" His voice boomed over me, making me feel small.

"You say you know so much, but I think you're even

blinder than I am," I snapped, the words slipping from my lips like poison darts.

"What's that supposed to mean?" He pressed through his teeth, making my heart pound. I couldn't tell him about what I knew, not yet, but the words sat heavy in my gut.

"I don't think you know half as much about what's really going on as you say. People are out there dying, and we have taken a major step back! I don't think we know near as much about what's going on as we say." I let that simmer, stuck between wanting Todd to understand the hidden meaning and not.

"Who exactly have you been talking to?" Todd's eyes were like daggers, prying the truth from behind my lips. I wanted to tell him everything, but decided against it, clamping the truth shut for a reason I wasn't sure of. "People *are* dying, Sam, why do you think we do what we do? But while everyone else is dedicated to fixing that, you're getting drunk and throwing yourself in harm's way to do anything but deal with your actual problems."

"I think it's time for you to go," I snapped back.

"Are you serious?" he asked, perplexed.

"Yes," I said.

"Fine!" He threw his hands into the air. "I can't ever win with you," he shouted, making his way to and out the door. I let out a breath I didn't realize I was holding before locking up.

I retried the little box, opening it once more to retrieve the picture. Again, I looked over Todd, his lighthearted stance seeming to resemble someone completely different than I saw now. My eyes were drawn up to the house number once again, *four-eight-eight-four*, the number not meaning much to me but sparking a curiosity I couldn't seem to push down. I powered up my old laptop, having to fish it out from under the bed.

The Mesozoic machine took forever to come to life, the sound of a facility fan seeming to propel out of it. Connecting to the internet, which was provided to all residents, was another nightmare, the speed testing my patience, but I pushed through. I didn't care how long it took. I was going to find out more about this woman, and if she was alive, I was going to meet her.

Chapter 19

THE WORN-DOWN home loomed upward in my vision. I felt so small, like a mere child, and it seemed as though the house nearly reached the clouds even though it was only a standard two story. I wanted to find out why Todd was so uncomfortable talking about Becca and exactly why she left. I clutched the photograph in my hand tighter for reassurance. I didn't know if this lady was even here, alive or if she would even know who I was, but this was my best lead. Something told me she hadn't left, but rather hunkered down and avoided the world. Maybe it was the way Todd talked about her, but I felt like he knew exactly where she was.

The wind picked up, tossing browned, fallen leaves against my jeans as I made my way up to her doorstep. For a half a second I thought about backing out. There had to be a good reason why no one told me about her. Why my parents never talked about her. Why Todd didn't seem thrilled to hear her name. Maybe she wasn't someone who could be trusted. Maybe that's why Todd had nothing nice to say when I asked about the picture.

Despite my worries, and against my better judgement, I reached out and banged the cold metal handle three times against the door anyway. The sound echoed throughout the trees surrounding her yard, frightening the resting birds and sending them into flight, away from the disturbance.

I looked around at the old paneling. The peach paint had all but chipped away, leaving the rotting wood exposed. There were clear signs of a termite problem, and, I gulped, rodent problem with little burrowed holes through the walls. A broken porch swing hung from one chain while the other lay in a pile on the porch, rusting away. I hugged myself, not from the malevolent breeze that whipped my hair but from the uncomfortableness I felt being here and not knowing why or what I was doing.

The house wasn't outside of the zone in the Deserted, but it was at the edge, and in a part of the city I had never actually been to. I knew some of the hunters who did their rounds here and it was normally quiet...until it wasn't. Even now no sounds came from the house as I stood there, all signs of life practically washed away, so I knocked again.

Nothing.

I was about to leave when I heard the lock get thrown, the sound resembling the lock on a dungeon. The door was yanked back. The only thing stopping it from flying open was the chain that was pulled taut, halting it in place. The abruptness startled me, and I stepped back, sucking in a shallow breath. No light shined behind the door, the darkness leaving me to guess who or what was behind it.

"What do you want?" a venomous voice snapped through the crack.

"I, umm—I'm looking for a Becca?" I asked, stepping forward, afraid whoever was there wouldn't hear me.

"There is no one here by that name," they quickly responded, immediately trying to slam the door shut.

"Wait!" I begged, jamming the tip of my boot between the door and frame with just enough time to stop the door from shutting. When I was sure it wasn't going to close, I moved my foot back, replacing the pressure with my palm to try and be less intimidating. "My name is Sam— Samantha Cordova. My parents were—"

SLAM. CLICK.

The door shut so quickly I couldn't finish what I was going to say. Defeat washed over me in a quick wave. After everything this was going to be a dead end. I had done what I promised myself I wouldn't do. I had gotten my hopes up. I stepped back, giving it a second to ensure they weren't going to open the door, before I turned to leave. I was almost off the porch when I heard that familiar sound again, followed by the chain being released. I turned as an older version of the lady in the picture appeared before me.

"Sammy?" She stepped out tentatively onto the deck wood, unsure of herself, her voice much softer than before, not resembling the voice at the door, but I knew they were the same person.

"Do you know me? Do you know my parents?" I couldn't help the words from rushing out of my mouth as I reset for another round of questions as she hesitated, but before I could ask anything more I was engulfed in surprisingly strong arms.

She smelled of dust and lemon as I was pulled in closer, my arms instinctively circling around her shoulders. Her arms felt slim around me and as I returned the hug to someone who was a complete stranger, I couldn't help but notice how fragile she felt under my touch, nothing like the woman I saw in the picture. Her shoulders trembled slightly, and I wanted to tell her it would be okay but stopped. I wasn't sure if she was crying or just weak.

"Come, come." She took my hand, leading me into her home.

The light flowing in from the door illuminated a maze of random stacks of junk. Dust had collected in a noticeable thickness, looking perfectly smooth except for a few fingerprint marks. The light left with the sound of the door shutting behind me. I let her steer me through the foyer and into a small room that was a little neater. A large lamp stood behind the couch, casting a yellow haze throughout the room, not quite reaching to each corner.

"Sit." She insisted, brushing papers off the sofa before patting it with her hand.

The leather crinkled under my weight as I sat down. The windowless room only had the door she pulled me through, sparking a claustrophobia I didn't know I had. Books were still stacked tall, but the layer of dust was nowhere to be seen. A single Victorian chair was angled in front of me, the dark wood polished and the mustard, floral fabric well taken care of. Becca didn't bother moving the papers from it and sat down, wringing her hands nervously.

"I'd offer you something to drink, but I don't really have much," she said, not ashamed, just matter-of-fact.

"That's okay." I assured her, ignoring the way my mouth dried up as if to mock me.

"How did you find me?" she asked, like she had been hiding.

"Well." I reached into my jacket pocket, retrieving the photo, and handed it to her. "I found this."

Becca stared at it for what felt like forever. Her eyebrows

pulled together as she studied the faces. I reached forward, pointing to her spot in the picture, not missing the way she pulled it closer to her like I was going to rip it from her grasp.

"That's you, isn't it?" I asked.

"I see," she said simply, not answering the question. "Your mother gave this to you?" She looked at me with gray eyes, her thin lips pressed together.

"Not exactly," I replied. "It survived the fire."

Her face twisted, but she didn't comment on it.

"This was a long time ago, when we decided to come together and create D.O.V.E.," she said. "We thought we were modern day heroes, trying to save people who couldn't do it themselves." When she smiled, I looked away, feeling like it was not for me but the memory she was playing in her head.

"You helped create D.O.V.E.?" I asked.

"I was part of it, yes, but the idea alone was your father's." She sighed. "He was always so gung-ho about saving the world. He was a good man. And your mother, she was his light, our light really."

My heart thudded painfully in my chest.

"So you were friends?" I asked.

"Oh yes!" Her laughter echoed through the room, lightening the air instantaneously. "We knew each other long before *they* ever came out. Back when things were so…" She searched for the word. "Simple."

"Why don't I know who you are then?" I asked, puzzling myself. I hadn't meant to be so forward, but I needed to know.

"I was always in the background. I was around, just not right in front of your eyes. I watched you grow, for a while anyway." She smiled. "I was part of a recruiting group. I helped build the stations across the country. I wished I could have been there for you, but I had a duty to the company. To your parents. Their goal was to make this a world where you wouldn't have to follow in their footsteps."

A light bulb went off. "Rebecca Sawyer. That's what Becca is short for?"

"The one and only." She grinned, flashing off slightly crooked teeth.

"Oh my God. You're a legend! They tell your mission stories every day at the academy. I grew up listening to how tough you were—are, I'm sorry." I could have kicked myself. Rebecca was seen as an equal to my parents, matching their skill and strategy abilities, but she was also seriously injured, ending her career. I looked closer at her eyes, noting the scar from her forehead to her cheek, and the haze that covered her pupil.

"It's okay." She lifted a small arm up and as if on cue fell into a fit of coughs. "I'm okay, just getting old." She tried to smile, but I could see she was being drained. "Don't mind the eye, it doesn't bother me none."

I looked away, embarrassed. "What happened to you?" I asked.

"There was a falling out between me and your parents. A difference of opinions. I wanted to stay on track with the plan, but the people who agreed were slowly changing their minds." Becca closed her eyes. "I had no choice but to leave."

"I don't understand, leave?" I wiped my palms on my jeans to clear the nervous sweat away.

"Todd." She whispered his name like a curse under her breath. "He wanted to lead the company, to make it into something it shouldn't have been, which I obviously objected, but the way he pitched it, it was like he—" She stopped abruptly. "Were you followed?"

"Followed? What?" I panicked for a second, listening closely for whatever sound she had heard. When the silence grew deafening, I looked back at her. Her eyes looked wild, searching for something, like it would materialize from thin air. The way she moved concerned me, jerky twists and turns, and I started to wonder just how much being alone had affected her.

"Shhhhhhh!" She jumped up, placing a hand on my shoulder. "Stay here." Becca disappeared out the door, leaving me in a stupor. As I sat in the room alone, sickness blossomed in my stomach. I didn't think she was well, and now I wasn't sure I should stick around trying to pry information about my parents out of someone who had already lost it.

I listened for her, for anything, but only silence returned, so I got up to follow. The house was darker than most tunnels I had been in, like it purposely blocked the sun to hide its secrets. I stretched my arms out, using my hands as my guide around the horde of items that had been accumulated over I could only guess how many years.

"Becca?" I wasn't sure why I whispered her name, but I figured I might as well play along in case she really was crazy. The last thing I wanted to do was fend off someone who already believed someone was out to get her.

My knee caught a stack of books, sending them toppling over to crash into the ground. I tried a half attempt at saving them, jutting myself forward to catch the cover of one, but it was no use, they scattered around the floor loudly until the last had fallen. I cursed under my breath, almost missing a sound I knew all too well.

The hairs on the back of my neck shot up, sending my

heart pitter-pattering into my throat. I held my breath, listening harder, hoping that whatever I heard was just my imagination. Tough luck because the sound of a feral vampire echoed throughout the house, originating from a place that was too close for comfort. I reached for my waist, retrieving the stake I thankfully packed, and used my other hand to feel for my surroundings faster, not worrying about knocking anything down. I needed to get to a window, I needed light.

My hand brushed against blackened glass and I prayed it wasn't a mirror. I reared back, ready to punch through it, but just as I was ready, I was ripped back before I could launch my arm forward. My body crashed into what I could only guess was more junk, sending items flying everywhere. I propped up on an elbow, trying to listen for the next attack.

I swung back, connecting my stake to flesh. The high-pitched wail forced me to cover my ears as I tried to retreat. I bumped into a lamp, sending it toppling down on me. I fumbled quickly with the shade, searching for the switch, as fast stomps collided with the floor, coming at me in an inhuman speed. I flipped the switch, sending the room into momentary light before the bulb blew, blanketing me with a perpetual darkness.

"Fuck!" I screamed out as I was tackled from the side.

We both tumbled together, fumbling for each other. I ended up on my back as claws dug into my shoulders. I bucked my hips up, trying to unbalance the feral straddling me and rotate my body out from under it. I scooted back on my butt, searching for my stake, which I had lost my hold on. Everything I bumped into that was light enough to pick up I threw in front of me, hoping to connect with the vampire and buy me time.

As my back connected with a wall, trapping me, I hurled another book forward as hard as I could. I knew it didn't connect but felt myself smile when I heard glass shatter. I knew the sun wouldn't hurt it after talking with Gray, but I hoped that living in constant darkness would at least make the sun bright enough to stun it and allow me to find my weapon. I looked past the creature that was now painted in the low lights of a cloudy day. It pulled back slightly, but was mostly unaffected.

"Well, great," I said, banging my head back against the wall in defeat.

The vampire attacked, coming straight at me. I pivoted to the side, deciding I'd have to make a run for it. Halfway up I saw my stake, perfectly illuminated by the soft light billowing from the window. I dove forward, rolling onto it and turning right as the feral connected with me. For a brief moment I wasn't sure if I had stabbed it or not as we both stood still. Without a word, it backed up and collapsed to the ground.

I bent over, breathing in deep, trying to dissuade the windedness I felt. I'd only been out of work for a few days, but I was already forgetting my training. No part of me was prepared for a fight. I looked up at the ceiling as I caught my breath, watching a spider scurry itself to a deeper corner of its web, away from the disturbance.

A quiet groan came from my left. Positioned in-between a dresser and wall was Becca, breathing labored, the soft rise and fall of her shoulders inconsistent with what had just happened. She leaned into the furniture, drawing on its sturdiness for support. My eyes trailed down to her hands, which tenderly clutched her chest. Crimson seeped through her fingers, dripping down her arms and onto the floor.

"Becca?" I called out as if I wasn't seeing things

straight. She answered with a bloodied cough. "Oh my God."

I ran to her, falling to my knees, my jeans tearing from the impact. I ripped my jacket off and pressed it into her abdomen, looking for a phone on the wall to call for help, but she reached her hand to my cheek, her blood trickling down my skin. Her cracked lips purpled quickly, but her eyes were still fierce.

"I need to get you help," I said, trying to sound calm, but she painfully shook her head, while clenching my face.

"Don't..." I waited for Becca to finish, but she just stared at me, unmoving, her eyes devoid of anything I had just seen.

"Don't what?" I panicked as her hands dropped to the ground. I gripped her shoulders, shaking her slightly. "Don't what?" I asked again, knowing she wasn't going to answer.

I knew as well as anyone would that she was gone. Her gaze had grayed over, making her eyes look like glass, and as much as I listened for her breathing there was nothing to be heard. I stared at her as if she was playing a prank and would awake yelling 'gotcha,' but there was no coming back for her. I didn't understand what she wanted to say. I didn't understand how I had gotten this close to finding some answers and now it was all for nothing. I sat back, not able to move, and stared and the body of a woman I knew nothing about, having the feeling she knew so much more than the time we had allotted her to say.

Why did she ask if I was followed? What would have given her the idea someone was out to get her? What was one of the most renowned vampire hunters in the world so afraid of?

What should I be afraid of?

Chapter 20

"SAM?" Gray's voice sent goose bumps scurrying up my spine. My fingers had just grasped the knob to my front door, the other hand holding the key still in the air as if his words had frozen time. "I tried to call," he said hesitantly.

"My phone's broken," I spoke to the door, thinking about the phone call I had just made from a pay phone, letting a crew know where to find Rebecca's body. I didn't know why I did it, but I asked them not to tell Todd. After a bit of hesitation, the boy on the other end of the line agreed.

"I know you said to stay away, but you're—are you bleeding?" His voice conveyed an emotion I was still uncertain that he had the ability to possess. Still, his voice sent my heart into an erratic rhythm, confusing me more than I already was.

Before I could deny it, his scent had surrounded me, immersing me in that minty pine smell I had grown accustomed to. His fingers gently tugged my still frozen hand down, encouraging me to turn and look at him. He made a sound through his teeth when I faced him, his eyes instantly finding my torn shoulder. The fire in his gaze made me suck in a sharp breath. The bleeding had mostly stopped, but the smell of copper clung to my skin and clothes.

"What happened?" he demanded.

"I went looking for someone, someone I thought might be able to tell me more about my parents," I said, not understanding why. "About Todd."

"By yourself?" He shot me a look.

"Yes, who else would I have had go with me?" I barked back, more annoyed than what I felt.

"Me! I would have gone!" He stared at me like I had grown a second head.

"Why?" It wasn't a question, but more of a challenge.

"Did you go looking for a vampire? Because those look like scratches." He urged.

"I didn't and yet they still seem to find me." It was a shot at him, and he knew it. He lowered thick lashes and exhaled in my direction. I sighed back at him and told him what happened with Becca. He waited there, in the hallway of my building, listening to every word, not interrupting for a moment.

"Why do you insist on putting yourself in danger?" he said finally.

"It wasn't intentional," I said, leaning back against the door. "But still it felt, I dunno, planned."

"Are you accusing me?" He jerked back.

"No, it's just I was so close to knowing someone who knew them, and it really seemed like she wanted me to know something." I closed my eyes and leaned my head back against my door. "It doesn't matter."

"It does to me," he said.

"Why?" I asked again.

He struggled to find the words as I waited for him to what? Confirm that he had feelings? That he was more than just a vampire? I knew better, but I still felt that hope in my chest. I held out hope that maybe, just maybe it was possible for this to be something of a dream, waiting for him to yell "gotcha" and make everything go away.

When he didn't answer I turned back and shoved the key in the lock, quickly turning it and the knob at the same time. Throwing my door open, I walked through the threshold. Gray's hand snuck out, gripping my shoulder to try and stop me. I hissed out when his fingers brushed the open claw marks in my skin, causing him to rip his hand back like he'd been burned. He stared down at the blood that coated his skin, my blood, unmoving. My heart picked up its rate in my chest as I prepared for his bloodlust to take over, but it never happened, just like he said. He clenched his fist together and tightened his jaw.

"You don't have to be alone anymore. I know you hurt. I know you feel like you can't keep people safe, but you don't have to worry about that with me. I am not that easy to kill." When he looked back up at me his eyes burned into me, making my body react against my better judgement.

Before I could argue he closed the distance between us even as I stepped back farther into my apartment. The door shut behind him and in an instant my back was pressed up against the wall and his chest was flat against mine. His hands snaked their way up behind my neck and without hesitation his lips were against mine. They were soft and hungry and as much as I was trying to tell myself this was a bad idea my own hands had already betrayed me and encircled his neck, drawing Gray in even closer. Everything I was holding onto snapped, and my cares and fears dissipated. In this moment I didn't care what he was, that this was wrong and that there was no going back, all I cared about was this feeling I had with him.

His skin, though slightly colder than my own, burned me to my core. Each breath filled my lungs with Gray's scent, the smell infighting something in me I thought would stay dormant forever. He pulled back from me, not completely but enough to catch his breath. I was disappointed, but the desire in his eyes had not dissipated.

"You weren't kidding about the broken phone, huh?" He tilted his hand to where it lay in pieces.

I laughed and pulled him back, this time initiating the kiss. He lifted me easily, as I wrapped my legs around his waist, hanging on as we drifted to the bedroom. We didn't dare to break our locked lips a second time as if it would throw cold water onto the moment and bring us to our senses, stopping us right in our tracks.

Gray lowered me gingerly onto the bed, taking care to lessen the contact with my shoulder. Only then did he remove his lips from mine, only to place sweet kisses on my chin and down my neck, one after another, each more tender than the last. I lifted my head to grant him access and let anything else that was scraping at the back of my mind go.

Our hands roamed each other's bodies, exploring our most vulnerable places. Like magic our clothes found their way to the floor and the only thing left between us was the longing for company. Gray paused to ask me permission with his eyes and I responded by pulling him close and in, arching in response to our merge. Sparks danced behind my eyes as the emptiness in my heart filled with something I had pushed to the side to be dealt with another day. When we were breathless and done, we still clung to each other like life preservers, begging the rough waters to not swallow us whole.

———————

THE SUNLIGHT WARMED MY SKIN, painting my eyelids orange. I struggled to pull myself from sleep, from the peacefulness of the night. I hadn't dreamed, a rare pleasure that was often not offered to me. My legs were tangled in the white sheets of my bed and as I blinked my eyes open, I found myself smiling without forcing it. I could feel the slow rise and fall of Gray's chest next to me. I refused to roll over and face him, instead tried to shallow my own breaths and stay still. My cheeks burned crimson as my senses came around, reminding me I was naked.

"Good morning," he said sleepily. Tracing his finger along the curve of my body, right over a scar on my back. I went rigid and he sat up abruptly. "Are you...okay?"

"They're ugly, aren't they?" I said, embarrassed.

"What are?" He seemed confused.

"My scars." I shrugged.

"Why would you think that?" He chuckled lightly, but I knew it wasn't to make fun of me. "I think they tell a story, each and every one."

I knew he would see all of my scars, scattered around my skin accompanied by the bruises and cuts from recent missions.

"They disappoint me," I stated.

"Disappoint you?"

"They are all from a time that I wasn't fast enough, or strong enough. They are all consequences from not being the best," I said.

Gray bent down and kissed the scar, a little gasp escaping my throat. "These are not from being weak." He kissed another, sending pulses of heat to the nether regions of my body. "You are strong, stronger than anyone else I know, but you're fighting a battle that should have never been started."

Anything I was going to say was abruptly cut off when Gray touched the healed slashes on my stomach. He noticed the change and covered them with his palm. Vivid memories were quickly playing in my mind, and what I let happen to Alec...

"What is this one from?" Gray asked tenderly.

I struggled to get my thoughts together. Gray gently reached up and pushed a layer of hair behind my ear, relaxing me enough to choke out what I wanted—needed to say. "It was from the last mission with Alec." My eyes trailed away, looking anywhere but at Gray's face. The shame I felt crawled its way through my skin, begging to be exposed to him as I absentmindedly tried to itch it away. He patiently waited for me to explain, but the lump in my throat made me afraid I'd suffocate before I ever got the words out. I laid my head on Gray's chest. His heart was beating steadily, which still surprised me. I had thought that it would be still, but it thudded against my cheek as if he were still human.

"As you know we have issues with our tracking abilities when the systems go dark. We had been following two ferals before our grid shut off. I thought if we got a team together and went in, we could bring them both back to the compound for studies. Everyone was so upset over Zoe, over the cure slipping through our fingers, and I just wanted to help."

Gray drew circles against my bare shoulder, encouraging me to continue.

"At first, we were all on board, but when the grid went down a few hunters hung back, worried we didn't know how many were actually there. Alec and I held our position since he thought it would be best to wait for backup, but we didn't expect anyone to be walking around there at that time of night. The lady was snatched so fast, dragged back into the building and her screams…" I swallowed.

"I couldn't wait, and I rushed in. The hunters were right to be worried, though, there were way more than we expected. Too many to fight and Alec tried to save me. Before I knew what happened I was bleeding to death and Alec was being dragged away."

Gray had stilled, as if the movement would stop me from continuing, but as I started to say it out loud it just came out in a rush.

"The thing is, he would be here now if I hadn't been so hasty. I jumped the gun and was caught off guard. He had to be there to protect me, like always he was protecting me and that's how they got him. By the time more of the team got there it was too late. Todd had warned me I wasn't thinking straight and needed to be rational and like always, I didn't listen."

"Sammy." He breathed into my hair.

I jumped out of bed like it had suddenly turned to lava, the sheets and his body scalding my undeserving skin. I didn't want his pity; I didn't need one more person to say it wasn't my fault because I already knew the truth. I threw on an oversized shirt I pulled from a dresser set that clashed with any feng shui that was going on in the room, pulling it over my head, acutely aware that I had exposed myself to someone who was until recently my enemy. I turned to look at Gray, his long torso stretched out on my bed. The only thing covering his—uh—well, was a sheet and it didn't leave much to the imagination. I slipped on some shorts, trying to act normal even though my heart was trying to escape my chest.

"Coffee?" I choked out as he moved to the edge of the bed, the sheet dropping dangerously low on his hips. "I'm gonna get some." I finished without waiting for his response, needing a reason to turn away. I entered the living room and it was…well, it was clean? Anything that had been broken was swept away, furniture moved back into their rightful places. Any sign that this room had ever seen something negative was washed away. "You cleaned?" I didn't know how to feel about it. "Unless I sleep clean and didn't know it."

"I think 'cleaned' is a bit overdramatic," he called back. "I picked up a phone that hadn't a prayer being in your possession."

He had a point.

"Sam, I wanted to talk to you about something," Gray said. I could hear him shifting in the bed.

"Hmm?" I asked as I walked the short distance to the kitchen to start the coffee. Just as I went to start the brewer there was a knock at my front door. It was so rare to hear anyone at the door, let alone this early. I tiptoed to the peephole, having to lift myself slightly to get a better view.

Oh no. No, no, no.

"Who is it?" Gray asked.

"Shhhhh!" I shushed him like my life depended on it. Actually, my life could very well depend on it because I'd have to leave the country if Todd knew Gray was here. I'd never hear the end of it. He knocked again. *What do I do?*

"Sammy, I know you're in there. Open up," Todd spoke through the door. I took a deep breath and unlocked the door.

"Oh, hey!" I said through a little crack. "What's up?"

"Are you going to let me in?" he said.

"Umm, well, you see I think I'm getting sick—" It didn't matter what my excuse was going to be, he pushed through the door anyway, forcing me to back up.

"Geez, can you put some clothes on?" Todd said, shielding his eyes as he shut the door behind him.

"Umm, last I checked you barged in, and these are clothes." I rolled my eyes. Todd looked uncomfortable but continued.

"I felt bad over how we left things. I wanted to come in and check on—Gray?" He stopped.

Great.

I turned to the room to see what Todd could see. Gray, standing in the doorway in—oh thank *jeebus*—pants. His chest was still bare as he leaned into the frame, not at all concerned about the situation, unlike me. If someone offered to fly me to a remote island to spend the remainder of my days that very second, I would have taken it no questions asked.

"What exactly is going on here?" Todd sounded...angry?

"It's not what it looks like!" I lied even though it was exactly what it looked like.

"Really? Because you're both half naked, in an apartment, alone. What else could it possibly be? You know I would have never let you live on your own if I'd known you'd make such stupid decisions." He growled, looking right at Gray, who still seemed unaffected.

"Okay, for one, I am an adult, so regardless if you like my decisions or not, they're mine to make and two, shouldn't you be glad I'm trying to move on and live again?" I crossed my arms over my chest but quickly reversed the move when it lifted my shirt too high. Gray raised an eyebrow and Todd all but turned around completely as if I had flashed him.

"I had another reason for coming by," Todd spoke to the wall. "I need you back. We are too short staffed to keep you away, even if I think it's for your own good. Unless you're too busy doing other…things."

I looked back at Gray, who had moved from the door to stand next to me. "Did something happen?"

"Team Delta was…overwhelmed last night during a mission," he said, throwing his hands up when my eyes started to bulge from my head. "No one died, but two of our hunters are going to need some time to heal."

"Is this permanent?" I asked, trying to not seem too hopeful.

"Let's take small steps first," he replied.

"Have you heard from Ruby?" he asked suddenly. "She didn't show up for work."

"Did you ask Elias? She seemed fine the last time we talked. I didn't think she was getting sick or anything." I didn't understand why he asked me. Now that I really looked at him, he seemed stressed. His hair was disheveled, and his normal pristine shirt wrinkled and unbuttoned at the collar.

"And when was that exactly?" he questioned, making me take a step back. Did he know I snuck into the building with Ruby's credentials?

"Are you sure?" Gray chimed in, addressing Todd before I could answer him. "She's been injured. Don't you think she needs to heal before being out there?"

"Gray!" I snapped. "I think I would know if I was fine or not."

He cast me a *really* look, raising his brow.

"Just after everything you have been through, I want to make sure you're ready." He smiled, reaching up to squeeze my elbow. "Still want me on your team?" he joked and I gave him a playful punch.

"If you can keep up," I said.

"Speaking of your assignment, Gray, meet me at my office later for a debriefing. Sammy, be ready for an assignment tonight. We've had an uptick in tagged. See me before you head out," he said.

"What do you mean debriefing?" I asked Todd's back, but he didn't stop and answer.

My heart was in my throat. Was Gray getting reassigned? All the stress I felt seemed to flow into Gray's body, making him rigid and awkward, something I rarely saw from him. He was always so relaxed and sarcastic, but now he stared at the door like it was about to be busted down any second by gun toting gang members. I wondered if he was trying to play it cool while Todd was here, but deep down he was just as uncomfortable about the chance meeting as I was. I felt like I had committed some sort of crime, so it made sense he would feel like the willing accomplice.

"What does he mean debriefing?" I asked again, looking at Gray.

"I am gonna head out and see what he wants. I'll meet you at headquarters, okay?" He slapped a quick kiss to my forehead, grabbed his things, and was gone before I could understand what had just happened.

"Okay," I responded to nobody.

Chapter 21

DESPITE THE TWO men in my apartment today, and their sudden departures, I was more concerned with the fact that Ruby wasn't answering any of my texts or calls. I visited the front desk to see if Elias was in, but it seemed he'd called in that day. They could just be playing hooky together, which I could totally understand, but I still wished I knew she was fine. Like the universe had heard me my phone chimed.

No more favors.

The message read, so I typed back a quick "I was just checking on you. I don't need another favor. Did you get your badge?"

Yes. Ruby responded.

She was clearly still not a fan of mine, but at least I knew she wasn't deathly ill or something and I could confirm that it was a call off to Todd, who I was sure would give her an earful for the no show.

Of course, when I got upstairs, I was tossed into a pile of paperwork and agreements. It felt like I had been fired and rehired. I had to meet with the onsite nurse to ensure I was capable of being in the field and that my injuries had healed up nicely. She clicked her tongue when she saw my shoulder but after about thirty minutes of pleading and a threat to start doing cartwheels in her office to prove it was fine, she wrote me a bill of health. Not a good one, but either way it allowed me to go back out.

Clutching my approval in my hand like a trophy, I headed straight for Todd's office. His door was already shut, which wasn't unusual, but what did throw me for a loop were the raised voices coming from behind it. I was pretty sure the only arguing that could be heard outside of this room was the arguments that happened when I was in there. I hesitated for only a moment before I knocked, the voices ceasing immediately. Todd cleared his throat and beckoned me inside. The tension in the room was palpable. Gray stood off center, his look unreadable while Todd's reddened face clearly said something was wrong.

"I am interrupting something?" I closed the door quietly behind me. "Should I come back?"

"No, actually I am glad you're here," Todd said. "I don't think you two should work together any longer."

"Listen, if this is about earlier, it won't affect my work," I said, my stomach dropping to my feet like I had swallowed a chunk of change. That metal tang clung to my mouth as I tried to wet my lips and figure out why I felt so panicked.

"The relationship is not appropriate, it's a conflict of interest. Anyways, now you don't have to—oh, what did you say? Pull his weight?" Todd said.

I looked at Gray, who shot me a curious look, and silently apologized with raised shoulders. I had meant that then, but that was before everything that had happened. I knew his secret; he didn't have to hold back anymore, and he could be a real asset to the team as soon as I convinced him working against the vampires would be better than with. I was still working out the finer details, but I was sure we could make it work.

"I know what I said, but that was before—" I tried again, searching for the words.

"Before what exactly?" He challenged, watching me closely like he knew I was hiding something.

"It just, well, I mean, it wasn't a problem before." I started slowly, walking toward him with my arms across my chest. I felt slimy for saying it, realizing I was starting to have a track record with my partners.

"I allowed it and look what happened. Neither of you could think rationally and now one of you isn't here anymore." Todd sighed and rubbed his forehead. "Don't you care about what people would say?"

"No," I said, not backing down when he frowned.

"Samantha," he said, exasperated. He looked back toward Gray, who had his jaw set, not contributing to the conversation. "This is what I mean about making bad decisions." He shook his head. "I'll make an exception tonight because we need all the bodies we can get, but we will need to revisit this and soon."

I decided to pick my battles and let it go for the time being and shift the conversation. "I got ahold of Ruby. Seems she's sick and she's sorry she forgot to call in," I lied.

"She'll have to be written up for the no call, no show," he replied.

"Can't you give her a break?" I asked. "I mean, should we be writing up our scientists considering the work they do?"

"That's absurd." He laughed humorlessly. "You realize, if you don't hold people accountable for their actions, they will just continue to disobey you. You have to nip it right away."

"There you go again showing you don't care about your staff." I rolled my eyes as Todd clenched his teeth. "They are people, Todd, not machines."

"Sam." Gray stepped closer to me, on edge. I figured he was concerned I might get into more trouble than I was already in. A darkness crept into Todd's face, but as soon as it had arrived, he pushed it back, storing it behind the professionalism I knew so well.

"I understand your concern." He moved back to his desk. "I know there are a lot of things above D.O.V.E. you don't understand yet, and it is partly my fault. These people are not your friends, Sam. They will be your employees and running this business successfully means having to make calls like this. You will learn that soon enough."

The way he went back to his work said the conversation was over. Gray lightly grabbed my elbow and led me from his office. He walked without a word to the elevators and hit down, with me trailing his every step. Once we got into the supply room, I couldn't take the cold shoulder any longer.

"What the hell happened between you two?" I asked.

"What can I say? He really was not happy about what he saw this morning." He was still short with me, not looking my way at all. I blew a stray hair from my face and sat heavily on a chair. I brushed my fingers back and forth on the corner of the stack of paperwork in front of me, unaware I was fidgeting at all. Gray's back faced me, his muscles showing through the light fabric of his shirt as he busied himself with cleaning weapons.

"Do you think Zoe's death was an accident?" I asked, the words shooting out like projectile vomit.

Gray's hands stopped moving as my words feathered down on him. His lack of movement was the only thing that confirmed he had heard what I had said as he kept quiet. My vision trailed the ground with uncertainty as I waited for him to acknowledge my comment.

"Do you?" He reflected it back to me, returning to motion.

"I'm not wrong, am I?" I said to the ground, pressing further.

He turned, and I didn't have to look up to know his eyes were unblinking at me. Insecurity coated my senses, making me feel like a child, but I still wanted to know, because something told me that Gray knew the answer.

"I'm not sure what you're getting at, Sam." He kept his expression blank.

"You asked me if I thought it was an accident, and I don't," I said softly. "I got the video, you know, and the last person to talk to her was someone I thought I knew really well, but now I'm wondering if I know anyone. Is Alana... like you?"

"No, she's not," he replied. "I am the only one assigned to D.O.V.E. right now."

"How can I trust you?" My fingers shot to my lips when I asked, like it was a forbidden question.

"There are a lot of people you shouldn't trust, Sam. Maybe you're right and I shouldn't be one of them." When I made eye contact with him, I didn't recognize the person staring back. "Take it for what it's worth, but I would tell you the truth on this."

"You say you're the only person assigned right now, but when does that change? We need to do something about this." I pressured.

"What would you have me do, Sam?" he barked.

"We could gather everyone. We wouldn't have to say how we knew, or be specific, but we could bring in more hunters and plan an attack. You'd be free!" I rambled, devising a choppy plan.

"You really think something like that would work?" he asked sarcastically. "That's the worst plan I have ever heard."

"I know it's not—"

"You don't know anything." He growled, frustrated.

"How could I?" I screamed, the sound bouncing off the walls, making him step back. "Everyone around me seems to have their dirty little secrets, so how could I honestly know anything?"

I choked on anything else that tried to make its way up my throat, turning on my heel to get as far away from Gray as I could. No more than three steps in fingers pressed into the tender nook of my wrist. The pressure wasn't painful, but strong enough to get me to turn and face him. His darkened eyes stared at me, somehow communicating that he shared in my pain, his own like the raging rapids of a river streaming behind his eyes.

Gray brushed hair from my face, tucking it neatly behind my ear. I didn't move away as he rested an unsure hand at my jawline. I looked back unblinking, trying to hide the fear that erupted in my stomach as I came to the realization that he, regardless of wanting me alive, was not being honest about everything. I had two options, out him or trust him, and though that loud voice of reason screamed at me every section I still chose the latter.

"People are dying, and it feels like I am the only person who cares." A tear slipped from the corner of my eye silently.

"You're right." He pulled us closer together. "I'm sorry.

I want to be open with you about everything, I just don't know how." He sighed. "You'd hate me."

"You're a vampire, and I don't hate you now. I feel like nothing could be bigger than that." I insisted.

Gray gave me a sad smile and bent slowly, the softness of his lips startling me more than the kiss itself. There was a tenderness to it, void of tension and longing, and rather filled with a desire to cure. I leaned in, breathing deeply, trying to inhale the moment to keep it sacred forever. I couldn't help but brush my lips as he pulled back from me, leaving me colder than normal. I searched his face for regret but only saw a matching question, but as quickly as it was there, it disappeared.

"You're deflecting," I said.

"A little." He shrugged. "But I don't think this is the place. Tonight, after we're done." He assured me.

"Do you promise?" I asked.

"How can I convince you?" His voice was rough as he stepped in closer, forcing me to back up into the table. It was cold against my back, as the heat from his look warmed my front. He locked me in-between both his arms, his lips teasing my ear. "What can I do to make you believe that I want to help?" Each breath I tried to take in to answer got lodged in my throat. With a deep chuckle he backed away, sending a knowing look in my direction.

"Where are you two off to?" Alana snuck up on us, making me jump.

"How long have you been standing there?" I asked nervously.

"Not long." She raised an eyebrow and winked at me. "Not long at all." My face burned as I looked toward Gray, who looked everything but back at me, a smile pulling at his lips. I busied my own hands to have a reason to not admit to what I thought Alana had seen.

"Oh, don't be coy," she teased. "Hiya, Gray." She sent him a wave as she walked to look at our coordinates, clicking her tongue like she knew I wouldn't be happy with the job.

"Hiya back." He laughed.

"Sam, can I talk to you?" she asked, getting serious.

"Sure," I said, walking away from Gray as she followed, aware he could probably still hear everything we were saying.

"Should I even ask you about your shoulder, because I'm pretty sure that was not there the last time I saw you." She looked me up and down, trying to find any other marks. I thought about fibbing, but knowing her she'd see right through it, so I just confirmed it was new.

"I feel like I need to apologize for the other day." She rubbed her elbow and looked away.

"It's okay," I said, still suspicious but not wanting her to know that. "I should have been more sensitive about what I was saying."

"You see, I—I loved her." Alana looked at me briefly before busying herself with checking my gear. I watched as she racked my gun and checked the chamber for the round.

"I know we all loved—wait." My eyes widened, under-standing washing over me. Guilt burning in my chest remembering how I got jealous thinking she was flirting with Gray.

"I-I didn't know. I'm so sorry." The pain was written in her eyes and I should have known, I should have seen it.

"I went to visit her because we had a date planned, but she needed to cancel. She had to button up her presenta-tion about her discovery. She was planning to meet with

Todd over it. She was really stressed and tired, and I was selfish." She wiped at her eye, the tear building there never having the chance to fall.

"It's not your fault." I found myself repeating the same words that had been said to me. She offered me a sad smile as acknowledgment and turned her back to the table, leaning lightly against it. I felt so stupid to bring up these painful memories, not caring who they affected while I forced my own narrative on what happened. The setback was huge, but the loss of someone so talented was an even bigger blow.

"Thanks, Sammy," she whispered and pushed off from her spot, her face changing instantly into the firm features I knew.

"Well, we have to get a move on, but I'd really like it if you'd want to hang out soon. Maybe coffee?" I asked.

"Sure." She smiled softly, but it didn't reach her eyes.

"Hey, Sam?" she said before we had gotten far. "Be careful, okay, the relays are acting up again." She had a faraway look but continued. "See ya." She gave me a slight wave as we headed back to the elevators. When I looked back, that strong façade vanished, leaving her shoulders to curl in on themselves and the pain to rack her body in steady shakes.

Chapter 22

THE CHAPEL STOOD out in the night sky like something straight out of a horror film, the building coming to an ominous tip that seemed to banish all light away. As I looked toward the point of the building, I realized the only thing that was missing from this scene was the flash of lightning shooting bolts across the roof from dark, pregnant storm clouds that rolled in out of nowhere. My skin came to life with ant legs as we crept closer to the front. The quietness was daunting. Even the breeze that had followed us here seemed to avoid the area altogether.

"Something is not right about this place." I walked forward but couldn't shake the waves of nervousness crashing into me as I looked at my tracker, the angry red dot that showed the tagged vampire had vanished from the screen. I hammered it in my hand a few times like it would solve the issue, but it didn't do much more than bruise my palm.

"Yeah." Gray's laugh carried, making me cringe in fear

someone…or something would hear us. "You have never been to church, that's what's not right!"

"Oh, like you spend so much of your free time here." I wanted to laugh, but I kept an unamused look on my face. There was something nagging at me about this building. "This place is just giving me the creeps," I said, looking around for signs of life, or the undead we were hunting. I sighed. "I thought vampires couldn't step foot in churches?"

Gray snorted as I followed him. "Do you believe everything you read in a book? Next thing I know you're going to tell me I can't enjoy garlic." He shot me an incredulous look.

"You can?" I asked, only half joking. "And what was that?"

"What?" He shied.

"That snort!" I laughed, forgetting to shush myself.

"I have no idea what you're talking about," he lied.

The door was slightly off its hinge, so Gray had to lift it and pull. The motion made an awful screeching noise that drove off the birds hiding in the nearby trees. They looked like ravens and that seemed like a bad omen. We entered the church, and I couldn't help but to admire the way the moonlight shone through the glass windows, painting beautiful shadows over the rotting wooden pews. The priest's podium stood tall, perched on a step that kept it elevated over the seats. Behind it were white candle sticks, standing close to each other at different heights, partially melted, leaving wax frozen mid drip.

A crucifix hung on the wall behind where the Father of the Parish would begin his sermon, covered in cobwebs yet somehow still appearing in perfect condition. Nails marks in the shiplap flooring told me rodents were in here with us and that almost made my skin crawl more than the idea of vampires hiding out in a church. Gray crouched down, running his finger over a dark substance, it sticking to his skin. He rubbed the matter between his thumb and fore-finger before declaring what it was. I already knew.

"Dried blood, probably weeks old." He furrowed his eyebrows. "Ferals are messy. If they were still here, we would know immediately."

"This is where the tagged was. The whole system is offline right now, but there is no way it would have made it past us without us noticing it, or it noticing us for that matter," I said. "It still doesn't make sense, though. I checked before we left, and it was relaying from here." The dread was rolling in like a thick fog, as my eyes landed on the smallest flashes of red, positioned carefully under the pews. The slick glass was cool against my fingers as I reached to pick up the tracker, painting my skin in momentary crimson. "Something's not right." I looked back at Gray.

"You'd be right," someone, not Gray, answered.

I turned on my heel, my weight bending the wood I stood on with a *pop*, to lay eyes on a vampire, fangs like Gray's extended, and looking awfully hungry. He was tall with slicked back, brown hair. He wore a tailored suit and looked exactly what I would expect a high-dollar bodyguard to look like, holding his hands gracefully in front of himself. A door slammed behind me from under the crucifix. Two more men sporting matching teeth stalked out from their hiding place, encircling us. Each one was dressed in a crisp suit like they were part of this guy's secret service. Gray backed up toward me as they closed the distance between all of us, herding Gray and me like cattle.

"Well, you were right, vampires definitely can enter a church." I tried to joke, analyzing my next move.

"It'll be easiest if you come quietly," the vampire in front of me said, ignoring my comment, his eyes deepening as he watched me. Everything about him screamed leader and the way the other two looked his way had me pretty sure he was running the show. He was the first one we'd have to take down.

"You're not taking him anywhere," I barked, widening my stance. They must be here for Gray, knowing he wasn't doing what he was supposed to be.

"Not him, *you*." The leader's eyes locked back onto me, moving over my body ravenously.

"Fat chance," I said, plastering my best amiable expression on my face. I racked my brain on how they knew we'd be here and exactly what they were planning.

"What's going on?" rumbled out of Gray like a warning.

"We have orders, Gray," he said lowly, not particularly feeling beat up about it.

"What orders?" Gray said.

Tension blossomed in the room like watching a flower bloom during a time-lapse, filling up the space and sucking out the air, making my chest seize. I took another step back, taking solace in the vibrations coming off of Gray's back, which brushed lightly against mine as he tried to see all three vampires. The stress struck me in waves, but knowing he was so close helped keep me calm. My fingers inched to my waistband. Though I was notorious for close combat, this situation seemed to need something more and a part of me was more willing to see tomorrow than I had used to be.

The metal was cold against my fingertips, turning rough as I slid my hand down the grip. The vampire pretended not to notice, but we both knew full well what I was doing and that it would quickly turn into a competition on who was faster. The gun wasn't as heavy as I was expecting when I yanked it from the holster, positioning it right at the heart of the monster standing before me. I wanted to laugh at his arrogance when he didn't attempt to move out of my way, knowing even with his speed he wasn't faster than a bullet. The trigger clicked easily under my finger, not giving the slightest resistance, but it wasn't followed by the familiar *bang* I expected to hear. Instead the click was the beginning and end. The vampire smiled at me like he knew in advance it would jam.

My brain went numb and only a name crossed it. *Alana.*

The safeness I felt behind me left, leaving the feeling of ice as I was yanked forward by the front of my shirt. I hadn't even seen him move toward me. The fabric ribbed slightly as he bundled the material in his fist, bringing me in close, his breath hot against my face. Gray yelled out but was quickly pulled back by the other two sidekicks this guy brought along. The ground dropped from my feet, leaving them to dangle beneath me.

"Well, that was unfortunate," he spoke, leaning into my ear. "But that's okay, let's have a little fun first."

"Yes." I smiled as I cocked the slide back twice more in quick succession and heard the jammed round move comfortably in place, letting my shirt hold my weight, and pointed the muzzle. "Let's."

Bang. Bang. Bang.

Silver plated bullets ripped through his chest, his fangs seeming to elongate as he hissed in pain. With a quick motion of his arm I was sent flying back into the struggle happening between Gray and the two goonies. With just enough time they stepped back, allowing Gray to open his arms, embracing me to try and slow my speed. The contact sent us both tumbling to the ground, but most definitely saved me from any broken bones. The gun was ripped from my palms on impact and scurried across the ground far from reach.

"Are you okay?" Gray asked, trying to look me over and keep an eye on the vampires simultaneously.

"I think so," I said.

"I need you to get out of here," he spoke quickly.

"I'm not leaving—"

He cut me off before I could tell him we could take them.

"Please," he begged. I gave a quick nod to his relief, even though I still had no intention of leaving him to deal with these guys alone.

Gray shot up, as I followed his motion at a slower pace, feeling the tug and pull at my side and shoulder, dusting dirt from my jeans for effect. The vampires stood like bowling pins, staring at us to see if we would attack. I tried to steal a glance at the back room they had to have come through to see if there was a doorway out, but the growl that echoed through the church told me I was caught.

"I wouldn't try that if I were you," the leader spoke.

"Did Akle send you?" Gray asked.

Akle? Their leader?

"You've been gone a while. Seems it's time to come back home," the vampire spoke. "We've been wondering when we'd see you."

"That's not my home, Dominic," Gray barked back.

"Formalities," Dominic spoke slow, flipping his hand upside down to show his palm. "She is coming with, Gray. With or without you."

"No, she's not." Gray growled, stepping protectively in front of me. I wanted to yell back that I didn't need protection but didn't think it was a great time to become distracted.

The two vampires snickered as Dominic looked at Gray like he was seeing him for the first time. A laugh burst from him, small at first but slowly growing into a boisterous sound that sent shivers racing up my spine. His humor stopped so suddenly it seemed to suck the air dry, turning my blood to ice.

"Get her." He snarled.

"Go, Sam!" Gray shoved me back as the room came alive, before advancing forward.

No. Way. In. Hell.

I ripped my stake out just as Gray linked arms with one of them as Dominic stalked him, clearly feeling he was the bigger threat. The other quickly dodged Gray's reach and headed straight toward me. I crouched down, strategizing as he advanced toward me. Our eyes locked, every place they darted to he took a step to meet them.

"This will be fun." A razor-sharp crescent lifted his face, the corners of his smile reaching his dead eyes as he lurched at me.

I sidestepped and grabbed my stake, thrusting my arm out to connect with his chest, but got nothing but air as he turned just in time to move again. The motion made me wobble on the balls of my feet just long enough for the vampire to copy my move, syncing its palm in-between my shoulder blades, sending me reeling forward into the steps leading up to the podium. I twisted at my waist, jutting out my armed hand in defense as he jumped on top of me. The sharp tip sliced through his shoulder like butter. The vampire hollered, retreating back a few steps and holding his wound tightly as blood dripped through his fingers.

Those black orbed eyes never left me as he recalculated my threat level.

"Sam?" Gray yell-panted as he tried to fend off both Dominic and his sidekick, managing to throw one to the ground before locking up with the other.

"I'm good!" I hollered back, trying to ignore the hit I saw him take, knowing that if I rushed that way, I'd be making things worse.

My opponent and I circled each other, gauging how to proceed. A strong right hook flew my way, slamming into the left forearm I barely threw up in time, followed by a right that I caught just as quick. I answered with a booted kick to his abdomen, expecting to knock him off his feet only to be surprised when a single step back was made instead.

"My turn," he taunted.

Quicker than I could react, his foot connected with my ribcage. I heard the crack just as my feet left the ground, sending me zooming through the rotten pews. I landed hard, splinters digging under my skin as I used the old wood to try and pry myself up, biting through the pain in my side. Within a blink he was in front of me again. Pressure around my neck increased as he lifted me up above his head, slamming me back down into the seat, wood exploding around me from the force. Pain erupted through my back, resonating back in my side where I was sure I had at least one broken rib. I coughed, trying to inhale the oxygen that was forcibly removed from my lungs from the fall.

"Sam!" Gray screamed out, but I couldn't form a response.

I crawled forward, trying to move under the pews, using them as an obstacle so I could put some distance between us. My head was swimming, and I needed to gather myself so I could block his next attack. I heard Gray yell out, making me pause, afraid he was hurt. Nails dug into my ankle, pulling me back in the direction I was so desperately trying to get away from. Dirt and rocks embedded into my stomach as I was dragged against the ground. I reached for anything I could get a grip on, faltering each time.

Sharp fingers burrowed into the back of my head, lifting me once again. I instinctively threw my hands back, trying to dig my own nails into his wrist to release some pressure to no avail. He turned me around, throwing my back onto a salvaged pew that by some grace didn't break under the force. The vampire stood in front of me, not disguising the insatiable hunger he clearly felt. Dots danced in front of him, making it hard to muster up a defense. His clawed hands bit into my shoulder and skull, prying them in opposite directions to reveal a pounding artery under delicate neck flesh.

"That's enough," Dominic spoke just as the vampire tried to bite into me.

He growled against my skin, breath hot, as my heart pounded uncontrollably. He hesitated before eventually obeying the order and backed up, leaving me on the pew. Wetness dripped from the side of my head, running down in a moist trail past my ear at a pace that confirmed it was not sweat. I looked up as the sidekick Gray was dealing with was pulling himself from what used to be the church's podium. Gray was struggling against Dominic's tight clench around his throat. Our eyes met, his normally relaxed features erratic as he frantically looked me up and down. Pain shot through my ribs as I adjusted my body. *Definitely broken*, I thought while trying to wheeze my breaths in with less audio.

"Well, as fun as that was, we don't wanna keep Akle waiting," Dominic said, releasing some of his grasp on Gray, who yanked away from the rest. He hurried to my side, no one stopping him, certainly convinced neither of us was in any shape to run.

"Are you okay?" I wheezed. Gray's eyes widened in anger at the sound. He had been clawed in the chest, the wound bleeding heavily, but it didn't appear to hurt him like it would have if he were human.

"I will heal," his jaw ticked as he spoke.

"What's going on, Gray?" I asked as he knelt next to me, lightly moving my chin from side to side to check the profile of my face.

"I don't know," he said, his eyes resting on an injury he didn't like.

Gray helped me to my feet, not rushing the motion when I paused to breathe through the sharp throbbing. I leaned on him slightly, trying to catch my bearings. The church was in shambles. Wood scattered across the floors like a tornado touched down in this very spot. The dust kicked up floated without direction in the air, giving the room a musty scent, making me choke down a cough. The stained glass of the cathedral painted a large cross that hung centered in the back with colors of the rainbow. It seemed too beautiful for the situation we were in, as those colors painted the faces of the vampires staring our way.

"Gray?"

He tensed.

"This isn't good."

"I know," Gray said.

Chapter 23

THE VAMPIRES LED us through the door in the back of the church, and then another door that led to the outside. I was trying to figure out how neither of us heard the vehicle pull up, or at least saw its lights. They could have been there the whole time I thought, but I never considered scoping the place out. I bit my lips to stop myself from crying out as I tried to pull myself into the back of the car. One of the sidekicks had already sat down in the back seat and grew impatient, yanking me forward. My rib jutted painfully into my skin, but I threw my hand back at Gray to tell him I was okay when I heard him growl.

Somehow, I was the one who got stuck in the middle. *Cherry on top.*

"Bag her," Dominic said, getting into the driver's seat. "No one touches her. Father will be displeased."

"S'cuse me?" I managed between breaths.

"Just go with it," Gray whispered into my ear, calming me.

I let them place some type of black out fabric over my

head, the smell of sweat and blood prominent in the material indicating this was not the first time it was used. I tried to see through it, but in the dark all I could make out was the random lights on the car dashboard. The car was unbearably quiet except for my breathing, which was still coming in jagged breaths as the adrenaline wore down, letting me feel my battered body. Gray kept his hand tightly on my thigh, drawing nervous circles into my jeans with his thumb. With every bump I'd bare down on myself, trying to limit my movement, closing my eyes against the keen feeling in my side. Gray would squeeze my leg in reassurance, and I hoped it meant that he was working on a viable plan.

I could only imagine my being a guest of honor was not a good thing, not when I had spent so long making it my prime mission to kill as many vampires as I could. I could tell we were nearing our destination because Gray tensed next to me and I doubted this was his first time going wherever we would end up. The car rolled to a stop and without a verbal cue everyone except for Gray and me got out. I yanked the bag off of my head, it snagging momentarily on a bobby pin in my hair.

"You're faster than them. Get out of here while you can. You can get backup." I rushed.

"Don't worry, I have a plan and it doesn't include leaving you." Gray looked so sure and it made my heart swell.

"What did they mean father?" I asked quickly, looking around the car to try and see what they were planning.

"That's what he likes to be called. He was patient zero and he believes we're his children." He voice was wrong, scared.

Just great, I thought to myself.

"Please don't die," I begged. He reached his hand out,

his fingertips brushing the line of my jaw. A look passed behind his eyes but before I could ask, I was ripped out of the back seat.

I grunted in pain, my stomach churning as those pesky lights danced in my vision. I heard Gray yell, but I was too focused on carefully drawing in my next breath to hear what he was saying. The next time I opened my eyes he was kneeling in front of me, searching my face. "Are you okay?" He sounded panicked, but I could only nod, not trusting my voice.

"Let's go," Dominic barked, not giving me any time to recover.

Gray helped me up. I didn't remember falling or asking to lean on him as we headed into what looked like an older museum. We walked past white columns that lined a runway to the back of the building. The light shone bright, reflecting off of artifacts from what I would have guessed with my limited knowledge in history belonged to the Romans. The place was impeccable, looking as if it was open just this morning for public viewing. There wasn't a speck of dirt or cobweb in sight. My shoes left contrasting marks on the polished ground as we walked forward, the sound of the soles hitting the porcelain echoing off the walls and back to me.

We came up on a section that had a mint condition throne, perched up in front of two more columns. It didn't seem to fit there, like it had been moved by command rather than layout. Dominic's finger called one of his lackeys, who produced a thick fibered rope. The vampire grabbed for my hand, though I quickly evaded it and moved back, swatting him away as he stepped for me again.

"Don't touch me." I growled.

"What is this? We're here, aren't we? Is that not enough?" Gray reasoned.

"I am almost sorry, brother." Dominic smirked. "Father's orders."

Gray moved in front of me, blocking the vampire from advancing further.

"You're not touching her." His voice dropped in warning.

"The hard way then?" Dominic snapped his fingers. The sound brought forth what felt like an army. At least twenty more vampires materializing from rooms and the corner shadows of the building.

"Wait!" Gray looked around, throwing his hands up, and lowered his head in defeat. "Okay."

I broke hearing him like that. He was so sure, so strong, but we both knew we had no plan, no backup, nothing to help us in this situation. It was the assignment with Alec all over again. Gray was moved to the side, the vampire pushing me back and forcing my arms to circle the pillar behind my back, securely fastening them with the rope. I thought about fighting him, but the sheer number of them and my injuries put me at odds the most addicted gambler wouldn't even bet on. Two more vampires slapped their hands to Gray's shoulders, probably understanding rope would do little to hold him in place.

The door opened and a middle-aged man only a little taller than me walked up. His graying hair was neatly cut, matching the color of his woven sweater. He looked like a professor, except his eyes were blank, absent of anything that made me think he was human. When I looked into them, as much as I didn't want to be scared, it forced fear to claw up my throat like the razored claws of a feral reaching for me.

"Gray." He spoke with a prominent Greek accent, looking down as him. The blood drained from me, leaving me frozen. I knew that voice.

"Father." Gray matched his tone.

"We have been a very bad boy, haven't we?" He clicked his tongue. "And this must be Samantha. You have no idea how long I have waited to meet you." He smiled with teeth that looked as normal as mine.

"That makes one of us," I shot back, refusing to look intimidated.

"Oh, now that I can imagine." He laughed like I'd told a joke, the sound oddly rich coming from a creature like him. "I took the liberty of looking through your things. I hope you don't mind." He snapped his fingers and one of his followers brought something over to him, which he took without looking at, not daring to let his eyes leave me. "I figured you wouldn't, since you had no problem spying on me." I took a steadying breath, but my heart pounded away regardless as his voice clicked in my brain.

It was him, in the lab.

I looked back toward Gray, trying to read his face. Had he lied to me when he said he was the only one who was assigned there? Did he know that Akle had been to the building and walked right alongside my uncle? I suppressed a shiver, thankful he left Todd alone.

He pulled out my stake. The stake my dad had given me. My lungs filled with air as he twirled the piece of delicate wood in his hand, eyeing it carefully, looking at it as though there was a hidden meaning in the meticulous carvings down the shaft. The way his fingers brushed *my* weapon sent waves of unease through me. His grasp on the gift felt so personal, like he was stroking my very soul.

Touching me intimately without placing a single finger on my body.

"It's beautiful." Akle's words were soft. He could have been speaking to a lover, but he was so transfixed on the stake that you couldn't misinterpret what it was about. It was only a statement, but my stomach rolled anyway. "As are you. You have really…grown into yourself." He eyed me carefully.

"Sorry, you're a little old for my taste," I bit out.

"I find it peculiar you say that, instead of dead." He raised his brows inquisitively. "And this"—he looked at the stake once more—"you have been driving this into the hearts of many of my children." His eyes snapped back to me, a fire igniting behind them.

Anger boiled in me, sending adrenaline through my veins. My parents would be so disappointed in me. I'd allowed myself to get caught up, and now the 'father' of these bloodsuckers was holding on to a personalized vampire killing weapon. Rope dug into the sensitive skin around my wrists, but still, I struggled against it, trying to quickly find a way out of this mess, and a way to get that through his heart.

I let myself catch another glimpse of Gray. He was standing up tall just behind a bigger, scarier looking vampire, who was clearly in charge of making sure he didn't make any rash decisions. Dominic kept close to him as well, eyes shifting from him to Akle repeatedly. Gray kept casting glances in the direction we had come like he was waiting for something. I could see he was trying to find a way out of this. I didn't know if he would be able to talk his way through this disaster, and it wouldn't look good if he tried to defend a human surrounded by his…his own kind.

"Akle…" Gray's words dropped off as his maker

snapped out of his gaze and met his eyes. "Father." He corrected himself, looking down.

"Hush, boy." Even with his thick accent, his tone made everyone in the room fidget uncomfortably. "You have no say here. I made my orders very clear to you, and yet you decided to play house with a human, a human who kills *your* kind."

Akle nodded toward Gray, prompting the men standing on either side of him to tighten their grip on his shoulders. He struggled against them but made little progress and stood still once again. He looked at me, pleading with his eyes, but for what I couldn't decipher.

Akle walked up to me, eyeing me like an unknown species, like I was the abomination and not him. With one swift motion he used my stake to brush through a piece of my hair, holding the strands against the wood and letting them slowly fall away as gravity forced them down. He leaned in slightly, staring deep into my eyes. "What is so special about you, human? You seem to have corrupted my son."

Before I could control myself, I spat in his face. I could feel everyone's gaze burning into him, but Akle's never left my face. I kept my head up. I would not be afraid of him. He took a silk handkerchief out of his pocket and wiped away my saliva from his face, smirking slightly. As quickly as he had returned the handkerchief back into his pocket, his hand connected with my face, backed by enough force to knock me to the side. I lost my balance, my knees giving way, but the rope ripped my arms back up, keeping me from fully falling. The woven threads burned my skin as I struggled to get upright and take the weight off my wrists. I didn't want to pick my head back up. Ringing blasted my ears as warmth dripped from my mouth, flowing heavier with every painful throb. Against my better judgment I straightened myself up and stared back, trying my best to put on a brave face to not give him the satisfaction he was searching for. I licked the copper from my mouth as fire raged behind my eyes.

"You act so very strong, but I can smell the fear rolling off of you like fresh dessert." Akle lifted his head up and took a deep breath, releasing it slowly. "Ah, you see, the quicker your heart races, the better you smell."

I looked toward Gray. I *was* scared, as much as I didn't want to admit that. I kept a brave face plastered on, but no part of it was genuine, and it faltered easily.

"Ah, so she does show fear." His laugh rang throughout the building. Akle rubbed his fingers on the tip of my stake. He had a slow, deliberate stride while he put some distance between us, calculating.

"Samantha?" He said my name like he wasn't sure I was there.

I didn't answer.

He turned back to face me. "What do you remember of your parents?"

"W-what?" The question completely caught me off guard.

"Your parents, do you remember them?"

My breath lodged in my throat.

"How about the night they died?" His smile turned my blood to ice. "Because I very much do."

Chapter 24

My face flushed of color, my body going hot and cold at the same time. Beads of sweat broke out across my forehead while I tried to wrap my mind around what he was saying. Hearing it from the source was different than hearing it from Gray, reminding me that this so-called Blood Society planned to steal them from me. Akle nonchalantly continued, seeming satisfied once he saw he had my full and undivided attention. I didn't know why, but I turned to Gray. He pressed forward, making little progress. He shook his head at me, again looking back to the door and pointing to his pocket. I bit my lip to contain the smile. Help was on its way.

"Your parents were making a real dent in my colony. Wiping out massive numbers of vampires almost daily, creating a business out of death. Paid killers." He looked at me like he didn't kill people, like his *children* weren't out feeding on humans. "My own soldiers, falling at the hand of two humans. Something had to be done." He reasoned, flipping his palm as to say, 'what else could I have done.'

Bile rose up my throat, burning my esophagus as I tried to swallow it back down. My heartbeat was erratic as my mind struggled to wrap around hearing this like it was bound to happen. He spoke like it was just business, nothing more, just as my being here was just a cause to an end. Humans had forsaken them and now it was their time to rise and our time to meet our reckoning.

"To be fair, love, I would have had you killed as well, that was my plan at least, but it seems your hiding skills match those of your killing skills now. Under the floorboards? I shouldn't have been so stupid."

How did he know that?

"It wasn't for the lack of help, however." He looked back at nothing. "You can come out now." He faced me once again. "Oh, you're going to love this." The excitement played across his face, his skin seeming to vibrate with the anticipation.

My eyes were playing tricks on me, they had to be as I focused on the face that entered through the door next. They had to be because that face had been present since my childhood, that face had been there to hold me when I hurt, to remind me I had someone in my life always. It was the same person I had just been silently thankful of being alive. Todd stared back, smirking slightly as he watched the wheels turn in my head. I wanted it to be a dream so badly, but I knew otherwise.

"Are you surprised?" he asked, voice sounding nothing like what my memory perceived it as. He wore the same suits I'd always seen him in, his skin a little more flushed than usual, but those same blue eyes boring into mine.

"Todd?" I asked as if it was some big joke. I forced my breaths out calmly even though I was too hot and cold at the same time, my clothing clinging to my sweat soaked body uncomfortably. I kept trying to adjust my hands, but the stinging sensation on my wrists reminded me I was bound here, unable to escape this nightmare, unable to wake up from the scene playing out in front of me.

"You didn't know?" he asked, like he expected me not to be shocked. "I have to admit your curiosity is what brings us here. You could have just left well enough alone, then so many people would be alive. Alec, Cindy...Ruby. This whole situation would have been avoided. It's been...a pain."

"W-what?" I didn't understand. "Ruby texted me today."

"You wouldn't understand, Sammy." The use of my nick name punched me in the gut. "I texted you today."

"Why?" Was the only thing I could force out of my dry mouth.

"I was never going to go anywhere, not in this world. Not while everything I worked so hard for was being credited to your parents. Everyone else had it all, leaving me to sit here and plateau." He shrugged. "Your father"—venom twisted into his words—"he had it all. The company, your mother..." Todd's look glazed over for a moment, taking him to a memory I couldn't see. "I didn't want to do it," he said convincingly. "But she didn't love me. She was never going to love me, not in the way I loved her. You have to understand how hard of a decision that was for me. We could have been a family."

Something clicked in my mind. That picture, the way Todd stared longingly at my parents—no, at my mother. Of course she would have rejected him, she had eyes for no one other than Samuel Cordova, but to kill them over it?

"You...you killed them? No..." My voice shook with the question even though I knew it was true, I knew long before he had to answer me.

"No, of course not. I mean, not personally," he said as if it made it better. "Please believe I never expected you to have to live without them, Sammy, I never wanted you to survive that night. All I wanted was what I deserved." His voice coated in jagged ice cut through me. "Even after that, a will. Like your father wanted to spite me even in his death. After everything I did, I would have to give it all up to *you*. You don't know the first thing about having this type of power. I couldn't let you ruin everything I worked for. Even so, I thought maybe it could work. You lived for the field work and I hoped you'd eventually come to your senses and realize you weren't fit to run the company, but every time I turned my back you were digging into places your nose didn't belong. It didn't matter if I loved you, you would still have to die."

"How could you!" I screamed out. I wanted to get my hands around his neck. I wanted to feel him take his last breath.

"You really mean to tell me you didn't already know?" He smiled, looking at Gray. "After I found out you requested those tapes, I was sure you were on to me. It wasn't a coincidence that they were turned off, Sam. Then I thought it was just unfortunate luck that you weren't at the facility when it was attacked, but after I saw you two together, I knew luck had nothing to do with it. I guess I underestimated your reach."

I looked toward Gray, who wouldn't make eye contact with me.

Todd's laugh cut into me. It was long and drawn out,

making his eyes water. "This is rich! Come on now, don't make me spill the beans for you—"

Gray tried to cut him off, but Todd just raised his voice.

"Oh, all right, I'll take the honor." He turned back to me. "He was in on the whole thing, Sam. Maybe even had a little of his own agenda." Todd winked at him suggestively. "I employed him! Although foresight says I chose wrong."

"Sam, it's not what you think!" He struggled, begging me to understand.

My cracked heart shattered. He knew about Todd? He knew Todd wanted me dead and never told me?

"That can't be true!" I looked back and forth between Gray, who refused to make eye contact, and Todd. My movements jerky like a caged animal being taunted from the outside. "I don't believe you?" It was meant to sound strong but came out as a broken question. After everything I was right, I couldn't trust him. I couldn't trust a monster. How could I when I couldn't even trust my own family?

"Maybe I am being too vague." He continued. "He had a simple task. You were already digging your own grave with your recklessness; he was just going to help push you into it." Todd sighed. "I was to play the mourning uncle, burdened with the responsibility of keeping the D.O.V.E. legacy alive. Although, we are going to have to change things around since he clearly lost sight of what his role was in this little story. I was thinking rogue hunter, looking to even the playing field against one of D.O.V.E.'s best or maybe partner turned vamp slays the last Cordova." He formed an imaginary rainbow in front of his face like it was displaying a headline before he tapped his chin, thinking. "I don't know, I am still working on it, but I'm sure I will think of something."

"What about Becca?" I asked, disbelieving.

"Oh! How could I forget!" He clapped his hands together, the sound traveling. "What a prime opportunity that was going to be. It couldn't have been any better, you finding that picture. I knew you'd search for her. I also knew that crazy bat never left her house, not since I forced the falling out between her and your mother. That one was my misstep. I should have known better than having one vampire sent your way, but it was risky with it being daylight, and they're not exactly subtle." He shot a scowl over his shoulder, earning him death glares from the vampires around him, but no one made a move to stop him. "Gray never did find what you took from D.O.V.E.," he said suddenly. "I really thought it was Ruby at first, but she cracked easy. So, what was it, what gave me away?"

"Nothing," I said, realizing when Gray picked up the apartment it was because he was looking for something... on Todd's orders. I looked up, a single tear falling freely. "There was nothing."

"Whoops. I guess I was a little paranoid, but you see how it was going to come to this eventually. Better late than never I always say." He shrugged.

Anger and heartache were fighting back and forth for a spot in my mind. Anger won. All I could see was red, the fury spilling into my mouth, escaping me like a venomous snake trapped in a corner. I couldn't feel my body anymore, all I could feel was the need to get to him. All of this for money, for what, power? Power over people who'd already lost everything.

"I. Will. Kill. You." My voice was quiet, my teeth clenched so tight they could shatter, but I knew everyone in this room would be able to hear me. "Both of you." I looked from Todd to Akle.

Akle stepped forward, in front of where Todd was standing. "I believe you." The tone in his voice did not reflect being threatened, rather just understanding. "That is why I am going to do what I should have done all those years ago."

Gray yelled something, but I couldn't focus on him because a piercing pain had started in my stomach, spreading to every nerve in my body in a slow, intricate route. I tried to take a breath in, but it lodged in my chest. I hadn't even seen Akle move, but now he was right in front of me, wiping his hand on that same handkerchief, staining it. When did he get his hands dirty? I barely heard the commotion to my right, the sound seeming too far away.

I tried to reach for the pain, but my hands were still strangled behind my back. An explosion sounded in the distance, but the more I heard, the farther away it seemed to get. I looked down and laughed, the movement excruciating, but I couldn't stop myself. My beautiful stake was sticking out of my stomach. I could clearly read the engraved 'with love' facing toward me like a bad joke. Blood was staining the light wood, dripping down onto the floor, accumulating into a pool with each drop. I hadn't realized I couldn't hold my head up as my knees trembled, threatening to give out any second.

I managed to pick up my head enough to see Gray struggling with one of the guards. Where did the other one go? And where was Akle? Todd? And was that Alana next to him? I was losing it and I didn't care.

My knees finally gave up, unable to hold me up the heavier I seemed to get. I fell, only to be caught by the rope that was binding me to the pillar, ripping my arms up so hard I was sure they would pop out of their sockets. The rope sliced into my skin even deeper, blood running up my arms in a slow stream, soaking into my shirt. It got really quiet. I guess that made sense. Death was going to be lonely.

The light touch on my shoulders was barely discernable through the pain. I didn't want to move. I just wanted to sleep. "Shhh, you're okay."

Gray? No, it wasn't, I was dead. Wasn't I? I wanted to tell him to go away and come closer in the same breath, but my lips wouldn't move.

There was a snap and my arms fell forward. My body wanted to follow, but Gray braced me and gently laid me on my back. I reached instinctively toward my stomach, but my arms were abruptly shoved down. I would have tried again, but they were too heavy to lift. It was like I was melting into the ground, slowly losing connection with everything around me.

"Don't move." Gray didn't sound okay. "I'm going to get you out of here."

I tried to protest, beg him not to move me, but he shushed me again. "I'm going to save you."

Didn't he see that he had killed me? Still, I wished I could smell him, let that scent surround me and drown out the copper that stung my nostrils, gagging me.

He put his arms under me and lifted me up. The move itself was so painful I couldn't help but scream out. My head rolled back and through a blurry lens I saw the vampire that held on to Gray, ripped apart, entrails nowhere near inside of his body. I couldn't believe this was how it was going to end, by the hand of the vampire king, with my own stake. I hoped they all looked like that, so I could die with some type of peace, even if it wasn't by my hand.

"Sammy, open your eyes! You're not leaving me," Gray pleaded.

My eyes were closed?

We had stopped and Gray was kneeling over me, his hand gripping my face roughly to get me to focus on him. He looked really scared too. I didn't know vampires could be scared. I coughed and felt warmth splatter across my face.

"Shit. Shit. *Shit*." Gray tilted me to my side to let the rest of the blood flow from my mouth before I choked on it. "I have to pull the stake out." He gripped the wood and as badly as I wanted to say no, I was stopped with another fit of coughing. I couldn't breathe, I couldn't beg him to stop. He yanked on the wood and I cried out. The scene played out like looking through a reel viewer. Each time I blinked it seemed like he was in a new spot, making me wonder how long my eyes were closing for.

He pushed down on my stomach, trying to stop the bleeding. I thought I heard something, but Gray didn't move, he wouldn't turn, and I couldn't explain why, but I didn't want him to die. I tried to warn him, but he was ripped off of me in an instant and thrown into a nearby wall. I could barely make out the fast-moving shape, but once Akle stopped long enough for me to see who Gray's attacker was, I knew this was the end for us both. Gray tried to fend him off, but he was stronger, faster, and from the looks of it more experienced than he was. Akle grabbed Gray's head, slamming it into the wall, the sickening crack bouncing off the surrounding walls. Gray fell, his *father* standing over him.

"You love a *human*? A blood bag? You are a monster and she is food!" Akle was growling now. "You would kill your own for what? Her! Can't you see it in her eyes, she wouldn't blink twice after driving her stake through your heart." He let out a humorless laugh. "You, my boy, are so naive, it pains me, your potential ruined."

"You don't understand." Gray started to stand on shaky legs. "I'm not like *you*." The word was drawn out as if he wasn't suffering from the effects of the same virus that turned Akle.

"Oh, but you are." He pushed him into the wall, Gray's head snapping back against the hard surface. "These humans changed us both. We're the result of their greed and indifference. Even now, we mean nothing, just another thing to eradicate so they can go back to their lives, follow the same vicious cycle. And you want to protect one."

"They're not all the same. She's not the same." Gray's eyes met mine, sparking something in my chest.

"You poor fool!" Akle growled, lowering his head. "You're a weak link. One I plan on disconnecting."

Akle plunged his hand into Gray's chest, his hand seeming to sink into the skin like it was nothing more than jello. Gray yelled out, gripping Akle's wrist to try and keep it from puncturing further. I wanted to beg him to stop, but my tongue fell flat against my mouth. The wood of my stake teased my fingertips, taunting me with what I should do. I gripped it in my hand, a peaceful resolve coming over me. With strength coming out of nowhere I managed to stand, my world swaying, making it near impossible to get one foot in front of the other. With the last of my strength I shot forward, praying I'd hit my mark.

Akle gasped, stepping back from Gray, leaning into me, into the wood sticking out from his back. Gray made eye contact with me over Akle's shoulder, his eyes wide, sweat trickling down his skin. His breaths were jagged, but I didn't know if it was from almost dying or seeing me standing there. I thought I heard Akle ask 'how' and I would have loved to answer, but as quickly as the strength weaved its way through my veins it was gone, and we were both falling back into blissful nothingness.

Chapter 25

"You can't let her die!"
"Sir, I need you to stand back! Someone grab him!"
"She's got a collapsed lung. Did it hit her artery?"
"Prep the room for surgery and get that code team over here!"
"Stay with me!"

THE RHYTHMIC BEAT dragged me into unconsciousness, just to have the stark smell of disinfectant that burned my nostrils to coax me out. I don't know how long I stayed like that, feeling like I was riding a rollercoaster of alertness and nothingness. Things came back to me in waves. My finger twitched. I wanted to stop it, but I couldn't feel anything else, so I just focused on that movement until it eventually traveled up my arm. As more of my senses came back so did the pain. It was bearable at first, but the more I reached for that beeping sound the more it hurt. Dark waters lapped at my ankles, enticing me to go under, but I pressed forward.

"Sammy?" a smooth voice called for me, but I couldn't work my lips. I was so tired.

The harsh light dried up the calling river I stood in. I tried to ignore it at first, but it never turned off, never stopped asking me forward. I squeezed my lids tight before testing them. The sounds were more prominent. I could feel everything. I groaned against my new world, shifting my body to get more comfortable with immediate repercussions.

"Don't move!" I was told. The hand that was placed upon mine was small but rough.

I opened my eyes, my pupils adjusting slowly as I tried to blink their way to clarity. The pale blue of my gown contrasted against the itchy, blanched blankets I lay on. The IV in my elbow ran down my arm, splitting into two lines, running up to its stand. I turned my head to the voice, still feeling lost and needing something to anchor onto.

"You're awake." A choked sob escaped Alana and she stood over me, looking down like I might disappear.

"Hey." I wet my lips, the feeling of the dry skin scratching my tongue. "What happened? Where am I?" The memory was just out of my reach.

"Oh, Sammy!" Tears freely flew from her eyes. The sight was so peculiar because she never cried like this. She rushed forward, landing on me, trying her best at a hug.

"Ow, ow, *ow*!" I sucked in a breath.

"I'm sorry!" She backed up. "I'm just so happy to hear your voice right now." She wiped her hand along her face, slightly smearing her mascara. "We didn't think you'd come out of this—" Her eyes widened like she'd said something wrong. "I mean, you did! So that's all that matters."

The events slowly crept back into my mind. The church, seeing Todd, finding out about Gray and killing Akle. I closed my eyes against some of the memories, but I couldn't will them to not be true. I forced my lids back open, peering into Alana's own swollen ones, searching for anything that would tell me she had betrayed me too. As hard as I tried to see evil, all I could see was my friend. Guilt washed over me as I remembered my silent accusation, followed immediately by relief that my gun jamming was just coincidence.

"Where's Todd?" I asked, afraid of the answer. If he was dead it would still hurt, but if he was alive it would be worse.

Alana grew quiet, picking away at the black nail polish on her fingers. "We don't know."

"What do you mean you don't know?" I sat up, pain erupting from my stomach. "Ah!" I gripped the bed railing, trying to ease it away.

"We shouldn't talk about this now! You need to heal." She gently pried my fingers from their hold and helped me lie back.

Once I had caught my breath I tried again. "How much do you know?"

She cast me a look and sighed when she realized I wouldn't give it up.

"We got there just as Todd—" She stopped to look at me before continuing. "Right as he let that vampire stake you."

I stared straight ahead, trying to muffle the flashback.

"We got a distress alert from Gray's phone. I just—I just wished we had been there sooner!" Her eyes begged for my acceptance, but didn't she know she had nothing to apologize for? It was me who should be apologizing for thinking it was her who had betrayed the company. "No one knew." She gulped. "No one knew they could look human."

"Todd did," I said matter-of-factly, omitting that I also knew.

"Sammy, I can't even begin to understand what you're going through, but we're going to find him." She promised and I smiled at her desire. She was there for me even when I had been so distant from her.

"You know, Gray's been here every day looking after you. I sent him out to rest right before you woke up." Her words dumped ice water onto my skin.

"Gray?" I said, not trusting myself to say more. Didn't they know he was one of them?

"Yeah, I almost had to drag him out. He's been so worried about you, Sam. I didn't know you guys had bonded like that." She laughed. "He said you killed patient zero. I had no clue there really was one, but the field is impressed and fully expects you to step up. Once you're healed of course. D.O.V.E. needs a new leader." She looked excited.

"I can't," I said, the words flying from my mouth.

"What?" she questioned. "Of course, not now but—"

I cut her off.

"Not ever, Alana, don't you see? I didn't know about Todd and I trust—" I stopped. I didn't know why, but I couldn't out Gray. He had betrayed me, convinced me to trust him, but he had played me the entire time. Still, the words caught in my throat. "I just don't think I can do it." I sighed, feeling exhausted.

"I understand," she replied. "Listen, we don't have to talk about any of this now. Trust me, the buzz out there is crazy with everything we learned. They are starting to check humans, seeing if they test positive for the virus. It turns out placebos were being sent to the people who live near the Deserted, making it easier to create more vampires. We don't know how many they got to yet, but everyone is working overtime." She squeezed my hand gently and got up to leave. "I'll be back. We can discuss more after you've rested."

"Alana?" I called out before she opened the door, head still reeling.

"Hmm?"

"Thanks, for everything," I said.

"Don't sweat it." She gave me a toothy grin. "Just get better so you can buy me that coffee, like you promised."

"Deal." I promised and she left.

The next days passed in a blur. Every hour I had nurses in to check my vitals, making sleep impossible. Gray had asked to visit but each time I asked the nurses to send him away. I wasn't ready. Alana stopped by each day, even helping me to convince the doctor I was well enough to walk around the hospital just to get me out of my stuffy room. I learned I had been in a medically induced coma for a little over a week, to try and let my body heal faster. Aside from a collapsed lung and needing surgery for the wound in my abdomen, I had also dislocated my shoulder from the fall, so I got to sport a limiting sling, which I complained about every chance I got.

It had been determined that somewhere between a hundred and two hundred people had been bitten. Some changing into ferals, some dying, and some living with their families, blending into the crowd. After everyone at D.O.V.E. was tested it seemed besides Gray and Akle, no one was actually a vampire, so Gray didn't lie...about that. Alana had convinced me to sit in the charge even though I didn't feel I had any business being a leader even if she felt otherwise, but I promised to until we could find someone to take it over for me.

My discharge day finally came, and I buzzed with anticipation. The staff wanted me to call someone to help, but I refused and signed my paperwork anyway. I wanted to get away from the smell of bleach and death as fast as I could. The air outside of the hospital could have been mistaken for the smells from a fresh garden as I took a deep inhale, ignoring the way my ribs protested. I took a step forward and stopped right in my tracks.

Gray.

He wore simple jeans and a cotton shirt. His hair was messy and the bags under his eyes told me he hadn't slept in days. He stood there, his presence acting like an invisible wall, not allowing me to unroot myself and move away. Anger washed over me with a hint of something else. Sadness, longing? I didn't know, but I knew I needed to get away from him.

"Sammy, wait!" he called after me as I stomped in the opposite direction. I ignored him.

Each step I took sent razor blades to my stomach. The skin was too tight for normal activities after being sutured together and I worried that my brisk movements would tear the stitches I'd been forced to promise, on three occasions, to be careful with. I paused every few steps to catch my breath and re-motivate myself to make it down the road to catch the bus home, not realizing how much strength I had lost being cooped up in the hospital. Gray's presence followed me close, but far enough I wouldn't be able to swing and hit him easily…as if I could in my state.

"Please let me help," he pleaded, still keeping his distance.

"I think you have done enough. Thanks," I snapped

back. I was too tired to fight with him the way I wanted to. He had ruined my entire life, well, worse than it was already ruined. I wanted to yell and scream. Shaking him and make him explain why he would allow me to believe he cared when really, I was just a job to him, a job he was supposed to let die. I didn't know why he saved me. He had his chance to fulfill his obligations and screwed it up, and I was going to make sure he knew that was the biggest mistake he had ever made.

"I swear if I thought it wouldn't put you in more danger, I would have told you." His voice sounded sincere, but I knew better than to trust him again.

"Yeah, you're right. Because sending me into an ambush was *definitely* the easier decision there," I said, biting the words out as the pain sharpened with each syllable.

"We—not just you—we were sent to an ambush. You know I had no idea. You know me!" Gray was just shy of yelling.

"There is no we. And clearly, I don't know you at all." I turned the corner, heading toward the city's center. "I thought I did." He stopped in front of me, and I jabbed his chest with a forceful finger. "I trusted you even though I knew better. You're a vampire, not a person. You are nothing to me." My words dripped venom and though he flunked back he didn't return the tone.

"I deserve that. I just want the chance to explain," he pleaded with me.

Church bells chimed, echoing off each building nestled in the shopping district, drowning out anything else he wanted to say to me. The sound sent the thin hairs at the nape of my neck up into a full salute. I felt eyes glued to me like I was standing under a limelight, but as I scanned through the people busying around us, I only found occasional curious glances, none of which seemed to be at the root of the unease that was quickly building in my gut. It chimed again, as if to mock me and my paranoia. My feet were rooted to their spot as a rush of heat engulfed my senses, traveling up my spine and sending little bugs scurrying across my skin. Gray moved forward, taking a few steps before realizing he didn't have my attention any longer, and turned to see what I was searching for.

I turned to the street, not sure what made me do it, but knowing somehow I needed to see what was there. The church bell rang one final warning as my eyes locked with another's. Those eyes, those familiar eyes drove into me like an unstoppable train, strong enough to steal my breath away. Everything stopped, the sounds of the city, Gray's voice, everything but the bees that took flight in my eardrums. The buzzing grew louder until I had to refrain myself from putting my hands up to the sides of my head to try and block the noise out.

It couldn't be him. It was impossible.

Alec stood still across the road, unblinking, his gaze piercing right through the very flesh surrounding my heart.

As clear as day, unchanged from the last time I remembered seeing his face. His stare was emotionless, watching me closely. Gray's voice sounded like he was under water as he tugged on my shirt sleeve, trying to get my attention, but I couldn't respond. I could barely breathe. The only thing I knew in that moment was Alec, and the fact that he was very much alive.

Acknowledgments

The list of people that helped make this story possible is endless.

First, a huge thank you to my father for not only being one of my biggest supporters but also never telling me to pick a "real" job. Next, to my husband who, even as someone that hates reading, was always engaged in what I was working on and telling me that he believed in me and my dream. Next up is my daughter, Emberly. You will never understand how your very existence allowed this book to come to fruition. Without you, I would have never had the courage or motivation to complete this story.

An endless amount of thanks to my editor, Emily, who not only had to work through my countless grammar and punctuation mistakes, but also gave me some of the best encouragement a girl could ever ask for! I also need to thank both of my younger sisters, Desiree who has always supported my dream and Lauren who was always there to help me work through writer's block and read through my work to tell me what was and wasn't working.

Last, but most certainly not least, a **HUGE** thank you to my beta readers, including my close friend Victoria. Without you all, this would have never come together in the way that it did. Please know this list is not all-inclusive. My appreciation reaches out to anyone who has ever supported me or encouraged me to follow my dream. This includes the writing community which is filled with some of the most sincere people I have ever met.

About the Author

B.B. Palomo is an American author from the state of Arizona. A writer at heart with a wild imagination, she has always had an affinity for the supernatural. Her debut novel began as a short story written in the fourth grade. While it was nowhere close to the writing prompt assigned, her teacher gave her credit anyway, noting the creativity B.B. demonstrated. This encouragement sparked her dream of becoming an author.

Even though B.B. was born in Arizona, she is not the desert heat's biggest fan. Give her the subtle crunch of freshly fallen snow under her boots any day. In school, B.B. often used the old trick of hiding a book within her textbook while pretending to follow along with the rest of the class, though she still placed significant value on her studies. After graduating high school, she moved on to study business management in college.

B.B. now works as a licensed financial principal by day and works on her novels and blog by night. She is a wife and a mother—to an amazing daughter and a few fur babies—but when she does manage to find the time to unwind, B.B. enjoys a tall cup of coffee to go with a great book, all while daydreaming about the next story she wants to bring to life.

To learn more about B.B. you can follow her at:

More by B.B. Palomo

The Department of Vampire Extermination Trilogy:

The Blood Society

Engraved in Blood *(August 2021)*

Other Books:

What Lies Beyond *(Early 2021)*

Stay up to date on new releases by visiting authorbbpalomo.com